The

Proposition

*A
Geek,
An Angel*

A novel

J. A. Jackson

I will always believe victory is the stuff I am made of...

Acknowledgments

I'd like to give out a big endless gratitude of thanks and appreciation for the wonderful support and editorial guidance of my editor the very knowledgeable Mr. Rossi V. Jackson.

I'd also like to say a special thanks to the incredible man in my life, my husband who believed in my writing and supported my dreams.

Also to my mother Dorothy Henson you blew the wind beneath my feet and made me enjoy learning, writing and living this life. God gave me you and you gave me unconditional love and support – Thank you.

Also a special thanks to my sisters Kay, Shelia and Marie. I am so grateful to you for your support and love. And to my brothers Ray and Eric I thank you also.

To my readers and fans I am forever grateful. Thank you.

For Rossi, Daddy & Mommy always….

Prologue

The soft gentle click of heels echoing against the marble floor faintly floated on the air.

Janeshia nodded as if waking out of a dream. She thought the heels clicking were part of her dream. She opened her eyes and looked around. There was no sign of anyone. She realized she wasn't cold. Someone had thrown a warm thick blanket over her. A heavy arm lay a cross her body. She was naked, lying crushed against the hard strength of a man's muscular body.

The man stirred and wrapped his arms securely around her. She snuggled in closer enjoying his warmth.

Slowly she adjusted her eyes and stared back at the huge picture perfect window in front of her. She watched the silvery moon slide from behind a blanket of clouds. It made her sigh with contentment. She started to close her eyes.

Startled Janeshia shifted. There was that noise again, the sound of heels clicking on a marble floor.

Instantly, bright lights flooded the room.

"What in God' name is going on in here?" A woman's shocked voice gasped as it sliced the air.

Chapter 1

A Challenging morning calls for strong brew...

Savoring the aroma of her morning cup of coffee Janeshia James took a sip, inhaled the aroma and closed her eyes content.

"Janeshia, you've got to fire that man! Aren't you the boss around here?"

Janeshia's eyes opened wide blinking frantically. The stressed out voice belonged to Tamara Bell, her assistant.

"Well Tamara," she mumbled wiping up a few drops of spilled coffee. "It sounds like you're having a bad morning. Normally I'm pretty busy this time of morning. But go ahead. What's up?"

Tamara walked first to the side table behind the door where a fully stocked small kitchenette stood. "You spilled your coffee. Here, let me pour you some more. I made a strong brew this morning, just the way you like it."

"Thank you," Janeshia said focusing her gaze on Tamara. "What's your beef?"

"Adam St. Charles is my beef. That insanely rude, egotistical, psycho-analyzing nerd brain man is driving me crazy!"

Janeshia nodded. "Didn't you used to refer to him as that Mr. Deliciously Gorgeous Brain?"

"Maybe, but that was the woman in me speaking. The one that loves to look at gorgeous men," Tamara sighed heavily. "I know he's good at what he does, and he is very good looking. But it's my job he's trying to tweak right now. And I'm not some computer virus," she shrugged.

"Are you sure you're not?" Janeshia teased. "I mean a computer virus that is?"

"No! I mean yes. I'm sure I'm not a computer virus. Stop joking. This is serious. Don't you want to know what he did to me?"

"Sure I do."

"That compulsive and obsessive computer geek decided to tweak my emails. He has corrected everyone I sent him this morning. And I've only sent him three. And they were one liners saying *please see the attachment*."

Janeshia inclined her head to hide her smile. "Just ignore him like you normally do," she said swiveling around in her chair to face the view. It was foolish for her to ignore Tamara when she was upset.

She glanced out of her window. The sky was so clear and blue. This had to be the hottest Friday morning ever this summer, she thought. She gazed across the valley. The Santa Cruz Mountains loomed into view. She marveled at their beauty. They were mesmerizing to behold.

"Oh look Tamara. Look at that cloudless blue sky. Doesn't it make you just want to take a deep breath and sigh?"

"Whew! A sight like that makes me want to cry, because I'm stuck here dealing with Adam St. Charles and all of his cryptic weirdness," Tamara exclaimed.

From the shadow of her window, she watched as Tamara walked to the end of the long window that occupied her office. This was Tamara's favorite. She watched her do her deep breathing exercises to calm herself.

"Feeling better now Tamara?"

"Yes, you know how to take my mind off of Adam. But I still think you should talk to him. And tell him his rudeness stinks, especially when it comes to that email thing. He needs to be reminded that he's human just like the rest of us."

"Tamara, what can I say that you don't already know about Adam? He can be a little trying sometimes, but please be patient with him. He did a great job getting that virus off of your computer that you got downloading music."

"Please talk to him," Tamara said marching over to her desk. "He likes everything about you. Do you know what I heard him say?"

"Tamara, you know how I feel about office gossip...."

Tamara didn't wait for her to finish. "He said you had excellent taste."

Janeshia flushed nervously. "You've got to be kidding. Adam doesn't pay compliments."

Tamara nodded agreement. "Oh, but this time he did. But I haven't told you the best part. Adam said you were not quite girlfriend material because of how much of a bad girl vibe you put out in that Halloween costume you wore last year."

"I was Cat Woman for crying out loud," Janeshia blurted.

"Yeah, well he thought that black faux leather spandex halter top jumpsuit you wore was way too "*Mistress Dominatrix,*" with an emphasis on the S&M. He said he thought you were going to hit him with that black leather whip you carried around at the Halloween party that night."

Janeshia regarded her with concern. "Excuse me, but didn't you pick out that costume for me? After, I gave you specific instructions not to pick out anything too sexy or too revealing?"

"Yes, I did but...." Tamara said quietly. "You are the one that wore it."

"Wait a minute Tamara, when I refused to wear it, you accused me of being a bad sport."

"Yeah I did," timidly Tamara rubbed her brow. "That was because I knew you had to wear that costume. You looked good in it, real good. And you achieved what I hoped. Which was to spook Adam," she chuckled. "You spooked him good. I knew he was afraid of cats."

"Tamara, you didn't tell me that."

Tamara shrugged. "That's not important. Let me finish telling you what I heard," she whined. "Adam said your personality was so altered once you put on the "*Mistress Dominatrix,*" Cat Woman costume that he believed it was your true personality and therefore he would never consider you as girlfriend material," she giggled softly. "Then Walker told Adam he couldn't spot excellent girlfriend material if it came up and slapped him in the face. Walker said you were perfect in every way; from your honey complexion right down to your superb figure, with your tiny waist and ample behind."

"Tamara!" Janeshia said dryly trying to interrupt.

"Wait a minute, there is more. I haven't told you the best part. Adam said he thought you looked like a tall Beyoncé," she laughed. "But Walker said your cheekbones were way more defined and that you were strikingly more beautiful than Beyoncé could ever be. Don't you get it? They were arguing over you."

A frown marred Janeshia's expression as she tucked back a lose strand of her long sable hair. "Wait a minute. You were talking to Adam St. Charles and Walker Perrault about me?"

Tamara smiled mischievously ignoring her as she continued. "That's not the point. The point is I'm telling you what they said," she said. "Oh and here's the best part. Walker said that when you two danced the samba together at last year's Gala Ball you were so graceful he almost cried. He said he could feel his fingers resting on your hip. He fantasized about your dancing for weeks after."

"Oh did he really?" Janesha frowned and leaned back in her chair. Her brows rose quizzically. "So Tamara you've been sitting around the office gossiping with Adam St. Charles and Walker Perrault about me?"

"Actually, I didn't mean he said; like we, the three of us were talking. It was more like I overheard Adam and Walker talking guy stuff when they thought no one was listening. Like I said earlier, I was eaves-dropping," Tamara nervously smiled.

Janeshia raised a brow. "So you admit eaves-dropping on their conversation?"

Tamara muffled a laugh. "Well…..... Okay maybe, alright, yes I was. But that really can't be defined as real eaves-dropping. Since I'm not in the habit of doing it, let's just say I was in the right place at the right time." She nodded her head. "Anyway the point is, we were talking about your talking to Adam and making him stop nick-picking on my emails."

"Wow, you are so amazing sometimes Tamara. So let me get this straight. You want me to talk to Adam about the emails that are annoying you. Yet you've been eaves-dropping oh his private conversations. And you don't see anything wrong with it?" she paused. "Or notice if it pissed the boss off?"

"Ah, okay If you have to put it that way," Tamara said.

Janeshia ignored her. "Besides, I think it would be better if you talked with Adam about the emails."

"I take it that's a firm no. You won't talk to Adam?" Tamara asked.

"A very firm no," Janeshia said tossing back her long sable hair that flowed from a center part, and turned back to stare out of the window. She was amazed at how warm the room was beginning to feel. Earlier she thought she heard the air conditioner moan. She stared out of the window and appreciated the view her eleventh floor window afforded of downtown San Jose, California.

Out of the corner of her eye Janeshia caught a streak of light. She stared out attentively. A sudden light burst into view. It shimmered golden, sparkling like a Fourth of July fireworks before her eyes.

All at once it vaporized before her eyes.

Tamara sighed heavily behind her. "Seeing a shimmering streak of white light blaze and disappear in broad daylight is showing you what is wrong in your life, so that you can set it right," she giggled. "That sort or rhymed."

Janeshia jerked nervously. She had forgotten that Tamara was standing there. "Wow! That was interesting'." She said with a shake of her head. "Where did you get that saying? Did you make it up?"

Tamara walked around Janeshia's chair and stood beside her. "It's a real one. I heard it somewhere before, maybe from an old gypsy or my mother."

Janeshia smiled nervously. She was sure she didn't want to get Tamara talking about her mother or gypsies. She changed the subject. "It is warm in here. I believe I heard the air conditioner groaning earlier. I hope it isn't going out," she wiped her brow.

"You're right it is getting warm in here."

"Tamara, please call building maintenance and see if they can check it out."

"Okay boss," Tamara said softly. "Is there anything else?"

Janeshia turned around. "By the way Tamara, you're great at your job, in case I haven't told you lately."

"Thanks," Tamara sighed.

"Oh yeah, getting back on the subject of Adam; don't forget to stand up to him about that email thing. He's done the same thing to me a couple of times," Janeshia nodded. "But when I finally stood up to him he stopped. Anyway, all I can say is, when you do be patient with him. He means well."

"Adam is just so annoying," Tamara shook her head in frustration. "That man really needs to get a life."

Janeshia could see this was going nowhere. She changed the subject. "One more thing, are there any messages for me?"

"No, but Mr. Walker Edmond Perreault is here," Tamara said. "Oh, I didn't tell you earlier because he said he was going over to talk with Adam for a few minutes."

Janeshia checked her watch and let out a sigh. The peace and contentment of her morning was now shattered.

"Don't worry. I'll tell him to knock real hard before he enters," Tamara joked. "Now that man is obsessed with you. He really likes you. He's looking very handsome today in a romantic leading man sort of way. But then he always does."

Janeshia threw back her head and snorted out a laugh, "Get real and stop being a diehard romantic."

Now, Walker Perrault is the one who really could use a hobby and a life," she murmured under her breathe.

"If you ask me, Walker has a hobby. I believe it's coming by here every day to see you," Tamara flashed a mischievous smile.

"I'm going to ignore that," Janeshia pretended to study some papers on her desk.

"Walker is dangerously handsome in a geeky sort of way don't you think?" Tamara blurted. "You like him. I can tell."

"My thoughts are always on my work Tamara, when I'm at

work. Unlike some folks I know." She looked away. "I don't harbor secret romantic notions about someone I work with or for, or overhear other people's conversations," Janeshia lied. She fussed with the papers in front of her. "Don't you have some work to do?"

"Yes and I'm starting with telling that egotistical man, Adam St. Charles, who thinks he's God's gift to a computer and this office, to go piss-off," Tamara said as she turned and walked toward the door. "But only if he bugs me again. And I'll do it nicely of course."

Janeshia watched her office door close. She finished her coffee in one gulp and placed the cup back on her desk. She leaned on her elbows in deep thought.

For the last three years she had achieved a number of her goals. First by being hired as the *Director of Silicon Valley Making a Difference Foundation* and then by maintaining and increasing the foundations multi-million dollar asset and investment portfolio, as well as increasing the foundations sponsor list. Because of her hard work and dedication the final out-come had meant that all of the programs the charity funds were well able to meet their annual budgets for many years to come. She only allowed herself one personal achievement. And that was purchasing her home.

Her thoughts traveled back. If Walker's mother Claire Marie Edmond-Perreault hadn't taken early retirement just before Janeshia applied for the directorship, she never would have achieved her first goal. Now, the only thing missing from her life were fulfilling some of her other personal goals and finding that special someone to meet, marry and have babies with. Maybe this was a tall order. She knew that part wouldn't be easy. She was a little bit too selective when it came to men. And to top that off her list of what a man should be was known to change daily. Still the major part of her "what a man must have" qualification was always running through her mind. Top of that list was that he had to be easy to get along with and be a great conservation. She knew Walker Edmond-Perreault, with his butting in and control issues and his trying to run the foundation, didn't fit those two qualifications at all.

Walker Edmond-Perreault held a PhD in chemical engineering and a Masters in economics. Many said he was a genius. Janeshia was sure he was a geek. Albeit, he was a very handsome geek; but he was still a geek, never-the-less.

She guessed that Walker Edmond Perrault's, being the only son from a wealthy family, influenced the lack of charm he possessed. He was highly intelligent, she had to admit. But a bit pompous at times. He was a man who was accustomed to being in charge and giving others instructions. At thirty six years of age he was a full ten years older than Janeshia.

The way he talked could irritate her nerves something awful sometimes. But she couldn't ignore the warm sensation that coursed through her body when she heard his name.

Janeshia shook her head, *"Talk about annoying,"* she thought. "Walker Edmond-Perreault wrote the best seller on being annoying."

The day had started out too perfect, Janeshia thought. It had seemed so, except for the possibility that the air conditioner might be going on the blink. She let the thought pass.

Her position as director *of Silicon Valley Making a Difference Foundation* meant she worked for Walker and his family. And if there was one thing she didn't do. She didn't date men she worked with. She made it a point to keep her distance from Walker from the first time she saw him.

Her mind wondered, remembering his deep green haunting eyes. Even now she thought of the way his eyes fit perfectly with his high lean cheekbones and strong nose. Under his uniformed geeky dark colored suit he radiated a primitive sensual quality that Janeshia couldn't always ignore.

Quick rapid knocking interrupted her thoughts.

"Ms. James, Mr. Edmond-Perreault would like to see you now, are you available? Tamara's voice boomed through the doorway.

Then Tamara moved a few steps aside.

Walker Edmond-Perreault stood at the threshold of her door.

"Good morning Janeshia!" came Walkers excited voice. "How are you this morning?" He stood with one hand in his pocket. The other hand he ran through his hair smoothing a loose curl back in place. The rest of his jet black rakish looking shoulder length hair was neatly tapered at the nape of his neck. His deep green eyes looked flawless against his olive complexion.

"Janeshia, I'm so glad you have time to see me."

Janeshia breathed out slowly at the sound of his saying her name.

"Hello Mr. Perreault. It's so good to see you again." "Now Janeshia, you know I asked you to call me Walker," he said slowly closing her office door behind himself. He quickly walked over closing the distance between them.

Janeshia found herself tensing up at the sound of his voice. She knew how critical Walker could be. She glanced up at him. "Sorry Walker, I forgot. Now what is this about?"

"Oh, you know. I was just checking on the Gala expense report."

Janeshia glanced up in surprise. "Yes, of course. Walker did you want the Gala expense report?"

"Yes, I do," he said.
"Oh then that's Adam St. Charles' report. He is handling that expense report. I believe it's at his desk."

Janeshia gazed absent mindedly out of the window.

"Oh, I know. I just remembered." His voice rasped out sternly. He walked over to her desk with a formal air. He put his black leather portfolio case down on her desk and unzipped it. "I have the report."

Janeshia looked back at the report. The report could take hours to go over.

Walker Edmond Perreault pulled a chair up and sat it right beside her. "My goodness it's hot in here. Did you turn off the air conditioner?" He asked without waiting for her to respond. "I need to speak with you because there's a very delicate matter that I need to talk with you about," he said leaning over and whispering. "But not here in the office."

Janeshia sighed. She felt Walker was sitting too close for comfort. They'd never sat that close before. She looked up and caught him staring back at her with those vivid deep green mesmerizing eyes of his. They were the strangest shade of green she'd ever seen before. She could have sworn she saw flecks of amber and bronze in his eyes. A shiver ran down her spine. "What are you talking about?"

Walker's handsome face was marred with a frown. He lowered his voice. "Look Janeshia we have a problem and since I know you've worked hard on this report I want to speak with you privately about it. The walls have ears you know."

Janeshia's brows shot up. "What, are you saying we have spies in my office? Come on Walker these are my employees. I trust them," she said.

"We shouldn't speak here on that topic. Not in your office. We should talk about this somewhere outside of the office," he said quietly.

Just then his cell phone rang.

"Hello! Mother, is everything okay?" He asked. "Good. Look mother I have to put you on hold for a minute."

Janeshia sat in silence watching Walker. She reached for the file he had in his leather portfolio.

Walker studied her and reached out closing his portfolio. He looked up at Janeshia.

Janeshia drew her hand back and looked back at him.

"Look Janeshia, I really need to take this call. It's my mother. She was ill recently."

Janeshia remembered Walker's mother Mrs. Claire Marie Edmond-Perreault as a charming elderly lady. She was always flawlessly dressed whenever she saw her at the Gala Events. "How is she?"

"She's fine," he said seeing her reaction. "It's just that she's under the impression......Oh never mind," he hesitated. "Look there's a huge discrepancy in that report. As director of this nonprofit it's your responsibility.

Janeshia shot him a questionable glance. Then tilted her head slightly to look past Walker and stared out of the window again. She pretended to pay attention to him.

Walker remained firmly planted in his seat. He cleared his throat. "You know Janeshia what I need to go over with you is a lot more involved than I thought. I think perhaps we should discuss this report more in depth over dinner tonight. What time do you think I could pick you up?"

Janeshia's attention returned. "I'm sorry Walker, what was that you said?"

"What time should I pick you up?"

Janeshia breathed out heavily caught off guard. "No, I can't go out with you. It's Friday night. I have to do laundry." She regretted the lie as soon as she told it.

Suddenly the phone in her office rang.

Walker took advantage of the situation. "Go ahead and take that call Janeshia it might be important," he said. "Besides I've got mother on hold."

Janeshia's eyes looked down and checked the caller ID. The name flashed Emergency Services. The call could be important.

Her telephone rang again.

Walker interrupted her thoughts. "So you're saying Saturday night would be better? You really should take that call. It might be important," he repeated.

"You're right Walker, I should get this. Hold on a minute," she said flustered reaching for the phone. "Hello-"

Quietly Walker rose quickly and walked to the door. "Oh, Janeshia," his voice called across the room. "Since its Friday and your laundry night. I guess our date will have to be tomorrow night then," he quickly said. "Don't worry, I have your address. I'll pick you up at 6:00. See you then," he said abruptly closing her door shut behind him.

Janeshia looked up stunned and frustrated as she cradled the phone to her chest. "Walker, hang on a minute, Walker....I...." Suddenly she realized Walker had already closed her office door.

Chapter 2

Once upon a time I called you friend...

Apprehensively Janeshia put the phone back to her ear. "Hello, this is Janeshia James speaking."

"Hello Ms. James, this is Harry Billings with the Systems Branch Incident Command Center."

"Yes, hello Mr. Billings is there something going on?"

"Yes, Ms. James. We note that it seems to be some sort of electrical surge occurring on the infrastructure. The electrical company states a transformer maybe out. They are aware of the power. And their crews are hard at work trying to isolate the problem. This is just a standard alert to let you know that if we have a power surge on our back up energy power, your computer systems may go out. But we have all your data files back-up in place. No data will be lost. I'll be monitoring and let you know if there are any problems."

"Okay Harry...."

"Look Ms. James, I'm getting a call on my other line. Let me call you back," Harry interrupted.

"Sure," she said hanging up the line. This morning was proving to be challenging in more ways than one. First Walker, now this, Janeshia was amazed at the morning she'd been having. She took a big gulp of her coffee. It had grown cold but it still tasted good. She was eager for a little diversion. She sipped it slowly.

Her phone rang out loudly again. She didn't hesitate to pick it up.

"Hello Harry?" she said softly.

"Hello Janeshia how are you doing?"

Janeshia's spine stiffened in surprise. She recognized the voice. It was Alice Couvertier-Trudeau, a voice from her past. She grew up with Alice. Once upon a time she thought Alice was as good a best friend as being friends with Jesus. One thing was sure; Jesus was a good child who grew up to be a good person, and Alice? Well Alice was a child once. That was one thing she knew was true. But Alice was a bully then. And she is a bully now. Bullies never change.

"What do you want Alice? I'm busy. And why are you calling me at work?"

Alice cleared her throat. "Hear me out Janeshia, it's important. We need to talk. I'm out of town right now. But I'm flying back home tomorrow night. Sunday is bad for me. Can we meet for lunch next week? Any day of the week is fine. We can go meet at El Burro's at the PruneYard. It's still your favorite right? I'm buying."

"How dare you..."

Quickly Alice interrupted. "Look Janeshia, calm down. I swear I'm on the up and up. I've changed. You should want to see it for yourself. In fact, I want you to see that. Please, just think about it. You have my number? It hasn't changed," Alice pleaded.

"Look Alice why should I want to see that you've changed? You should respect that I don't give a damn if you did change anyway?"

"You're right, you shouldn't care. But I do. That's why I want you to see that I've changed." Alice said softly.

"It's not like the two of us are great friends," Janeshia replied. "Anyway how did you get my work number?"

"I called though the main number. Look, that doesn't matter. The most important thing is that you should have lunch with me. We are friends......" Alice pleaded.

"That's a preposterous notice Alice and you know it," She abruptly interrupted. "We are not friends. I don't know where you got that."

Alice interrupted her. "Look we're not kids anymore. Why can't you get over stuff we did as kids?"

Janeshia blurted. "Look Alice, did you forget about bullying me?"

"Oh for Christ sake Janeshia, you need to grow up!"

"I am grown up. I'm over it. I'm an adult now," Janeshia said tersely. "I think you are just an adult bully who wants to hurt other people!"

"Bullying...No.... I mean. Look, I apologized about all that stupid kids' stuff. I swear," Alice said apologetically. "Meet me for lunch, you'll see I've changed."

"Sorry Alice, but I'm not a gullible stupid kid any longer. Goodbye!" She hung up the phone abruptly. Just like Harry had done to her earlier. She hoped that sensation would make her feel better. But it didn't.

The loud whiny death of the air conditioner seemed uncanny. It gurgled loudly before going silent. Maybe they shut it down to save energy. Sure that had to be the reason. It would allow the backup generated energy to last longer.

Chapter 3

Once upon a time and that Eavesdropper ...

An hour later Janeshia pushed back the wayward strands of her hair and sighed softly. The air in her office was becoming unbearable. She knew her makeup must be suffering. She checked her compact and quickly wiped the shine from her nose and forehead.

Normally she was always in control. But the heat of the room increased her tension. This had certainly been a strange morning, first with her encounter with Walker Perreault and then dealing with the worst person from her childhood, Alice Couvertier-Trudeau.

The lights flickered and then went out. They quickly came back on. Then the lights flickered again several times before the whole office went dark.

"What?" She exclaimed.

Her office door opened quickly.

"Tamara, what happened?"

"It's a total power outage. The whole building is out now. Even our backup generator has died. My computer died."

Janeshia swerved her chair over to the light by the window. "Harry Billings called earlier and said that he'd bring the computers down if we had a power surge, I guess he did."

Tamara walked over and stood by her boss. "Yeah, well one of the building maintenance technicians just called. He said another transformer blew out somewhere. Apparently this is going to take a while to fix, from what the Tech says. It could be hours."

Janeshia glanced up at Tamara. "I can tell what you are thinking. You want to leave right?"

Tamara smiled shyly, "Yes, I have a few personal things I really need to take care of."

"No problem, tell you what, let everyone know it's okay to leave early. Then stop by Adams's desk and tell him I'll need the section report on the financials for the last quarter. He can just leave it on his desk. I'll pick it up later. Be sure to tell Adam he can leave early as well."

"Sure, no problem," Tamara said. "You have a good weekend Janeshia. See you on Monday."

Janeshia quickly got up and pulled the blinds up to let in more light. She sat down at her desk, determined to go over the ledger and files in front of her. She concentrated.

Adam St. Charles was a tall man who knew he had a mesmerizing effect on women. His eyes were brilliantly dark and cool. His hair jet black and wavy with curls that lightly tapered at the nape of his neck. He was gorgeous. But he appeared not to register that fact.

He stood silently in the doorway and studied Janeshia.

Finally he spoke. "Excuse me Janeshia. I see you're off the telephone."

She turned at the sound of Adam St. Charles' voice.

"Boy it gets stuffy in here when the powers out," he said. "I hear you wanted the section report on the financials for the last quarter. Oh, and are you done reviewing the Gala Report?"

Janeshia glanced up at him. Men like Adam could sometimes be impossible to deal with. His eyes smiled back at her. The sun's rays flickered bright sparks off of the gold rimmed spectacles he wore. She studied him. There was something about his smile. He wore it like it was a disguise.

"Oh darn, no I haven't finished reviewing the Gala report. But I do need the section report on the financials for the last quarter. Do you have it with you?"

He handed her the report. "Yes, here it is. But if you don't mind I was hoping to speak with you about the Gala report. There are a few things I'd like to point out to you."

She glanced at her watch. "I can spare a few minutes."

She watched his eyes. His dark eyes watched her like a hawk.

Janeshia found the Gala report. "What did you want to show me?"

Adam sat down. He briskly got down to business. Flipping the pages of the report and pointing out facts. He spent the next fifteen minutes going over it.

Finally Janeshia checked her watch. Being around Adam too long alone made her nervous. "Look Adam, I don't want to waste your time. Is there anything specific you want to bring to my attention?"

He cleared his throat. "Yes, yes of course. You need details for the foundation board meeting."

His expression was hidden from her by the long lashes guarding his eyes. He felt sorry for her. She held the leadership position. A position that he felt was best suited for a man.

Adam flipped the pages and pointed. "Here are the signatures. I even have Bob Green's signature. He's the most popular news anchor in San Jose, California. I'm sure," he said warmly. "Even from an accountant's or banker's point of view, his presence will have positive effects on the foundations cash donations. Every part of this report is in order. The board of directors will be impressed."

"It sounds like you really have taken care of everything Adam," She smiled glancing up at him quickly. She caught him staring back at her with a crooked smile.

"As you know I'm fully capable, when I see what needs to be done. I get it done," he said with a bit of hostility in his voice.

Janeshia looked in his eyes. She tried not to stare at the small scar just below his left eye. She knew Adam St. Charles was self-conscious of it sometimes. But she also knew he was capable of handling every situation. He could be bluntly rude, a bit arrogant and scornful at times she thought. But he was smart, hardworking and very intelligent. His insensitivity to the feelings of others could be annoying sometimes. And she also knew that Adam was the sort of man who had a slight bit of trouble in taking direction from a woman. But normally he made an effort to keep this part of himself in check.

"Well, I do trust the decisions you've made so far," she said forcing a smile.

"Was there any doubt?" Adam condescendingly asked. He removed his glasses and wiped away some non-existing dust.

"No….I Ahhhh" she nervously grimaced. She was irked by his cool aloof manner. "It's just that I'm the boss Adam and sometimes I just need to check on things. That's all."

"You're right. You are the boss," he said. "You know what's best. Do you mind if I admire the view from your window."

"Sure," she laughed to cover her annoyance. She didn't want him thinking she was staring and turned away to stare back at the report on her desk.

Adam walked to the window and stood there. The deep blue of the sky held him. "I hope I didn't upset you Ms. James, you know my confident manner was one of the things you liked most about me when I interviewed for this position. I really do admire you. In fact, you could say I'm your greatest fan."

Janeshia knew he was just saying that for her benefit. She felt the need to explain. "I'm not upset with you Adam. I just needed to know if anything unexpected could happen that we haven't considered. I only asked because I'm having dinner with Mr. Walker Edmond-Perreault. And I wanted to be clear on all the details just in case he had questions," She assured him.

At the mention of Walker's name, Adam turned and raised his eyebrow and walked back to her desk. He studied her. "I thought you needed the information for the board of directors meeting?"

"Oh, I do at that Adam. But first I have a business dinner to go over everything with Walker. One could say it's like having dinner with the board."

"Ahhhh…….Really?" He frowned. "But I met with Walker earlier. We went over the report and he seemed satisfied with my explanations. As a matter of fact, he stated the report was excellent. Better than any he's seen produced by this office in a while," he replied with heavy irony. "Janeshia, it's not like you to mix business and pleasure. Especially to further your career," the tone of his voice held a conceited annoyance. "It's one of those things I have admired about you," his lips curved into a sneer. "I could have dinner with Mr. Perreault and answer any other questions he may have. Would you like for me to go instead."

She was thunderstruck by his comments. She knew that dating her boss was in no way beneficial to her career. And she didn't need Adam pointing it out to her. She cleared her throat hoping to hide her reaction. Sometimes Adam St. Charles could be a hand full. "No....No... Adam I can manage. Besides have you forgotten Mr. Perreault is your boss too? He gives the orders we just carry them out," she checked her watch. "Why are you still at work? The power is still off. And it sounds like everyone has left for the day. I'm sure you are anxious to be somewhere."

Unnoticed Adam stood behind Janeshia for several seconds and said nothing as he glared back at her. *I'm here because you know you want me, his thoughts reasoned to himself.*

Finally he adjusted his glasses and shook his head. "No, I'm not anxious to be anywhere," he drily replied.

She looked at him in surprise. She took charge of the situation at hand and eyed him sternly. "Well you should leave. I insist. Go on. Take advantage of the power outage and have a long weekend too. Everyone else is. In fact I'm just about to leave too."

Janeshia dismissed Adam without a glance and turned her attention back to the papers on her desk, stacking them neatly. She was in a world of her own as she fumed, restraining herself from running after Adam to strangle him with her bare hands.

She turned to retrieve her purse and brief case from the cabinet next to her desk. She slammed the cabinet drawer shut and jerked up in surprise.

Adam didn't move as he silently stood by her desk.

"What's the matter Janeshia? You look like you're about to faint.

"Is there anything else Adam?"

He adjusted his stance but remained where he stood. "You really should let me go out to dinner with you. You never know with Mr. Perreault," he hesitated. "Forgive me for saying so but a lady like you shouldn't be left alone with a man like Mr. Perreault. He might try to rape you or something."

"I beg your pardon?" She coughed out astonished.

"Look Janeshia, isn't it obvious? I already went over this report with Mr. Walker. Can't you see he has other ideas?"

Janeshia lost her patience and stood up and walked around her desk. The encounter with Adam was making her tense. She needed to take the upper hand. She quickly walked to the door and held it open for him. "Look Adam," she emphasized leveling her hand toward her door. "I really need you to leave, right now. You have a good weekend," she said dismissing him.

Adam walked to the door and paused. He had to have the last word. "You know Ms. James, men and women can't just have dinner and be friends. The man always thinks that he just might get lucky." His eyes locked with hers before he walked through the door.

Janeshia slammed her door forcefully behind him. The gesture was rude. But she didn't care. She walked back to her desk and sat down slowly. She breathed out trying to get her emotions in check. She swiveled her chair to face her view.

The room seemed hot and stuffy as she took in her view. She steadily gazed at the glass pane in front of her. She realized the window seemed strange as she stared through it.

All at once the vision hit her hard. Her eyes just stared off into the window. Deeply within her mind she felt and heard the pounding hooves of their horses before she saw the men riding the horses.

Two men sat proudly erect and rode the horses hard, deep into the misty forest of wild terrain. Her eyes grew wide as she saw clearly the path they took into the wild forest of thousand year old bald cypress and old pine trees, spreading far and wide. Low cascading branches hung over their heads. A misty, velvety cloud swung low and drifted onto the ground around their horses. The valley rolled ever far, deep and wide. The two rider's bodies shadowed against the moonlight of a midnight deep blue crystal clear sky. She saw that one of the men stood out. His body's frame was tall, strong and lean. His muscles were tight and his facial profile showed that he was majestically mysterious and handsome. The bright moonlight hit his eyes for a moment. She saw that they were a deep vivid green. Her heart pounded and her breath caught in her throat. It was as if her heart knew him and had always known him. Her breathe caught in her throat.

Standing alone against the stark of midnight she saw there was a woman that stood off in the distance waiting for the two riders.

The woman stood confident, determined and strong against

the chilled night wind. She wasn't old or young, or so it seemed. She was wearing what looked like a colorful flowing scarf. It's kaleidoscope of colors softly bellowed out all around her.

The two riders rode closer and closer to her.

The effects of the colors bellowing around her, acted like a mysterious spell being cast.

The woman's voice lured them to come closer in a coarse, smoky, erotic and eerie, voice. Her song escaped her lips. It was sad against the wind, and it was a mysterious song.

> "Shadow of those who walk in the heavens above......
> *"Oh light of the radiant white she dove*
> *She watches sitting way up high from afar*
> *For tonight she waits to see her shining star*
> *Oh sing to me oh Golden One*
> *Oh sing your song, and make the night moan*
> *Sing to me oh Angel of God's Light*
> *Sing to me and give me sight*
> *As the stars come out on this faithful night*
> *Show forth this man of her hearts pure delight*
> *Before the dawn the night do chase*
> *Bring forth the one she loves*
> *Come now and show his face*
> *I call forth unto thee make haste, make haste!"*

The woman's thick smoky coarse laughter echoes into the night. And just as quickly as the vision came it went away.

Janeshia's vision was so vivid and real.

The sharp ringing of her telephone jarred her out of her vision.

Janeshia blinked her eyes hard twice to make sure she was wide awake, she heard herself saying "I'm wide awake...I'm wide awake....yes...yes I am. And that guy on the horse was that guy real? His physique was so deliciously beautiful. Could such a man exist?" Her thoughts raced.

She quickly reached for her phone.

"Hello"

"Hello Ms. James, this is Bud from building maintenance. You sound strange. Are you alright?"

"Yes I'm fine," she lied. "What's happening with the power?"

"Well, it looks like the power is going to be out for the rest of the day. Most folks have already left the building. I was just calling to let you know in case you haven't heard," he said.

"Thank you for calling Bud. I think I'll be leaving early too Bud. Good bye."

Chapter 4

You should want more out of life...

After she hung up the phone, Janeshia sat at her desk. Her thoughts wandered back to the vision that she had earlier. Puzzled, she rose and walked over to the window. She tried to make out the vision's meaning.

Soft tapping on her office door startled her. She turned around quickly and took a nervous step. She thought she was alone in the office.

The door to her office slowly crept open.

"Janeshia are you alright?" Walker Perrault stood in her doorway with a worried frown on his face.

Her frightened expression greeted him. "Where did you come from?"

Walker came forward and stood next to her. "Oh I didn't mean to scare you Janeshia. I was standing in front of the building at the little hot dog cart having a cup of coffee when I heard about the building's power failure. I thought I would come back upstairs to check on things," he said. "You look a little peaked. Is everything okay?"

"What?" She murmured looking at him. Her eyes held his. He looked every bit as good as Tamara said earlier. The sunlight accentuated the chiseled lines of his jaw and high cheekbones. He had the face of a man not easily forgotten. Her heart raged as she stared back at him. Her eyes fell on his lips. She swallowed hard and breathed out slowly.

Time seemed to stand still between them. All at once the only thing Walker could think about was that he needed to touch her. He closed the distance between them and reached out and touched her face.

"Where did you come from Walker? I thought you had left," she said as her lips trembled.

He put his arm up and touched her shoulder. "I guess I was a little worried about your being up here all alone." He pulled her close and hugged her. "God, I wouldn't know what to do if anything happened to you."

Janeshia felt a jolt from the care and concern in his voice. She didn't know why his strong arms made her feel safe and warm. She laughed nervously, loving that he was worried about her.

"Say Walker, why all of this concern for me," she said softly against his shoulder.

Walker pulled back and tenderly looked down at her. "I'm concerned because I saw Adam St. Charles leaving. He hinted that he may have made you upset. Did he say something to make you upset?"

His care and concern overwhelmed her. She sighed, feeling a warm glow running through her.

"Janeshia," he softly said her name and leaned in closer and smiled at her. His charming smile caught her off guard. It made her heart pound. "You are so beautiful."

She didn't step back.

And then he lowered his mouth to hers and he kissed her. His kiss was soft at first and then it increased harder, stronger and bolder.

Janeshia didn't know what came over her. Maybe she hadn't kissed a man in so long that she was hungry. She tried not to think about it as she leaned her body closer molding it to Walker's.

Walker's hands traced her body and she arched eagerly under him.

The sharp ringing of her telephone broke her out of her trance, as she stumbled back and walked past him. "We shouldn't be doing this. I don't know what came over me," she explained. "I've got to take that call. It might be important."

Walker's hopes dashed when she pulled out of his arms. "Janeshia, what about what was just happening here?"

She was irked by his cool aloofness. She tried to remember what her best friend Larissa London was always saying about coolness and aloofness. Her thoughts raced. She could have sworn the two traits were what Larissa often said were part of criminally minded men who preyed on single females. "Look Walker, I don't know what just happened. But it wasn't supposed to. I work for this foundation, for your family. Don't you remember?"

She put some distance between them. "This isn't what you think. The heat affected me or something. I never date the boss!"

"It wasn't dating. It was just a kiss."

The phone rang again. She was glad for the distraction. Urgently she marched to her desk. "Walker I need to take this call."

Agitated he walked to the door. "Damn it Janeshia, I don't know what you are afraid of," he said as his thoughts raced. *You should want more out of life, he thought.*

More than a little taken back, Janeshia stared back at him. "Walker can't we talk later? Let me take this call ...."

"Don't worry. We're still on for Saturday night!" He yelled before slamming her office door.

Chapter 5

Hook, line and sinker....

The morning dragged on, with the power out. Less than an hour later Janeshia walked out of the lobby of her office building. The sun shining on her face felt good.

The parking garage loomed ahead of her. She pressed the automatic start button on her slick black Cadillac STS. Before she opened her car door she noticed something on the windshield.

She leaned forward and reached for it. Her gold bracelet caught the sunlight.

Janeshia's deep green eyes sparkled happily at the beautiful array of Blue Violets flower bouquet attached to her windshield wiper. A small heart shaped card was attached by a satin blue ribbon. There were no words written.

She looked around her. No one was there. She quickly opened her car door and got in. She tossed the flowers on the seat next to her. She locked her doors and engaged the engine key.

Sitting in her car, with too much time on her hands, she grabbed her cell phone and thought of her best friend. She quickly dialed her number.

Larissa picked up on the first ring. "Hello Larissa."

"Oh, hey Janeshia," Larissa said. "What's up?"

"Oh…. Larissa you know me. Always looking to play hooky and take the Caddy out for a ride. Want to go with me or have lunch or something?"

"Sounds like you had a bad morning and you need some cheering up. Okay, but we have to do lunch first and then go for a drive. I'm starving."

"Yeah, well sure Larissa."

"But you'll have to wait. I have a short meeting. It should not last more than twenty minutes, or a half hour tops. As soon as it's over we can leave. Where are you?" Larissa asked.

"I'm headed for your office building right now. I can wait for you downstairs in that pretty little park in front of your building."

Larissa laughed out loud. "Sounds like a plan. If you meet any single men, grab one for me."

"Men? What's that?" Janeshia joked easily. "I'll see you shortly my best friend."

Several blocks away, at the very moment Ramsey Montgomery stepped out of the building, he breathed out a sigh of relief. He quickly put on his shades to shield himself from the sun's rays. The heat of the hot sunny day felt wonderful, after the tense meeting he'd just left. He walked lazily for the small green park. The deep green grass felt as soft as a pillow under his feet. Several women openly stared as he made his way across the small park.

Ramsey Montgomery was a man of confidence. He hadn't been born to money but he had acquired it. And through his genius he controlled a great deal of it. The confidence money brings oozed through his every pore. He was a man accustomed to people being in awe of his powerful presence. He was smooth and perfectly at ease and in complete control in any situation. There was a quality to his being that dominated his presence. He was extraordinarily handsome and knew it. His hair was wavy and black and cut close tapered to his neck. He had brooding mysterious slanted eyes he hid behind dark glasses.

A woman walked up to Ramsey real close. "Damn you look

sexy mister," she murmured.

Ramsey shook his head and walked on. He knew his body was ripped tight and toned. It made him look taller than he actually was. He was proud of the way he looked. He knew people loved to watch him, especially women. He often watched them watch him. But he didn't care. He had his pick of any woman he desired. And he was selective. Few women were worthy of his time.

He was only a few yards from his favorite spot. He walked on like a man on a mission.

Ramsey sat down on the bench under the tree in front of the pond. This was his favorite spot to unwind after a meeting here at this building. He blotted out the meeting and everything that had happened that morning. Even the sounds of the traffic disappeared. He set the timer on his watch and relaxed his mind. Then he closed his eyes and savored the moment.

Twenty minutes later, the soft chiming of the bell on his watch awakened him. Ramsey opened his eyes and checked his watch. The hands on the dial sat precisely at 1:25 pm. He shook his head and yarned. Slowly his eyes caught sight of a beautiful woman standing in front of the pond. He watched her stare out over the pond for several seconds and then turn and walk away.

At precisely one thirty p.m. Janeshia walked past Ramsey Montgomery. She didn't even notice him as she walked across the lush green grass in front of her best friend Larissa London's office building. The fresh air of the open park comforted her. She quickly found a bench to sit on.

Janeshia sat poised with her back against the bench taking in the beautiful flowers. Her mind wandered. She paid no heed to the people around her.

When the man came up and sat beside her she hardly gave him a glance.

"What's the matter? Did you have a rough childhood? Or did you just have a bad day?" A man's voice softly asked.

"Huh?" She grunted.

"I walked by you just now and greeted you with my best hello and you didn't even smile," the man said.

She turned to make eye contact. The man wore the dark motorcycle shades that were very popular. They hid his eyes. "Look mister, I didn't hear you, okay?"

The woman's eyes held him. Luminous green almond shaped eyes that haunted him and drew him in. Her beauty took his breath away. He gazed back at her curiously. He had to draw her in to wanting to talk to him. He had to be kind to her. "Oh, I see so is that your way of saying hello back?" He didn't wait for her to answer. "I thought a beautiful unforgettable woman like you, could say hello in such an unforgettable way that it drove a man completely insane just wondering what her name was," he joked lightly.

His irresistible grin caught her off guard. She knew the rituals that men and women used to meet each other. But this guy had perfected his art. He was the kind of man a woman could fall for hook, line and sinker, she thought as she fought back a smile and stared at the stranger. "Do I know you? Normally, I don't talk to strangers."

He reached behind her ear and magically produced a half dollar. "Well, maybe if I introduce myself we will no longer be strangers," he said. Did you know somebody once said *happiness is not for the frail of heart?* In any case I guess I just want to enjoy my day, have a little fun today and see what being polite will do for me today. By the way my name is Ramsey Montgomery."

The old magic trick he used broke the ice and made Janeshia smile. She was delighted with how he'd broken the ice. Not to mention she still loved that old trick. "Okay, in keeping with your quest to be polite today. My sincere apologizes for being rude earlier. My name is Janeshia. Janeshia James," she smiled.

"You are very beautiful Janeshia James," he said tilting his head and looking over the rim of his glasses. He smiled. "See I'm not crazy, just a gentleman who happens to love admiring a pair of very fine green eyes on a beautiful woman?"

Janeshia fought back a smile. "Oh how lovely. I thank you for the compliment." She cleared her throat. "You know Lana Turner once said *a gentleman is simply a patient wolf.*"

She shrugged. You could tell a lot about a man by the way he carried himself. She checked him out. This man was intelligent, handsome, sexy and very well educated. He was something else too. He had the kind of face she liked looking at.

His smile grew wide. He leaned his eyes over the rim of his sunglasses to get a better look at her. "Ah, you've got me there," he said. His eyes were as exotic as his voice. His voice had a strangely distinct accent.

"So Mr. Montgomery?"

He interrupted. "Please call me Ramsey," he smiled.

"Okay then Ramsey. If you don't mind my asking, what's your accent?"

He chuckled. "It's kind of weird huh? It's vaguely French with a slight London, Bronx flair. I kind of moved around a lot as a kid." He smiled. "I like your accent. It's Californian, huh?"

"You've got me there," she said nodding a smile. He'd broken the ice in the, "getting to know a person better", ritual. He had another point in his favor. Maybe they could find some common ground. She thought.

"Do you work around here?" They both said simultaneously.

"Ladies first," he said.

She studied him. He had a nice smile. "No, my best friend does. I'm waiting for her now."

"Unluckily, no I don't work around here," he said. "But I wish I did so that I could see you more often." As he spoke his eyes fixed on hers. He could tell what she was thinking. "You're wondering what I do for a living right?"

Janeshia nodded. "Yes, that was going to be my next question."

"Well my undergraduate and graduate degrees say I'm a highly trained Engineer. But if you look at what I currently do, then you'll probably call me a professional sitter. I sit on the board of directors at several venture capital companies. In fact I just left a meeting," he gestured at the building in front of them. "That's why I'm sitting here trying to unwind. I have another one this afternoon."

"Impressive," she exclaimed. "That's the same building my best friend works in."

Ramsey cleared his throat. "Do you work nearby Janeshia? I mean what do you do?"

"Yes I work; I can see that's what you were asking. I'm a director at the *Silicon Valley Making a Difference Foundation*. Perhaps you've heard of it?"

"Oh, yes I have," Ramsey's eyebrows rose. "That's the reason you looked so familiar to me. I attended the Gala event last year with a good friend. Impressive! If you don't mind my borrowing your word," he chuckled revealing his beautiful smile.

His compliment made her blush. She quickly added without knowing why. "I like giving back and helping others." Her thoughts raced. *"I must be getting desperate. This man gave me a compliment and now I want to tell him my hopes, my dreams and my telephone number. What's come over me? I like him."*

Ramsey ran a frustrated hand through his hair. "Janeshia, do you mind if I ask you a question?"

"Sure."

"Is there someone special in your life? Like a say a husband or a boyfriend maybe?"

"Why?"

"Because, pardon the old line, but you are the kind of woman I've been looking for. I believe I could fall for you hook, line and sinker."

Janeshia shyly smiled and raised her brow and let her eyes wander back to Ramsey's face. She was just going to answer him. When she looked past his face and saw the woman walking towards them. Her shoulders tensed.

"Janeshia, are you ready to go to lunch?" Larissa London's voice called out.

Larissa London was Janeshia's best friend. As usual she was dressed in a stylish high powered attorney's suit. She was slender with good bone structure, a head full of brunette hair and rich deep tan complexion. She was also a lawyer who had a knack for spotting men who were losers and liars.

Janeshia's gaze traveled to Larissa's shining bright eyes. She always felt like a social outcast compared to her best friend Larissa.

Janeshia looked back at Ramsey. But there was nothing she could do to shield him from Larissa. Her spine straightened. Quickly she said. "Look Ramsey, I need to explain my friend....."

Larissa whistled out loudly. "Whew! I smell money! And he's tall, handsome and a hunk of a man!" She sniffed the air hard. "Oh, I believe I smell a CEO." She said checking him out over the rim of her sun glasses. "Janeshia who is this?"

Janeshia went to open her mouth.

Larissa looked him up and down. "Oh never mind. I've seen you before. You have a board meeting in my building. You're Ramsey Montgomery, right?"

"Yes," Ramsey said rising and extending his hand.

"Well Hello Ramsey, I'm Larissa London, attorney at law,"

she said in a breathless tone.

"We were just talking," Janeshia nodded. "I mean not about you Larissa, but that Ramsey has a meeting in your building."

Janeshia stood and stared between her best friend and Ramsey. She figured at any moment Larissa was going to start interrogating Ramsey on his intentions. She braced for the worst.

Larissa and Ramsey glared at each other like two old rivals.

Finally Larissa breathed out. "So you seem to have all your own hair Ramsey and no grey. And you don't look like you're balding yet." She paused. "You know a little grey hair means you're more trusting. I'm guessing you're not married. Are you in the market? For a dating I mean. Ah…..Well at least your being a CEO means you're not a serial killer. Can't steal their money if they're dead huh, got to keep them alive" Larissa chuckled.

Janeshia was quiet. She never felt so embarrassed. She checked her watch. "Well….Ah we need to get going."

Larissa nudged Ramsey. "Come on I was just joking."

Finally Janeshia spoke up. "Larissa shouldn't we get going? It is your lunch hour."

"Yeah, I need to get going too," Ramsey murmured. "Janeshia, it was nice talking with you and your friend, Larissa," he said as he slowly backed away.

Janeshia nodded and glanced his way.

He stopped abruptly looked back at her. He smiled softly and nodded before he turned and walked off.

Janeshia waited until he was out of earshot. "Larissa how could you? That was rude even for you."

Both friends watched Ramsey's back as he walked out of view.

Annoyed and disinterested Larissa spoke. "I don't know why I did that. There was just something odd, familiar and strange about him. He reminds me of someone, I can't place it right now but I will," flickering a glance at her friend. "You like him, don't you?"

"What?"

"I can tell by that look on your face Janeshia."

Janeshia bit her lip. "I really like him. I hope to see him again."

Startled by her friends revelation Larissa turned and studied her friend. "He has strange eyes. Don't be so trusting of a man with strange eyes."

"He doesn't have strange eyes," Janeshia said. "I think he has wonderful eyes, plus he's handsome. And he's got smooth words. I love his smooth words."

"Smooth words you say," Larissa rolled her eyes. "You know, I wonder if Jack the Ripper was as smooth as silk right before he slashed his victim's throats."

Janeshia shook her head. "Stop being so morbid Larissa. I can tell you were impressed by the guy. You have to admit the guy has character. He oozed it."

Larissa shook her head. "He oozed CEO character, that's not real character; that's a cross between a banker, an accountant, a clown, and a maniac depressed alien from another planet. But I don't think it was his real character," she placed a hand on her friends arm. "Come on, let's get going, your cousin Greystone James called after I hung up with you. I told him I was meeting you for lunch and he insisted on joining us."

Chapter 6

The character of a man....

The modern setting, Venetian plants and terracotta ceiling of the Citrus Restaurant at the Hotel Valencia at Santana Row added to the uplifting atmosphere.

The party of three friends sat on the patio just past the bar area on the second floor.

Janeshia had trouble concentrating. Her mind wondered over and over again back to meeting Ramsey Montgomery.

Greystone James slowly sipped his glass of wine and studied his cousin. "So Janeshia, your buddy Larissa told me you have a date tomorrow with Walker Perreault. He finally got you to agree to go out with him. Is he the reason for the smile on your face?"

Larissa snickered. "Right now Janeshia's mind is on one of the most powerful venture capitalists in the valley, Ramsey Montgomery," her expression was arrogant. "The man who wears the mask," she spit out his name venomously.

Greystone James almost choked on his wine. "No kidding? We are talking about that Ramsey....The Ramsey Montgomery?"

Janeshia sneered at her two friends and took a bite of her salad.

"The one and only. You know he has some kind of board meeting in my building." Larissa shrugged and took another sip of her drink. "Say Greystone, why don't you fill your little cousin in about the man?"

"Damn, Janeshia doesn't have a clue?"

Larissa shook her head. "Sorry to say it Greystone, but she doesn't."

"Well it may come as a shock to you cousin. But Ramsey's got a pretty bad reputation as a powerful, ruthless player in the venture capitalist game." Greystone cleared his voice. "Not to mention. I think he's a social climbing antisocial kind of guy, if I do say so."

"What else do you think about the guy Greystone?" Larissa asked.

"Huh, I don't know, I heard he can be cold and unforgiving. He never shows any emotions, no kindness, nothing," Greystone said grimly.

"Well, he was very nice to me Grey," Janeshia studied her cousin astonished. "You know I have a system for studying people that's nearly fool proof?"

"Yeah, well reading a book entitled how to read someone in 30 days does not count," Greystone said firmly. "Oh yeah. I just recalled something, let me tell you cousin. I heard this story about a girl Ramsey dated a few years back. He was engaged to her as a matter of fact. But for some reason he called it off. She refused to give him back the engagement ring. And he hired a team of lawyers and forced her to give him back the ring and pay his attorney expenses." He hesitated. "The guy can be as cold hearted as they come."

Larissa grimaced. "Or an absolute lunatic. Dating or even knowing Ramsey is risky business."

Janeshia looked up in astonishment. "So what you both are saying is that Ramsey is way over my head. Well, I think the two of you are wrong. Besides, the guy has not committed a crime. All he did was make sure he got his engagement ring back. He probably paid a lot of money for it."

Larissa glanced at Janeshia and shook her head "See what we're up against Greystone. I told you she needed help in the love department. Walker finally got her to agree to go out on a date with him and now she's trying to sabotage it by pretending to be interested in another guy."

"Is that so?" Greystone shook his head. "You're quite sure my cousin is attracted to Walker?"

"Yes!" Larissa tilted her head. "She could never be in love with a cold-hearted guy like Ramsey Montgomery. Besides, I've seen the way Walker looks at her. He gives her that look of love at first sight and now they get to have their first date together."

"Come on Grey. Don't listen to Larissa. You know the attorney in her always embellishes the truth. I have a meeting with Walker that happens to be occurring while we are having dinner." A slight frown showed on her face. "And where do you get that *"love at first sight"* junk Larissa? The only reason I agreed to it in the first place was because I wasn't paying attention at the time Walker asked me."

"Hmmmm, like how you're not paying attention right now to our telling you who the real Ramsey Montgomery is?" Greystone sighed.

"Exactly like now!" Larissa exclaimed.

"Stop it Larissa. At least I don't date married men," Janeshia said bickering like a sibling.

"I didn't knowingly….." Larissa glanced at Janeshia with a rueful smile. "Okay I lie. I did date a married man. But in my defense how was I supposed to know he was married? He didn't even have a ring shadow or even a slight discoloration on his ring finger?"

Greystone cut in. "No ring shadow? Of course you couldn't tell the guy was married."

Larissa shrugged and piped in. "I did threaten to tell his wife when I found out he was, remember? I set the guy up to go straight."

Janeshia let out a chuckle. "Yes you did a major job of embarrassing the guy; I'll say that for you. I'm still laughing at how you just happened to have lunch with the guy when, Mildred Pearson, the brilliant divorce attorney walked by. And she pretended she remembered the guy from the fund raiser gala. She made such a fuss about knowing the guy's mother in law and threatened to tell on him if he didn't rethink his adulteress ways."

Greystone tried to keep from smiling. "Ladies quit trying to change the subject," he complained. "Now Janeshia, what happened to all of that business savvy you learned in college? You're telling me you let Walker ask you out on a date. But it isn't a date."

Janeshia put down her wine glass. "Well, I never said Walker asked me out on a date. As usual cousin, my best friend has put that idea into your head."

"I assumed it was a date because, when you called, you said you had a date," Larissa nodded.

She swore under her breath. "What I said my best friend….Oh never mind. Maybe I did say something like that. But what I really meant to say was that when Walker asked me, I wasn't paying attention. Otherwise I never would have agreed."

Greystone interrupted their bickering. "Yeah, I've had that happen before to me too. That's how I ended up dating my last girlfriend. By not paying attention. I walked smack into her and we ended up dating. In fact I think it's the best way to meet a person worth dating, don't you think?"

Janeshia took a sip of her wine, "Maybe it is for you Grey, but when it comes to Walker it doesn't work for me. Even Tonto had way better social skills with the ladies than Walker will ever have. And being private alone with Walker wouldn't be a date. It would be an ordeal, a very painful ordeal, just like having major surgery without an anesthesiologist present."

"Oh Janeshia, that is such a cruel thing to say!" Larissa said.

"Ferociously cruel!" Greystone echoed.

Larissa leaned on her elbow. "I'm sure if you gave Walker a chance, it could be one of those sweet innocent encounters that turned into a wonderful long term romance. Walker is intellectual and smart. He's mature, funny and loveable in a geeky sort of way. And he's such a sweet man. The kind of man that's ready for the settling down," she said waiving her hand. "That's how real love greets you in a guy like Walker. The guys I meet never end like that. My guys are always the kind you just want to have hot sex with. If you can believe it, it seems that's all I can attract."

"I believe it!" Greystone and Janeshia said simultaneously. The two cousins laughed out loud together.

Larissa looked at them both disapprovingly. "For reasons you two romantic simpletons will never understand, I use sophisticated sensitive female radar of discernment before I agree to date someone. That's why I date so infrequently. Now I have sex a lot because that's an easier thing to do. A guy just has to get my heat sensor levels up," Larissa snobbishly said.
"And I'm ready for a good romp in bed."

Janeshia laughed and shook her head. "Oh how I know that to be true!"

Greystone choked on his glass of wine. "Wait a minute you two. As I recall, we were not taking about a moment of passionate sex. We were talking about dating. And the kind of dating that leads to marriage."

"Oh please Greystone! Women know men don't do anything but talk about sex when we're not around," Janeshia joked. "Besides, you have had these conversations with Larissa and me before. Don't act so snobbish now," Janeshia joked.

"Janeshia is right. Besides, we are talking about good clean sex and I use a condom always," Larissa giggled.

A reluctant smile appeared around Greystone's mouth. "You two ladies are still lucky I have lunch with you," he said lifting his glass in a toast.

The Three friends laughed together.

Janeshia sat down her glass of wine. "Grey, if we were talking hypothetically, and speaking of a man's character," she shrugged embarrassed, "Which one would you feel had a better character, Walker and Ramsey?"

Larissa put down her wine. "Here…Here Greystone, please tell us, which man would you say was the honorable man for your cousin to have good clean passionate sex with?"

Greystone rubbed his temple. For some reason the image of that question didn't settle well. "If you are asking me to tell you which man is better at sex, you can both forget it. It's not my business and I don't care!"

"I meant character. True character," Janeshia added. "Come on Grey darling cousin. What's your opinion?"

He remembered back to the summers he spent with Walker. "I've known Walker a lot longer than I've known Ramsey," he hesitated. "I've only attended a few meetings with Ramsey." He hoped they didn't sense his lie. "Walker and I shared a lot of growing up. We shared a lot of classes together, for instance we did summer camp together for years and we took a summer engineering program together from middle school through high school," he nodded.

"Oh Really?" Larissa said. "I didn't know that."

Greystone tilted his head. "Oh, I recall Walker and I did meet Ramsey one year at Science Camp. The three of us did a project together," he paused. "To tell the truth, I spent way more time with Walker. I got to know him really well. Because of that I do feel I know him more personally. Walker, I can honestly say is a man of honorable character. His character is the best kind, loyal, steadfast and trustworthy. I would trust him with my wife if I had one," he hesitated and breathed out slowly. "I don't know Ramsey at all in terms of personally knowing his character. That one time at science camp isn't enough time, I think, to really decide that. I do know he is powerful. And he is very knowledgeable and important in his field. In character, I can't say. In importance, power and status, he is revered."

Larissa smiled. "And so a man's good honor defeats duplicity."

Janeshia asked suspiciously. "So, what does that have to do with anything? None of us know the kind of man Ramsey is."

Larissa opened her mouth to object and then thought better of it.

Janeshia interrupted. "Oh never mind Larissa," she muttered. "We'll be at it all day if we let you continue to talk."

Larissa's face registered surprise. "Now wait a minute. Oh I get it," she grinned. "Our girl here wants her cousin to get her some information. And she knows her cousin is the best man to help her out."

Janeshia made a face at her best friend. She turned her attention back to her cousin.

"So Cousin Grey, do you think you could strike up a conversation with Ramsey the next time you see him? I know you can do it," she encouraged him. "You could just mention knowing me. Tell him I'm your cousin. See if he asks for my phone number. Or better yet, just give it to him. What do you say?"

"Yeah Greystone, check out the man's character for lumps, bumps and all other shadiness," Larissa added.

Greystone rubbed his face and chuckled nervously. After several moments he finally replied. "I don't think you should get your hopes up about my seeing Ramsey again, I hardly ever do. In fact, I think you should keep your date with Walker. And I hope it turns into a possibility or at least an adventure."

"Please Grey, do this for me!" Janeshia asked.

"No!" Greystone said firmly.

Janeshia's face registered surprise. "What are you saying?"

Greystone shrugged and looked firmly back at her. "Janeshia, I'm not going out of my way to try and find Ramsey to match make for you. You should know better than to ask me that. You remember what happened the last time I did that?"

Janeshia raised an eyebrow. "No, I don't Grey."

"Oh, I can't believe you sometimes cousin," Greystone murmured."

"I know Brendan and Lynn both still won't talk to Greystone, "Larissa said smugly. "And their divorce was final a couple of years ago." Larissa sadly shook her head. "Janeshia, the attorney in me cannot believe you sometimes. Let this one go."

Chapter 7
Smooth as a.....

Several hours later across town, Adam St Charles smiled back at the woman sitting at the table across from him.

Adam took a deep breath. He was glad he had gone home, showered and changed his clothes. He oozed a suave arrogance in the starched designer jeans he wore. It added to his commanding presence. He was handsome and he knew it. The woman across from him stared openly. He could tell she wanted him to come over and talk to her. But he wasn't interested. He had just paid his bill and was ready to leave.

The crowded restaurant in Westgate Shopping center, off of Stevens Creek, was just the cover he needed. He checked his watch and dialed the number. The phone rang. It rang again.

Adam was about to hang up when a man answered.

"Well I'm waiting" a man's voice bellowed into the phone.

"I've got some news that I know you will want to know about."

"Oh... don't tell me over the phone. I'm upstairs in our regular location. Get up here now!" The Mystery man's voice yelled.

"I'm coming," Adam assured the man.

Adam walked briskly through Macys and headed for the parking tower. He took the stairway and quickly made his way to the third landing. He trotted over to the Black Mercedes and tapped on the window. The doors unlocked and he got inside.

He was out of breath when he got in.

"I wish you wouldn't run like that Adam, you might arouse suspension," the mysterious man said. His foreign face looked back at Adam over the rim of his dark glasses. "At least today you're clad in jeans and not a suit. Taking my advice and dressing down a bit?" He replied without waiting for a response. "I'm glad. I'd much rather believe I'm doing business with a sane, normal, over achiever. Rather than an over hyped, frantic yuppie pup in a suit," he paused. "So what do you have for me?"

Adam St Charles breathed in deep. "I.....I...." He sucked in another breath and wiped his nose with the back of his hand.

"Well go on."

Adam slowly choked out. "It's Janeshia......I think she suspects something. She's got the IT department double checking the computer system every night. Harry Billings, one of the managers in our IT department. He contacts her daily with some sort of updates," he paused. "He's got connections. He came highly recommended by the Systems Branch Incident Command Center. That's the company owned by her cousin Greystone James. Harry gets back to her every day regarding anything strange that comes up over the system." He cleared his throat. "I.....err'...Look, I don't think we should do anything for a while. We don't want to arouse anyone's suspicion."

The man in the dark sunglasses hesitated and tilted his head to stare out of the window. "You are smart Adam. Here is your money," the man said handing him an envelope.

Adam felt the corners of his mouth widen into a smile. The money made him happy. He checked the envelope. It wasn't the full amount.

"Maybe with time you might become a smooth criminal. But not now," he rubbed his chin. "And I agree with you. We'd better stop everything for a while."

"Agreed," Adam replied with a nod.

"Hmmmm." The mystery man rubbed his brow. "And your cover? You made sure it wasn't flimsy? You know Janeshia James is a very smart lady. She could figure this whole scheme out. You have been watching her? Making sure she hasn't caught on?"

Adam shook his head. "Those extra employees I've been paying a salary to never existed on paper. There's no way Janeshia or anyone else can trace them. I made sure of that." He smiled smugly.

The mysterious man chuckled softly. "You are a pretty smart man Adam."

Adam's eyes grew solemn. "I followed her before I came here. She's having lunch right now with Larissa and her cousin Greystone. That's why I feel we should not deposit any more money into the accounts. Not for a while anyway."

A slight accent escaped from the lips of the mysterious man. "Greystone James huh," he replied. "Now there's a smart man. Maybe too smart," he frowned. "Adam, you were right to stop the operation. We don't need to attract notice."

He growled. "Oh and Adam, don't try and contact me anymore. If I need you I'll get a hold of you. We don't want anyone tracking anything back to me."

"What about the rest of my money? The full amount isn't here."

The Mystery man said nothing he just started laughing. "Adam….Adam you haven't completed the job yet." He growled low and reached underneath his seat and pulled out a large brown paper bag. "But here is a little extra. To show you I believe in what we're doing."

Adam took the bag and reached inside. His fingers slid over the bills quickly. "Hmmmm this feels like fifty thousand dollars!"

"Ah that's what I like about you Adam. You can count. I threw in a little extra to keep your mouth closed. Besides, there's much more to come when you finish the job. Right partner," the corners of the mysterious man's lips pulled up into a smile.

"Yeah, right partner," Adam said. "What am I to do next?"

"Just be available when I need you. In the meantime don't draw any unnecessary attention to yourself. Just keep acting normal."

Chapter 8

Old familiar feeling...

Greystone strode into his office and shut the door. He sighed heavily sitting down at his desk. What he thought was going to be a routine lunch date with his cousin and her best friend now troubled him deeply.

The old familiar feeling balled up in his stomach. He hated to feel this way. He knew his cousin Janeshia liked the guy. He could tell by the way her eyes had beamed. He didn't want her blindsided by this guy. Hell, he didn't know a thing about him. Only what he remembered most from that camp that summer. Even his memory was feeble. Ramsey Montgomery was smart. That he did remember. He thought back. His mind drifted.

That night was strange and wild way back then as the group of boys sat by the fire telling ghost stories and trying to scare each other.

The tall lanky boy they called Slick had started the run of

magic tricks. Slick had jet black hair and looked like his father could have been a vampire. He stood up and pulled out a thin wide black blanket. It was odd. When it was his turn he stood up. Some kid did a magic trick instead of telling a ghost story. And that was how it had started.

Greystone remembered that the hairs stood up straight on the back of his neck when Slick did his magic trick.

It started with Slick Dickerson, the tall lanky kid with jet black hair and braces, started doing an eerie trick making his fingers smoke. It was pretty standard stuff if you'd taken chemistry. Even Greystone knew how the trick worked.

When it was Ramsey's turn, that's when stuff got ghostly frightening. A shiver ran through the small group of friends as they sat there watching Ramsey perform his hypnotism routine. The boy that had agreed to be hypnotized was named Isaiah Fifth.

Isaiah Fifth was the husky boy with the freckled face and reddish orange hair had said that night Ramsey Montgomery had hypnotized him, that Greystone would never forget.

After Ramsey had put him under Isaiah told the story of who he really was. Ramsey wanted to show the group of boys that Isaiah was really in a trance. He asked him a series of questions.

"Isaiah can you hear me?" He asked.

"Yes I can," Isaiah said.

"Where are you?" Ramsey walked slowly around him.

"I am where you sent me. I am in the place with the big window." Isaiah said.

"Then go to the room where the Angels stay with the children until they are born," Ramsey commanded.

"I am going." Isaiah's face contorted into a frown as if he was traveling through his mind. His eyes remained closed. "I am there….I am there now."

"Describe the place," Ramsey said.

Isaiah's eyes were still closed as his head tilted toward the sky. "It, it's bright and so full of light, but the light is not blinding. It's just pure and clean."

"Good, now do you see yourself before you were born?"

"Yes, but there is someone standing here beside me Ramsey and he wants to speak to you."

In an instance Isaiah's face twisted before our eyes and rays of light beamed from it. His voice changed from the cracking voice

of a pre-teen and sounded low and authoritative.
"Ramsey......Ramsey....

Ramsey seemed to jump out of his skin from the sound of the
voice. He popped his fingers several times. "Wake up Isaiah....Wake
up."

Some camp counselors told them that it had been just a gag
that Ramsey had performed. They told the kids it had been nothing
but a standard magician performance. But Greystone had always
been amazed at the spiritual coincidence.

Slowly Greystone woke up out of his fog. His logic told him
he should stay out of it. But he remembered the way Janeshia's eyes
sparkled when she asked about him.

If nothing else, he felt he should get to know the guy again.
Better this time. Just in case. He quickly dialed the number. "Hello,
this is Greystone James. I'd like to speak with Mr. Montgomery,
please," he said firmly.

"One moment please," his secretary said.

The line was quickly answered.

"Hi, Ramsey Montgomery is that you? It's Greystone James.
Can you talk?"

A few minutes later, Ramsey couldn't believe his luck. He'd
just learned Greystone was the cousin of that gorgeous woman
named Janeshia he'd recently met. His mind went straight to
Greystone's gorgeous cousin Janeshia. He remembered her well. Her
beautiful smile, striking good looks and superb figure was all he'd
thought about since he'd met her. Now he'd made contact with her
cousin. He thought quickly how to steer the conversation to his
advantage. "Hey Greystone, your company needs some of my
venture capitalist funding?"

"No, I don't need your venture capitalist money," Greystone
replied with a soft chuckle. "I just think we should have lunch
together and catch up. You did ask me before, remember?"
Greystone swirled around in his chair listening attentively.

Ramsey hesitated a few seconds. He didn't want to appear
too eager. "But this weekend is booked solid for me."

Greystone laughed. "I've got to have a life too. I'm not
available this weekend either," he replied.

"What about Monday?" Ramsey asked.

"Okay, you've talked me into it," Greystone said switching
the phone. "I've got just the place. How about that new Steak

Restaurant at Santana Row?"

Ramsey hesitated for a few seconds then switched the phone receiver in his hands. "Yes I love LB'S Steak. Let's say 1:00?"

"That's good for me. I'll see you then," Greystone said swiveling around in his chair and hanging up the line. He hoped he wasn't making an enemy.

Chapter 9
Meet the neighbors…

That Saturday evening Janeshia found herself tensing up as she checked her bedroom clock. In just two hours Walker Edmund Perrault would arrive to pick her up and she hadn't even dressed yet. She still wandered around her bedroom in her bath robe. She pulled the belt tighter and wondered if she could call him and cancel. Maybe it wasn't too late. She eyed her telephone sitting on the night stand and went to reach for it. Slowly she dialed the number and listened as the phone began to ring.

All at once her front door bell rang out loudly. She shrugged and hung up the phone quickly and made her way to the front door. She reached for the handle and opened it before checking the security hole.

Janeshia ushered out a surprised gasp when her eyes registered who was standing there. "I don't believe it. You are two hours early."

Walker Edmund Perrault pushed his way inside holding a huge vase of flowers. "I didn't want to give you the opportunity to cancel our date."

"But I'm not even dressed yet." She hesitated. "And it's not really a date," she said standing there holding her front door wide.

The door across the hall from her's opened abruptly.

She looked up and straight into the curious eyes of her neighbor.

Mrs. Olsten walked over quickly with a curious gaze in her eyes. "Hi Janeshia, you didn't tell me you've been dating a young man. My…My, he is a handsome fellow isn't he? And he's brought you such beautiful roses. Are those violets too?" She giggled winking back at her. "Are you going to marry that young man, Janeshia?"

"Hello Mrs. Olsten." Janeshia loved Mrs. Olsten. She was a sweet old lady that always looked out for her. "Is everything Okay Mrs. Olsten?"

"Don't look now Janeshia, but Mrs. Harvey's door is still ajar. You know Mrs. Harvey thrives on gossip. You'd better get inside with your young fellow." Mrs. Olsten smiled up at her.

Mrs. Olsten looked up at Janeshia and cleared her throat. Her eyes twinkled as she put her finger up to her lips to silence Janeshia. She spoke out in a clear voice. "Mrs. Harvey stop being nosey and leave the young people alone. Besides, if you leave your window too long you might miss Mr. Wong taking his afternoon shower."

All at once Mrs. Harvey's door clicked shut.

Janeshia looked back at Mrs. Olsten and smiled.

"Don't keep your young man waiting Janeshia. Even if it's not a real date, enjoy every moment. You never know. A fake date might turn into a real date right in front of your eyes."

Mrs. Olsten slowly closed her front door.

Janeshia bit her lips and looked back over her shoulder. She was amazed at how much that old woman knew without being told. She caught Walker out of the corner of her eye, standing behind her and watching her.

Walker smiled back at her and took her hand. The gesture was simple but complex.

"Well come on in Walker," she said, yanking her hand away from his, but not before desire shot through her.

Walker had waited patiently to see Janeshia all day. He knew he was early for his date. He gazed down at her tenderly. "These are for you," he said handing her the vase.

It occurred to her how remarkable Walker was in so many ways. He had the kind of spirit she found easy to get along with.

"You might as well have a seat while I get dressed."

The hallway opened into her living room and she placed the vase on the coffee table. "Have a seat Mr. Perrault."

"Please call me Walker." He smiled. "Oh my, what a strikingly beautiful room this is. I can see it holds so much of your wonderful personality. You know Albert Einstein said *to know that which is impenetrable to us really exists, manifesting itself as the highest wisdom and the most radiant beauty. This room is* so beautiful. Just like the woman who created it," he softly smiled.

Janeshia shrugged. Walker always did have an odd formal way of talking. His words seemed to march to a beat all their own.

"Oh, I'll take that as a compliment," she smiled. "Thank you."

Her formal living room was painted in a very soft, elegant, warm, deep gold, with white linen on the crown molding floor base. The formal dining room stood directly at the far end. The formal dining room was divided by a large walkway that led on the left to a great room and gourmet kitchen.

Janeshia had mastered eye catching details that looked elegant, different and expensive.

"That's an interesting coffee table," he said curiously peering down at the hand carved legs with ball and claw feet. "Is that a Chinois figure in the scenery?" Walker asked.

She smiled softly, "Why yes it is."

"I believe they call that a *chow* table. I'm impressed. As a matter of fact we seem to have similar tastes in decor."

"How wonderful I'm sure. Maybe I should take another decorating class," she said with a condescending smile.

"I'd be happy to take a class with you," he suggested.

"That would be fun I'm sure but no....No, thank you," she said abruptly.

He heard the acid tone in her voice and could detect the hint of mockery in her voice. He cleared his throat. "Ah, Ms. James do you have any refreshments?" He asked.

She stared back at him a frown marring her brow. "Excuse me?"

He shrugged and smiled, "I mean a drink; my throat feels a little dry."

"Oh, I'm sorry for not thinking of that. Yes I do. Would you like coke, diet coke, orange juice, I may even have some milk if you like."

Walker shrugged. "Being that I'm kind of nervous and all. I guess asking for something stronger is out of the question?"

"No, I mean yes I do." She shook her head. "Never mind I don't know why I feel I have to explain. Look Walker I have a bottle of port. Well really it's my father's. I mean he brought the bottle over for a family dinner here. Oh never mind," she said walking to get the bottle.

She retrieved the bottle.

Walker smiled. "Will you please join me in a glass?"

Janeshia grabbed two glasses "Okay, but don't say I made us late for dinner."

She watched as Walker poured.

He couldn't take his eyes off of her. "Remember I'm early, so we have plenty of time," he raised his glass. "I'd like to make a toast to the only women I now could have taken on running the foundation and doing it so well. To the sweetest, loveliest woman I know who loves Blue Violets. Here's to you Janeshia."

Their glasses clinked.

The two of them drank, in silence.

Janeshia's eyes glimmered with appreciation as she finished her port. It made her feel warm inside.

Walker filled her glass again.

She gulped down a big swallow and stared back at him. The port was making her feel warm inside. "Thank you for that nice compliment Walker and thank you for the very lovely vase of Blue Violets," she said. Something occurred to her. The Blue Violets someone had left on her car windshield. "So Walker you wouldn't know anything about an array of Blue Violets with a small heart shaped card with no writing, that were left on my car windshield would you?"

Walker's eyes sparkled as he looked back at her. The guilty look was all over his face.

"Explanation please?" She finished her port in one gulp.

Walker poured her another glass.

He glanced back at her through his thick curly lashes. His fiery piercing gaze bore into her. His eyes held hers relentlessly. "Yes, I'm guilty of putting those there," he said caringly. "I asked

Tamara and she said you loved Blue Violets. Once I knew they were your favorite, all I could think of was that they would brighten your day."

She could feel herself losing control. She felt Goosebumps from his honest admission. If he touched her now she didn't know what she would do. She tried not to stare at his lips. It was really getting hard to try keeping things just business between them. Flustered, she said the first thing that popped in her head. She regretted her words before they even got out. "Oh really? How do I know you weren't just staking me?" She went to turn away.

"Hang on a minute. I wasn't stalking you," Walker said as his protective instincts showed in the tone of his voice. It was tender and protective. "I just wanted to make you happy. I didn't mean any harm. I promise. Did it upset you?" He reached out and gently touched her shoulder.

Dangerous emotion crept over her at the feel of his touch. Something warmed in her heart. She could have sworn her heart was murmuring "*rescue me I need your loving.*" She smiled softly with her thoughts. His expression told her he was telling the truth. The man was making it hard for her not to like him more than she already did. Her eyes lingered on his lips. Those lips she had dreamed about.

She looked up at his eyes. What she saw staring back at her wasn't what she expected. She could have sworn it was desire greeting her.

"*Janeshia,*" Walker whispered in a husky voice. He'd wanted to touch her all over. He tried to restrain his hands. He reached out and framed her face with his hands.

The feel of his touch sent shivers down her spine. Maybe it was the glass of port talking but she really wanted to kiss him.

His deep green eyes looked longingly into hers as he gently pressed his lips to hers.

He broke the kiss. "I'm sorry, I couldn't help myself."

She didn't plan it but her fingers reached out and touched his lips.

His arm slid around her bringing her body close. His mouth lowered again slowly until it reached hers. His lips trembled as they came down on hers. Fierce and hungry, she softened to his kiss. She parted her lips wanting more. He pushed his tongue deep into her mouth and her tongue danced with his.

He moaned and came up for air. "Oh Janeshia I knew we

were going to be lovers."

She drew a ragged breathe. "Oh it would be great wouldn't
it?"

Walker kissed her ear. "Do you want to go to your bedroom
or would you like to do it right here? Don't worry your loyalty to the
foundation is safe with me. I won't let our being lovers get in the
way of your position with the foundation," his mouth gave a moan.
"In fact, if our love making puts you in the family way, we just
consider that your position with the foundation is forever. In fact, I'd
consider it a consequence of action."

Janeshia felt something cringe inside of her. "What do you
mean by that remark?" His words broke her out of her trance. She
pulled out of his embrace.

"I'm just saying you already have the job. So what we're
doing now won't complicate things. I won't put this off in the office
gossip grapevine if you won't. We'll just consider this scratching an
itch. Or consider....."

The heat of passion vanished. She felt so ashamed. She
pulled out of his embrace. "Why you arrogant overbearing,
conceited, rude Geek of a man," Janeshia murmured.

"What?"

She took a deep breath. "Walker you are totally out of line?"

"Wait a minute. You wanted me too," his thoughts raced. He
had to fight his instinct to keep from grabbing her and making her
change her mind. "What did I say that was so wrong?"

"I'm not going to sleep with you to keep my job. Maybe you
should leave."

"Look Janeshia, I just don't understand. I didn't......" He
couldn't believe it. He had said something stupid. He'd been so close
to having the woman of his dreams. He couldn't believe he may
have messed up. He studied her. "You think I was serious about
what I just said. I....I....." He didn't want to say something that he'd
regret.

"Look Walker why don't you just leave."

He wanted her. "Leave? Leave? I can't leave. We are
supposed to go to dinner. In fact we are supposed to meet some very
important people tonight," he nodded and hoped she didn't see
through his lie. He hesitated and swallowed hard. "Look, I apologize
for any misunderstanding. I may have gotten off course here. But
tonight is a business dinner, and you will attend. In fact I insist upon

it."

Janeshia fumed. "Oh really? I assume this is another consequence of action?"

Her response provoked his rage. He intended to teach her a lesson. "Yes, it is! So go and get dressed!"

Chapter 10
My Favorite Geek....

A half hour later Janeshia returned wearing her favorite black studded hip fitting tunic and jet black jeans. She carried her lambskin black leather jacket with the full faux fur collar.

"You look stunning. And that jacket will keep you warm," Walker smiled. "It's a good thing too, because we're headed towards San Francisco."

A few minutes later they drove away from her building. Janeshia sat in silence.

"Where did you say we were going?"

"I didn't." Walker shrugged. But sensing her tension he said quickly. "We're having dinner at Kingfish. It's a favorite restaurant of mine."

Janeshia turned her head and studied Walker.

The only thing Janeshia knew well about Walker Edward

Edmond-Perreault was that he was the son of a wealthy family of influential people who held a longtime commitment and a sponsorship relationship with the foundation that she worked for. He was highly intelligent and a bit pompous at times. He was a man who was accustomed to being in charge and giving others instructions. Other than that she really didn't know him.

Sitting in the car so intimately close to him gave her the chance to see him from a different angle.

Janeshia pretended to look at the speedometer to check his driving. She coughed softly and turned her head to study him.

In the dim light of the car she could study him as lights bounced back from the headlights of cars passing by gave her a chance to catch the shadows of his prominent high cheek bones. In the dim light of night he looked remarkably like the late actor Gregory Peck.

She thought back on the many meetings they had together. It wasn't hard to remember them. She could see him clearly. He was a handsome man and a man she remembered who could be fair and just. Sometimes to a fault. She hated to admit it, but she almost thought that he seemed sexy in the moonlight.

One thing Janeshia thought was a fact. Walker didn't look at all like someone who would enjoy Kingfish. Maybe he wasn't the stick in the mud kind of guy she thought he was.

Her eyes darted quickly at the speedometer again and then back at him.

All at once Walker reached out his hand and caressed hers softly. His touch felt sweet, yet erotic.

"Am I driving safe enough for you?" He asked tenderly. "Or are you just having a sweet dream that is yours alone?"

Janeshia froze instantly. She wasn't sure if it was from the warmth of his touch or how close he came to reading her thoughts.

Walker cleared his throat softly. "We're almost there. Is the car warm enough for you?"

She drew in her breath. "Yes."

Janeshia didn't speak again until they turned off highway 101 in San Mateo. Walker took West 3rd Avenue.

They pulled into the restaurant's parking lot and found a space. Walker got out of the car and held the door open for her. His polite gesture made her smile.

They entered the restaurant and were led toward the stairs.

The room was crowded.

"Walker, if you don't mind, I'll just go to the ladies room. I'll only be a minute." Janeshia smiled.

"Of course, I'll wait for you."

Janeshia quickly made her way to the ladies room. She walked to the mirror and stood gazing at herself. She looked at the black studded top. Her gold dangle tear drop earrings sparkling and glistening back at her made her heart shaped face appear elegant and classic. She turned around quickly and almost collided with a young woman. Once Janeshia looked closer the woman wasn't as young as she thought. Her titian colored hair framed her face like it had been carefully and masterfully done so to achieve the most flattering effect. A huge diamond ring sat on her left hand. Its brilliant light glistened off of the ceiling light fixture. The woman was older, much older than she appeared. She was dressed in a form fitting dress that accented her every curve.

The woman stared back at Janeshia. "Oh Miss, is that Walker Edmond-Perreault with you?"

Janeshia paused and steadied her gaze. The woman had to be over six feet tall. "Have we met before?"

The woman and Janeshia exchanged a look.

Janeshia turned away. She didn't want to appear rude. She pretended to need to fix her face.

"No I don't believe we have," she smiled. "My name is Elizabeth Desmond."

Janeshia noticed the points that reached eye level. She cleared her throat. "Hello Elizabeth, I'm Janeshia."

The moment seemed awkward.

All at once Elizabeth looked at Janeshia and said, "Honey don't let these magic bullets scare you. They're just breasts. I come by them naturally. I was born with them." She smiled easily. "You know it's hard on a woman with big breasts not to be stared at. If it wasn't for the natural valley of my breast a lot of folks would just think that I was a cross dressing man." She laughed out. "Oh, go ahead and have a laugh at my expense. This is the part where most folks do," Elizabeth said. "I would if I were you."

The moment felt tense. Nervously Janeshia cleared her throat. "Is Walker a friend of yours?" She asked.

"Yes and no. You see," Elizabeth mused. "I know Walker's mother well. You're the woman in the photo with Walker? I'd know that face anywhere Janeshia James, you look exactly like yourself."

"I'll take that as a compliment," Janeshia said.

"You know each year Walker's mom shows the Gala Event photos to our luncheon group." Elizabeth patted her hair in place. Her voice oozed a cool admiration. "I'll say this for you, you've got skills on how to date and get a rich man. You should give lessons."

Janeshia's mouth went dry. "I beg your pardon?"

"Oh I didn't mean any offense," Elizabeth said softly. "I was just wondering how long the two of you have been dating?"

"I'm sorry but whatever gave you the idea Walker and I were dating?"

A puzzled look crossed Elizabeth's brow. "You're not here on a date with Walker?"

Janeshia winced. "No, we're not on a date."

Elizabeth coolly smiled "How very fortunate for me, please understand, nothing that happens from this moment on is personal."

"I don't get your meaning."

"Believe me sister you will," Elizabeth said firmly as she brushed past. Her pungent fragrance rose up between them like a shield of armor on a knight in battle.

Janeshia took a step back.

Elizabeth laughed coarsely as she walked out of the door. She stopped and turned her head. "Oh by the way Janeshia, it was very nice meeting you."

Janeshia breathed out slowly wondering what all of that had been about.

Her brief encounter with the woman named Elizabeth wouldn't darken her mood.

A few minutes later she returned to join Walker. He was standing at the bar. He grabbed her hand and placed a drink in it. "Janeshia I hope you don't mind. I ordered an N'Awlin's Hurricane for you. I thought after that long ride you could use a drink."

The warm touch of Walker's hand felt good. "Yes, thanks," she said lifting her glass and taking a sip. The drink felt good on her dry throat. She licked her lips. "So what did you order for yourself?"

He grinned. "I'm just having a Weed Wacker. It's a house specialty. We can still order wine with our dinner."

She turned and studied the décor. The walls held a large collection of authentic Louisiana folk art. She found them interesting.

She took another sip of her drink. "Walker, can I ask you something?"

"Sure."

"Do you know a lot of people in this area? I mean, do you come to this restaurant often?"

He sipped at his drink. "I did grow up not too far from here; my mother has several good friends who frequent this restaurant. Why do you ask?"

"Oh no reason," she murmured taking another sip of her drink and realized how little she really knew about Walker.

Walker watched her take another sip of her drink. He needed to touch her badly. "Our hostess is ready to seat us now, Janeshia. Come," he said taking her hand and placing it on his arm.

The feel of his hand touching hers sent a shock wave through her system.

Their alert hostess noticed her eyes as she seated them. Their table was located right next to a cozy fireplace.

Candlelight added to the ambient experience. Soft music filled the air. The sitting arrangement forced Janeshia to sit closer to Walker.

Janeshia stared around the room. It was very cozy and inviting and made her smile.

The two of them never spoke.

Their waiter came by and took their orders.

Janeshia ordered the Jambalaya with a hot tea and lemon to warm her up.

She watched attentively as Walker's lips moved when he ordered the Braised Short Rib Gumbo with a bottle of Sonoma Coast Pinot Noir. His lower lip was larger than his top. She'd never noticed before how sensual his lips looked.

The drinks arrived quickly.

Janeshia breathed out as she sipped the warm tea. She looked around herself and loved the warm romantic feel of the place. The setting was warm and inviting as she slowly sipped her tea and became relaxed and comfortable.

The whole event was not lending itself to be a business dinner.

Walker slowly sipped his wine and smiled softly watching her. He thought she was the most beautiful woman he'd ever known.

Janeshia watched him lick his lips as he took the first sip of his wine. The movement was so sensual and powerful that her heart skipped a beat. For some reason her eyes seemed to linger too long watching Walker sip his wine. She loved the way his lips moved.

He smiled softly looking at her. "You seem to be enjoying your tea. You know, watching you sip it is making me jealous."

Janeshia cleared her throat. She felt it was her duty to keep the business dinner on track. All at once she blurted. "Did you bring the reports with you? The ones you wanted me to review?"

Walker rubbed his brow. "Oh the reports, I have them. But I believe I left them in their folder in the car. I'll give them to you when we finish dinner.

Janeshia raised an eyebrow. It was just as she thought. Walker didn't have any reports with him. She quickly shook out her thoughts and brought her mind out of the fog she'd been under.

Just then dinner arrived.   Janeshia stared at the plate of food placed before her. The aroma was exquisite…the smell reminded her of summers when she'd go back home and her family ate together at New Orleans' famous *Acme Oyster House*. Janeshia closed her eyes to reminisce. The whole experience was taking her back. She was happy and deep into her thoughts when she heard Walker say.

"I see you're enjoying your food. I hope everything is to your liking?"

Janeshia took another bite. The taste was exquisite. Her eye lashes fluttered and her eyes danced enjoying the burst of flavors on her tongue.

Slowly she cleared her throat. "The food is great. I'm impressed."

"You're shocked that I choose such a place?"

Janeshia's eyes glittered back at him. "Amazed!" She paused pushing her hair out of her face. "I didn't know you like Creole and Cajun food."

"We have a lot in common," he assured her.

"How would you know what I have in common with you Walker?" You don't know anything about me."

Walker cleared his throat, "Your family is Creole. So….I have been told."

"Been told?" She gulped and pulled back. His comment

irritated her. She could feel her temper rising. She kept her eyes steady as she looked back at him. "We don't have any friends or associates that I am aware of. And I hope you haven't been asking my employees, about me."

"Look that's not the case." He glanced at her. The moment wasn't going like he'd planned. He cleared his throat. "You know, you and I both work a great amount of time. Neither of us make time to have much of a social life. I was just remarking that we seemed to be having a good time and that's a good thing. Don't you think?"

Janeshia grew quiet and just kept eating. She didn't want to admit that he was right.

He could tell her mood had changed swiftly. All that he'd ever hoped for was to not have just a working relationship with her. Things had been going real well. "I hope you don't sit there in silence all night. I didn't mean to upset you.

She continued to ignore him. She took another bite of her food and stared around the room.

Walker inclined his head and smiled back at her. "Let's start over. I didn't bring you here to match egos."

"I beg your pardon," she said with a mouth full of food.

"Ok maybe that didn't come out right. But you shouldn't talk with your mouth full." He smiled amused.

"You're not the boss of me at dinner Walker." She opened her mouth wide and chewed then smirked with a glance. She knew she was being rude but just couldn't seem to help herself.

All at once a woman's sexy throaty seductive voice sliced the air. "Why hello Walker Perrault. My you look handsome tonight."

Janeshia and Walker choked on their food in unison.

"Walker it's so good to see you." Elizabeth's voice oozed out with sexual tension. She flashed him a dangerous smile that would have melted any man.

Janeshia stole a glance at Elizabeth. Elizabeth's gaze was fixed on Walker's face.

"Elizabeth, what a surprise to see you!" Walker exclaimed with a hint of desperation. He sighed heavily, "Funny meeting you here. I haven't seen you in a long time."

Janeshia looked on curiously.

Walker nervously cleared his throat. "I'm here with a date. Elizabeth this is Janeshia James. Isn't she very beautiful? He didn't wait for her to answer. "Janeshia James this is Elizabeth Desmond, a very good friend of my mother's."

"Janeshia and I met earlier," Elizabeth replied coolly.
Walker smiled uneasily and glanced between the two
women.

Elizabeth Desmond swayed over and pulled up an empty
chair and sat closer to Walker. She leaned her elbow on the table and
leaned in real close. "Walker, from my understanding, Janeshia tells
me the two of you are not here on a date," she blurted out.

Walker breathed out, "Elizabeth don't you have someone
else to bother?"

Elizabeth Desmond leaned forward making sure Walker
noticed her overflowing cleavage. "No not really Walker. You see
you're my favorite Geek," she sensually cooed.

Janeshia averted her eyes from Walker's and looked up at
Elizabeth in surprise. Her throat felt dry. Now she knew what
Elizabeth had meant. The woman was openly flirting with Walker in
front of her.

The moment was awkward with silence.

Janeshia looked up at Walker. "Walker maybe you two
would like to be left alone?"

"Christ no!" Walker exclaimed. "Janeshia, please don't leave
me alone with this woman. This isn't what you think it is."

A quick laugh broke from Elizabeth. She flashed a wide
wicked white grin. "Well now, of course Walker and I would like to
be left alone. How thoughtful of you Janeshia. See, I knew you were
a very understanding person when I met you earlier."

Walker didn't want to be rude. "Listen Elizabeth, maybe you
misunderstood. I'm having dinner with Janeshia. Haven't you ever
heard that two's company and three...." His annoyance evident.
"Well let's just say we don't need you to tag alone."

Janeshia was on the verge of saying something but closed her
mouth watching Elizabeth openly ogle Walker.

Elizabeth provokingly fluttered her eyelashes. She leaned
closer to Walker. Her gaze lingered on his lips. "Oh Walker don't
you know I just love it when you get angry. It makes me hot all
over," she licked her lips.

Walker was openly annoyed and embarrassed.

Janeshia smirked out a laugh watching Walker squirm.

"So Walker are you up for some instant action tonight?
This woman is available now or right after dinner if you like."

"No Elizabeth that is out of the question." He turned his eyes. "Can't you see I'm having dinner with Janeshia? This is so disrespectful of you."

"I don't like the way that this is being handled but I really don't care, Walker," Janeshia said drumming her fingers on the table.

Elizabeth burst into a raucous chuckle. "You see, Janeshia understands and besides she doesn't care. Come on now Walker, let's just call her a cab and make sure she gets home safely?"

"Again the answer is no Elizabeth!" Walker declared with a murderous intent in his eye.

"Oh come on Walker please. I'll make it worth your while," Elizabeth pleaded.

The moment was tense.

"For Christ sake woman the man said no!" A man's voice coldly sliced the air.

Elizabeth's grin died quickly. Fear took its place.

Walker looked up quickly. A wide surprised smile spread across his face. "Pierce Abram! It's so wonderful to see you again."

Pierce Abram was a tall man, with a commanding presence and a pleasing face with soft blue eyes that crinkled in the corners as he closed the distance between them.

"Walker," Pierce said as the corners of his mouth etched with deep laugh lines. "I thought I saw you coming in earlier. I knew it was you when Elizabeth never returned to finish that drink she was having with me. She never could resist you," he said pulling Elizabeth to her feet.

Apprehensively Elizabeth said. "Pierce darling I was just on my way back."

"Yeah, I know darling. I know how hard it is for you to find your way back so I figured I'd just come and get you," Pierce shrugged. "By the way Walker, that's a real beautiful lady you're dining with tonight."

Pierce Abram glanced over at Janeshia and smiled. "And she has class and manners. I love that in a woman."

Elizabeth Desmond hung her head in silence.

"Pierce Abram this is Janeshia James," Walker said making introductions.

The two men nodded agreement at each other.

Pierce Abram smiled again and with his free arm gave

Walker a soft mocking punch. "Whew! I might sound ridiculous for saying it again but your date is really something special. She's beautiful."

"Well thank you," Walker smiled and grinned back at Janeshia. "I really think she is special too," he said, as he reached across the table and took her hand.

Walker's remarks caught her off guard. But his touch made her feel something deep inside stir. Her thoughts raced. She smiled back at him.

"I can see you two would like to be alone Walker. Elizabeth and I will get back to that drink we were having. Won't we Elizabeth darling?" Pierce held Elizabeth's hand firmly and pulled her along beside him.

Elizabeth turned around slowly and looked over her shoulder. Her hips swayed seductively as she walked away.

Women like Elizabeth Desmond made her sick.

Janeshia stared back at Walker.

They were both silent.

Walker winked at her. "Thank goodness she's gone."

Janeshia managed a smile and shook her head. "Walker I never knew you were such a magnet for the ladies."

"That makes two of us." Walker said chuckling lightly.

"Well, I hope you don't mind it if I don't like her?" Janeshia said.

"Nope darling, I wouldn't mind at all. In fact, let's drink a toast to not liking Elizabeth Desmond," he said raising his wine glass in a mock toast.

"She kind of ruined the evening," Janeshia said cautiously.

Walker sipped his wine slowly. The lines on his forehead sat into a sad line. "Yes she did," he shook his head sadly. "I had plans to wine, dine and woo you with my charming delightful personality and then Elizabeth Desmond shows up and ruins the whole spirit of the evening.

Janeshia opened her mouth to say something then abruptly closed it. For some reason it bothered her to see him so down. She thought back remembering something her father said to her when she'd been disappointed on her first date. *We have to accept things we can't change. Sometimes it is not wise to fight with fate.*

"Don't you think life has a pattern?" She hesitated. "I mean I heard that things happen that we have no control over and that we just have to accept that it was fate."

Walker turned and gazed at her. He reached out and touched her hand.

Her fingers tensed from his touch.

"I'm sorry tonight's evening didn't go as you planned," he said. "Come on Janeshia, I'll take you home. You and I both have had a great shock this evening. Dealing with Elizabeth Desmond has been known to put a few people in the hospital. Thank God Pierce Abram's saved us when he did."

Chapter 11

Romance underfoot…...

That Sunday morning time seemed to move slowly as Janeshia stood staring out of her large balcony patio window. Her brow lifted in interest as a warm breeze blew back the curtain. She reached out her arm and pulled the patio door closed.

She occupied the tenth floor of a spacious North San Jose high rise. It afforded her some of the best views of the mountain range of Mount Hamilton.

Janeshia turned around and surveyed the room. She stood with her head bent to the side admiring her home. The large luxurious condo reflected her likes. The room was beautiful. Rich warm tans, ivory and creams were graceful and charming to lookup on.

"Larissa did you know this rug is called romance underfoot?"

Larissa shrugged not paying her any attention. "Yes, you've told me that a hundred times, if not more," she said flipping through a magazine.

Janeshia smiled softly as she looked down at the extra-large wool rug. The floral scrolls in warm soft gold, ivory and tan looked like something romantic. The rug set the flow of the room. It lay beneath a Black lacquer, hand carved Chinois figure coffee table. The table was framed between a large ivory overstuffed and cushioned sofa that was flanked by two Ascot chairs in a soft pearl gold color with black throw pillows. Her formal dining stood directly at the far end of the room. An extra-long black lacquer and glass dining hutch divided the room. An ivory gold and metal crashing wave sculpture hung in six divided pieces above the hutch.

The room felt exquisitely serene, sophisticated, glamorous and romantic, she thought.

Larissa closed the magazine. "Well, how did your date go with Walker?" What did he want?"

"I couldn't say for sure but I think he wanted some woman named Elizabeth Desmond or rather Elizabeth wanted Walker."

"So Janeshia are you telling me Walker is a babe magnet?" Larissa sat her coffee cup down on the Chinois figure coffee table. "Hmmmm from the look of that frown on your face, he must have wanted this Elizabeth woman bad."

Janeshia sat on the floor in her favorite spot by the Chinois figure coffee table. "Ah….No well what I didn't tell you was that before we left my condo. Walker sort of made a pass at me."

Larissa mischievously smiled. "What, did the Geek King squeeze your hand or did he try to kiss you?"

Janeshia stiffened as her friend gazed back at her. "It was more than that; we both had been drinking some of that port my dad left here. Maybe I had too much. I sort of kissed him," she said as her eyes glazed over. "But none of that matters. Like I said at the restaurant that woman named Elizabeth practically threw herself at him. And she was just so rude and forceful about it."

Larissa looked up and studied her friend. "If you sort of kissed him it sounds like you've got some hot-to-trot, well, hidden feelings for Walker. That needs to be scratched. If you know what I mean," she paused. "You know you've always been such a romantic, believing in all that fairy tale jazz. All it took to show you that you really like Walker was to see Elizabeth trying to take your man."

"Oh come off of it Larissa. That is not what I said. I knew you would put your own spin on things. You always take things out of context."

"Hmmmm, I don't have to take anything out of context. Just

watching you sitting on the floor rubbing your hands ever so gently across a rug called *romance* and smiling gave you away."

"Who told you this rug was called romance?"

Larissa shook her head. "You forget Janeshia I was with you when you bought it," she took a sip of her coffee. "You know what I've been thinking?"

"No, what?" Janeshia asked

"Oh, that maybe you should have had yourself one hot and spicy dinner entrée," Larissa emphasized. "Spicy hot in fact."

Puzzled, Janesha gazed back at her friend.

"I'm not talking about spicy food. I'm talking about you're going to bed with Walker," she shook her head. "The next time you go out with him and if he really doesn't mean anything to you; then just sleep with him and get him out of your system. But if you do sleep with him and you can't get him out of your system, try marrying the guy. It would stop him from ever coming down to your job and brothering you again!"

Frustrated Janeshia gritted her teeth and stared back at her friend. "Larissa, how did we get from talking about how weird my dinner date was with Walker to you're talking about Walker and me getting married?" She rubbed her brow. "Anyway Walker is a dead issue. I don't date my employer."

Larissa chose her words carefully. "So then who are you going to date? You don't have any other prospects. You haven't heard from Ramsey have you?"

Janeshia looked up at her friend in surprise. "Well, not yet anyway. "But I should have a date with Ramsey soon."

"Really? Did he call you?" Larissa walked over and sat on the floor by her friend.

"He sort of called. He left a message with Tamara, telling her to let me know that he called."

Larissa curiously looked on. "So did he leave his number?"

No….No he didn't leave his number. He told Tamara to tell me he would call again soon."

Larissa laughed shaking her head. "Get real Janeshia! He didn't leave a number you won't be having a date!"

Larissa laughed again.

Chapter 12

Spoiling Lunch...

That Monday at a half past noon, Adam St. Charles
nervously walked past the restaurant and peeked in. His eyes eagerly
scanned the window. Finally his eyes found the object it searched
for. Janeshia sat slowly eating her meal. He smiled thinking how
beautiful she looked. He noticed she was reading. Quietly and
cautiously he walked in and approached her table.

"Do you mind if I join you for lunch? I'm buying of course,"
he murmured.

Janeshia glanced up. Adam's new suit caught her eye. He
smiled softly back at her. Today his mood didn't seem hostile.
Maybe he was just there to have lunch. "Oh hi Adam, sure you can
join me. But you don't have to buy lunch."

Adam sat down quickly and looked over the menu.

Their waiter quickly came over.

"I'll have what she's having," Adam said. "But substitute the
chicken for salmon, please."

Janeshia smiled as their waiter walked away. "I should have

ordered the salmon. I order chicken all the time."

"Salmon is my favorite. Next to a good steak," he said.

"Oh, by the way, I've been meaning to tell you I like the new suit," Janeshia smiled.

Adam's eyes warmed brightly. "Thank you." He hesitated and felt the need to explain. "I caught a great sale at Macy's."

"That's great. I love the sales at Macy's," she said taking a sip of her water.

A few minutes later the waiter quickly returned with Adam's food.

The silence drifted between them as they ate.

Janeshia felt the need to speak. "How's the financial report on the After School Tutoring program coming along?"

"Great," Adam said taking another bite of food. "The numbers are on target."

"I knew they would be," Janeshia quickly assessed Adams mood. She knew Adam St. Charles helped take care of his younger brother and sister. His sister was in her second year of college. "How is your sister coming along at college? Don't forget to make sure she sends in her yearly status report. We do want her to keep getting her scholarship monies."

He burst into a wide grin. His conversation wasn't going the way he wanted. He definitely didn't want to talk about a pretend sister he made up. "She's doing great," he grinned. He hoped his lie would never be discovered. He cleared his throat and lied again. "She really appreciates that scholarship. So do I….."

Adam didn't want to get off the subject of why he was having lunch today. His mood shifted. He smiled softly. "Look, I really didn't come here to discuss my sister's college tuition. How long are you going to make me wait before you give me details about the dinner meeting you had with Walker the other night?"

Janeshia tried to ignore him.

Adam took the offensive. "By going out to dinner with Mr. Perrault you've basically put an end to your privacy," he picked at the food on his plate. "You know there is a rumor going around the office that you have a crush on him, but that he's really just putting up an act so that he can keep you running the foundation successfully?"

Janeshia felt a faint heat heighten her cheeks. If he was trying to annoy her he was succeeding. She shrugged her shoulders. "And

Adam are you the someone whose going around spreading gossip?"

Adam laughed out a nervous denial. His dark eyes held a menacing expression. "No….No, I refuse to participate in idle office chit chat. Besides I didn't over hear this information at work. I observed it." He kept his eyes on hers. "I saw how you looked at him at the office. So how long have you had a crush thing on Walker?"

Janeshia looked at Adam. She felt an uneasy sense of fury building. "You are way off base Adam."

"Am I? I figure I need to know how you are being perceived by some people in the office. You do want to know? Or do you care that your mannerisms are interfering with your working relationship in the office?"

Janeshia stared back at Adam. Sometimes he made her feel like a piece of meat and not a person. "Look Adam, my personal life or crushes are none of your business."

"You know some folks are referring to you as being Walker's private little outlet," he paused. "So are you still telling me there is nothing going on besides business between you and Walker Perrault?" Adam's thoughts raged. *"Or is he getting some overtime in the sheets?"*

Janesha took a sip of water and tried her best to ignore him and hold her tongue. Adam St. Charles was annoying, but he was good at his job. She didn't want to think about the delay it would cause if she had to begin interviewing for someone knew to do his job. They sat in silence several moments.

"So Janeshia aren't you the least bit concerned about what I heard? Don't you want to know who said it?"

"No Adam, I don't want to know who said it," she disarmed him with her expression. "I've had enough of office gossip. Besides, you're spoiling my lunch."

Adam went to open his mouth.

Janeshia interrupted abruptly. She rose. "Oh, Adam I've changed my mind. You should buy me lunch," she said standing throwing her napkin on the table and rudely taking her leave.

"But Janeshia……Ms. James!" Adam called after her in vain.

Adam meekly sat back in his chair. Jealousy tormented him.

"Bitch," he muttered viciously under his breath when he knew she was safely out of distance.

Chapter 13
Roses will make you spellbound...

Janeshia walked out of her way going back to her office. The forty five minutes allowed her a chance to work off a couple of calories and burn off some stream. At almost two o'clock she returned to her office. She acknowledged Tamara's presence before closing her office door. She sat perched in her chair gazing out of the window when a knock sounded on her door.

Tamara opened the door. "An urgent package just arrived for you express." She smiled tilting her head at the oriental vase she held in her hands. "This sure cheered me up. It looks expensive."

A black silver leaf fishtail vase was decorated in an intricate art deco design held an arrangement of white zinnia and blue periwinkles. The arrangement sent a bold message. Someone wanted to be Janeshia's friend.

Janeshia and Tamara looked at each other.

"Who are those from?" Janeshia asked.

"Beats me, unless you want me to read the card?"

"No, I can do it myself. Tamara please put them on my desk."

She waited until Tamara closed her door before reading the card.

Dearest Janeshia, "I will always feel you were a friend that was brought to me by angels. I still want to have lunch and talk. I want you to know that I believe you. Lately I have been remembering a lot of what happened in the past. And it made me thoughtful.

The other day I was reading Edgar Allan Poe's Stanza. The one that says, "Of what in other worlds shall be –and giv'n In beauty by our God, to those alone Who otherwise fall from life and Heav'n." And it made me think of something that you once said.

Janeshia you once told me. "Which of us have known with pure heart what happens in our brother's nightmares? For that which happens late in the night springs forth as truths in the glow of daylight?"

When you spoke then I didn't understand. But now I do. What you meant was that what one person sees is often seen by other persons as plain old lies. I say this now because now I do understand. I now see how what you said fits so true to life. Especially what you said about Sheba, I believe you now.

Please call me. You have my number. I hope you like the flowers. I wanted to get your favorite blue violets. But the lady at the flower shop assured me blue periwinkle were the way to rekindle an old friendship. Your devoted Best Friend Alice

Janeshia laid the card on her desk and grunted out in anguish. She shook her head trying to clear her thoughts. She didn't want to think about that. Sad raw energy shot through her. She trembled as the old memories flashed through her mind. She closed her eyes tight summoning the old memories to fade. She felt the coldness settle into the pit of her stomach as a tear rolled down her face.

Moments later, a heavy knock drew her attention. Things couldn't get any worst today she thought.

Her door opened without warning and Tamara rushed in frantically pushing the door behind her, bolting it with her body. "I beg your pardon Ms. James, I tried to tell Mr. Perrault you were busy but he won't take no for an answer."

Walker Perrault pushed past Tamara. "Like I told you Tamara, Janeshia and I have an appointment. She's expecting me." His face turned into a frown at the anguish he saw on Janeshia's face.

Tamara looked puzzled. "Janeshia are you alright? You don't look so good."

Walker watched the sadness in Janeshia's eyes. Her vulnerability overwhelmed him. Her eyes didn't hold their usual sparkle. He stood spellbound, torn by the desire to pull her into his arms and comfort her. A familiar sense of sadness gripped his heart. He hated to see her this way.

"Yes.....Yes of course I'm fine. Walker is right. We did have a meeting. I almost forgot. You may go Tamara. I'll call you if we need anything." Janeshia quickly composed herself.

Walker pulled a chair closer to where Janeshia sat. He took a tissue from the box on her desk and gently wiped the tears on her face. "I hate to see you so unhappy Janeshia. If you need to cancel today's meeting I will understand," he said tenderly.

Janeshia's eyes locked with his. She wondered if he was whispering something. She shook her head, trying to clear her thoughts.

His voice came in clearer. She heard him say, "If you need a shoulder to cry on or a listening ear, I'm a great listener."

The last thing she needed was to have a relationship with her boss. Especially a boss she found very attractive and caring. "No, I'm okay, thanks. Let's go over those reports," she smiled wryly and quickly regained her equanimity.

For the next hour and a half Janeshia and Walker sat talking about the business of *Silicon Valley Making a Difference Foundation*.

Their time together today had been remarkably productive.

Janeshia quickly recapped their discussion. "Well Walker I've noted the changes you want on the end of the year reports. I'll make sure they get included," she said.

Walker had been pacing around the room. All at once he returned to his seat and pulled his chair closer. With warm eager eyes he gazed at Janeshia's face.

With his eyes on hers Janeshia's gaze locked with his. She wondered idly what it would be like to kiss his lips.

Walker leaned in closer. Heat flickered brightly in his eyes. His lips curved in a warm smile. "Are you feeling better now Janeshia? I love it when you look happy," he said. "Please promise me that if anyone upsets you again you will let me know about it? I want you to know I am here to help you in any way that I can."

She swallowed hard and breathed deep. "All right," she said as her pencil trembled in her fingers.

His hand captured her trembling fingers.

The warm feel of his touch overwhelmed her. She became aware of a heat building inside. She liked his touch very much. Her mind seemed like it was in a fog. She wondered why strange things seemed to be happening whenever she was around Walker.

Walker leaned closer. His mouth paused right in front of her. He wanted her.

Janeshia hadn't expected this. She thought he was going to kiss her. "Oh my God! Look at the time," she said quickly regaining her equanimity. Nervously she rose and strutted toward her office door.

Reluctantly Walker followed behind her.

Janeshia paused to open her door and held it wide for him.

He smiled smugly noting she was ending their meeting. He quickly stated. "When I pick you up this Saturday I'll try not to be late or too early."

"What?"

"I'll try not to be on time," he said.

"What do you mean, early?"

"Remember early, at the beginning of our meeting I mentioned it, and you shook your head in agreement. Didn't you hear what I said?"

She didn't want him to know she hadn't been listening to a word that he said. "Yes....Yes, I remember," she lied.

"Good, then I shall pick you up Saturday; let's say 6:00 o'clock."

Chapter 14

A powerful presence…

Ramsey Montgomery steered his black Jaguar into the parking garage. He found where Janeshia's car was parked. Her black raven Cadillac CTS made him smile. She loved black cars, so did he.

Ten minutes later, Ramsey made his way into the building lobby. He was a man of confidence. A man accustomed to people being in awe of his powerful presence. He was smooth and easy going; perfectly at ease and in complete control in any situation. There was a quality to his being that dominated his presence. It sent a message of power that people were drawn to. He relished in the power manipulating others gave him. He knew he was superior in intelligence to anyone. He was a genius. His eyes quickly glanced at the gentlemen's name tag. He'd remembered where he'd seen the name before, at the security intelligence conference on homeland security held last year in San Francisco California.

Ramsey prided himself on his photographic memory and his powerful presence. Some people thought he was arrogant. But it was just this lethal combination; when applied with a head for business, which made him a man capable of getting others to do his bidding. Handling the elderly gentleman sitting behind the security desk would be easy. Then he smiled the smile that he knew got results. "Forgive me for interrupting Mr. Joseph. I believe I met you before at the conference on homeland security. I'm impressed with your security software."

Joel Joseph grinned wide. "Well I'll be, Ramsey Montgomery; you're a sight for these old eyes of mine. What brings you around here?"

A half hour later, Joel glanced up at the symbol on the door. It was the right door.

The sudden knocking on the conference room door broke the quietness of the moment.

"Yes."

The door quickly opened. "Hi Ms. James, I hope I'm not interrupting you?"

Janeshia swiveled in her chair. "Hello Joel. How are you this evening?"

Joel Joseph was the head of security for their building. His smiling brown eyes beamed back at her through black framed glasses. His heavily coffee stained teeth formed into a grin. "I have a gentleman here who says he's a close friend of yours. He insisted I bring him up to you. I hope you don't mind."

Joel stepped aside and Ramsey Montgomery stood in the threshold. She noticed he was only a few inches taller than Joel. His cool eyes studied her. Their gazes connected.

She sucked in a deep breath and rose. "Ramsey? How on earth did you know where to find me?"

Ramsey nodded his head. He quickly walked over and extended his hand in greeting. His other hand held a pink bakers box. "Good evening Janeshia. I apologize for barging in unannounced like this. My flight just arrived a little under an hour ago. I drove past your building and hoped you were working late. I hope you don't mind my dropping by like this." He eagerly extended his hand as he explained.

The moment was awkward.

When she didn't respond he shook his head. "Please don't

get the wrong impression. I'm not stalking you. I just really hoped you were like me, working late. I don't want to make you uncomfortable."

Janeshia's pulse raced. Quickly she grabbed his hand in greeting. "No, of course I wouldn't think that," she exclaimed with breathless surprise. She held his hand longer than she should have. She was aware of the warm sensations of his touch. She didn't want him to see how glad she was that he had found her. She finally let go of his hand.

Her eyes sparked as he gazed back at her.

Joel nodded approvingly glancing between them. "Well, now that we've established that Mr. Montgomery is not a stalker, I should be getting back to my desk. Security in this building is my number one priority. I don't want to leave the closed circuit security monitors unmanned for too long," he said.

"Yes, you do that Joel," Janeshia said without taking her eyes off Ramsey.

"So how are you this evening?" Ramsey asked.

"I'm fine." She said smiling like the cat that just caught the mouse.

Ramsey looked back at her with interest. "Oh by the way, these are for you. I didn't know which one was your favorite. So I had the baker mix up something he calls a *Lady's Delight*," he said handing her the pink bakery box. "I brought napkins too."

Janeshia sat the box on the conference table. Her nimble fingers untied the string and opened the box. "Wow, I see two sugar cookies, two Fudge Brownies, two oatmeal raisin cookies, two lemon squares, two shortbread cookies, two Snicker doodles and two Macadamia Nut Chocolate chip cookies," she smiled. "You've made sure you covered everything a girl could love."

"I love fresh baked cookies myself," he said licking his lips. "As a matter of fact the smell coming from that box has been making my mouth water."

The man looked sexy and charming licking his lips. Janeshia nervously bit her lip as she stared at him.

"Well, aren't you going to offer me a cookie?" He playfully asked.

She offered the box to him. He took a Snicker doodle heavily laced with sugar. She watched as he devoured it in two bites.

"Your favorite I suppose?" She tenderly asked.

"What gave me away?"

"The sugar crumbs you have all over your face," she suggested.

He grinned. "Where? Get it off for me please?"

Janeshia grabbed one of the napkins Ramsey brought with him and gently went to wipe the crumbs from around his mouth. Her finger softly touched his face.

He tilted his head and his lips gently kissed one of her fingers. "Did I tell you that you are beautiful and tormenting at the same time? And that I'd like nothing better than to kiss you?"

She drew in her breath as he leaned in and softly kissed her. His quick movement sent waves of warmth pulsating through her. She reached up and touched her lips where he had kissed her.

She watched as he smiled a dangerous grin. Butterflies began to form in her stomach. One thing was for sure, she didn't work with Ramsey. There wouldn't be a problem if she had a relationship with him.

Ramsey's mysterious eyes watched her. Their intensity never wavered as if they were casting a spell.

The air conditioner clicked on with a sudden rush of air. The breeze lifted papers on the conference table and brushed them to the floor. Their movements woke Janeshia from her fog. She cleared her throat and reached for the papers.

Ramsey beat her reaching for the papers. He placed them back on the table before her. "Oh I almost forgot this is for you also," he said reaching into his pocket. A tiny white box was revealed.

Janeshia's fingers trembled as his hand brushed hers as he handed her the box.

Touching Janeshia sent shivers up his spine. He needed to touch her again. His hand reached up to comb a lock of her hair behind her ear.

"More gifts?" Janeshia moved nervously away and fumbled with the box. She pulled out a strange shaped stone. "It's beautiful! What is it?" She asked stroking the egg shaped stone. "The stone makes me feel so happy."

"The egg shape represents both the male and the female from where all creation was formed, like Adam and Eve. It's great as a paperweight." He sighed. "I figured it was the perfect gift to ask you out on our first date. So how about it my little Eve where would you like to go Saturday? We can do whatever you like."

She looked up in surprise. A date with Ramsey was everything she wanted. The sudden realization that he was asking her out tomorrow shattered her moment of happiness. She had already agreed to go out with Walker. "This Saturday? Tomorrow?"

"Yes, of course tomorrow night."

"But I can't," she sighed. "However about Sunday or next Saturday?"

Ramsey stood abruptly. His eyes flashed furiously. "This can't be happening. I made plans for tomorrow," he hissed out bitterly.

"We can meet for a date on Sunday," she suggested.

His eyes probed hers. He reasoned. "I can't change the time. I'm only available tomorrow night. Can't you cancel whatever little old thing you have on your schedule?"

Flabbergasted she stood. "You don't even know how important that little old thing is that I have on my calendar. It's a work meeting that I can't miss," she corrected him.

He laughed out humorously. "Mine is work related also." He paused. "I know I want to go out with you. And you want to go out with me. And I have to go out of town. I leave early Sunday morning. I won't be back for at least several weeks. Look, I'm a game player," he said begrudgingly. "My point is, let's put it down in dollars and cents. You could cancel what's on your calendar. It can't be worth that much in dollars and cents, while my meeting is worth millions."

Janeshia was irritated and annoyed. "Then I guess you should leave now. We wouldn't want you to lose millions on my account," she fumed. "Besides, I don't like your attitude Ramsey Montgomery. Maybe we shouldn't go out on a date at all!" She quickly began compiling words of protest in her head. She went to open her mouth.

Ramsey regretted what he said as soon as he saw the glint of rage forming in her green eyes. She was like a drug he couldn't get enough of. He knew this was not the way of handling things if he wanted to get anywhere with Janeshia James. The best thing to do with her now was to do the unexpected. "Oh, I'm so sorry. I didn't mean it the way it sounded. Please forgive me Janeshia. I do apologize for my bad behavior just now," his eyes pleaded. "Come now, you weren't taking me seriously? I just had a bad day at work and was letting it come between me and the woman I want to know better."

"Oh," she said with a baffled content expression.

He studied her for a moment. She seemed to be buying what he said. He pushed the envelope. "You should be flattered I even want to have dinner with you." He grinned lecherously. "I'm on the board of several wealthy committees. I could make it worth your while. I can make *Silicon Valley Making a Difference Foundation well on its way to easy street.* And I can make you the most influential director this valley has ever seen. If I were you I would play the game with me and reconsider having dinner with me tomorrow night."

"Well, you're not me!" She said fuming. "I can't believe this," She muttered under her breath and slowly packed up her things.

Ramsey rubbed his brow. He realized that he had pushed the wrong button. He tilted his head slowly studying her. She wasn't like any woman he'd ever met. Any other woman would jump at his offer. He needed to change his strategy if he wanted her to like him enough to go out with him. "I'm sorry, again," he muttered under his breath.

Janeshia glanced back at him flustered and upset.

He realized she probably hadn't heard him. He fought his instincts from reaching out and touching her. He cleared his throat searching for the right words. "Janeshia, sometimes I let my tongue run astray. I still like you very much Janeshia and I hope you still like me. I'm so sorry for what I just said." He drew a deep breath. "I'm so sorry if I made your meeting feel less important than mine. I hope you still like me enough to consider giving me a rain check on going out with me sometimes."

Janeshia's eyes flashed at him. She didn't answer.

"Your eyes tell me I still have a chance," his features softened. "And I'll take what I can get. I guess I'd better go." He turned and walked to the door.

The next thing she heard was the conference room door closing.

Chapter 15

Wants, needs create an embarrassing situation ...

That Saturday night, the cold night wind from San
Francisco Bay whipped by chilling the air with its windy breath.

Janeshia stared up at the sky and studied the stars as Walker
drove his car leaving San Francisco.

She studied him. Dangerous emotions churned inside her
when she looked back at him. Visions of trust and hope crept into
her mind.

Walker checked his rear view mirror and then noticed her
staring. "What?"

"I can't believe it," she sighed.

"What are you talking about?" he quickly looked at her then
turned his attention back to the road.

"Oh, that we had dinner, sat together for over two hours and
you were civil the whole time," she smiled wide. "I'm not upset
about that. In fact I just wanted to give you a compliment."

Walker smiled softly with his thoughts. *"I live for watching
you smile Janeshia. Therefore I am a very content man."*

A few minutes later, Walker took the Junipero Serra exit and the sign for Burlingame's Prestigious Country Club Manor Estates came into view.

"Very impressive town, I've never seen so many luxurious estates in one place before," she complimented nodding her head.

Walker's voice resounded joyously. "Yes this is a very fine town. I know the area well."

Janeshia excitedly smiled. "I wish I lived here or knew someone who lived here. For no other reason than to be invited to one of the fabulous house parties these folks must give."

Walker's grin nearly split his face. "That's good to hear. I have to make a quick stop."

Janeshia gasped turning her head to look at him. She sat back and watched as the lavish homes went by. *Expensive champagne and the best caviar had to be what folks who lived here were used* to, she thought.

They drove down a twisting curving canyon road.

Walker slowed down and turned into a rustic charming elegant drive way with a wrought iron locked gate with thick pillars of stone sitting on either side of it. Janeshia noticed a voice monitoring system located on the left hand side. Walker didn't even use it. He pressed a button located on the dash board of his Mercedes and the gate slowly opened.

Janeshia gushed. "I didn't know you were rich enough to live here." As soon as her words were out she regretted them.

Walker only shrugged his shoulders.

The road led to a beautiful home sitting perfectly on its very own hill. It stood perfectly alone. The car's lights shone on the home and made it look stately and majestic in the dark.

Walker turned off the ignition. And walked around and held her door.

Janeshia noticed immediately the quietness of the night and the isolation of the home.

Walker could tell Janeshia was uneasy. "Don't worry my dear. I'm just stopping by to pick up something. Just relax."

Walker reached for her arm and led her toward the massive front door.

For the first time that evening she felt the need to stay close to Walker.

The house was a breath-taking rich blend of English and French designs.

Opulence and luxury greeted her. "While I'm amazed," she said. "This room is even more beautiful than the outside."

"This is no room." Walker said grabbing her hand. "It's just the foyer.

She glanced up at the Foyer's oval, high-domed ceilings and nodded.

"Come on I'll show you the rest of the house."

Walker led Janeshia down an impressive hallway.

She felt like she was Dorothy in the Wizard of Oz, shaking in her shoes as her heels clicked on the marble floor. "Is this the part where the girl is supposed to start screaming for her life?"

"Janeshia," he whispered huskily.

"Yes."

"No horror movie jokes okay? I just want to show you something."

Finally he led her into a beautiful room where paneled walls set off the delicately carved statuary. He walked her past a massive fireplace that sat in the center of the wall.

"There," he said softly. "Do you notice anything?"

Janeshia walked over and stood in front of the massive ten foot high and ten foot wide window. She felt the massive window tower over her as she beheld a breathtaking view of vast night sky, as a luminous magical full moon met her gaze.

The moon rose higher and right before her eyes and the stars twinkled brightly piercing the sky as she watched. She stared back in a dreamlike state as the moon slowly cast its spell. At that moment she felt a stirring as old as time. She was a woman who only wanted to be loved.

"Enchanting!" She exclaimed letting out her breath slowly as she walked in front of the sofa sitting in front of the window. "God this view is so deliciously beautiful. Whoever designed this room thought of everything? Look, there is a warm blanket to curl up under and look at the moon," she said. "Just look at that full moon cascading over the foot hills. It looks just like the ones in the movies."

Walkers' eyes beamed. Slowly he walked over and stood in front of a full table top bar. He poured a clear liquid from a crystal decanter into two glasses.

"Oh my goodness! Those paintings are fabulous," she exclaimed noticing the fireplace. She studied the two paintings hanging above it. One was of a baby crying with a hand reaching. The next was a woman crying reaching towards the baby. The look on the mother's face planted an indelible memory of true love in her mind.

"You like them?"

Enthusiastically she walked closer. The painting was vivid and life-like.

"Yes, what's there not to like?" Her lips twitched studying the paintings. "I think it's the most beautiful part of the room. It has such feeling it makes you want to cry."

"Well, I think that was the effect the artist was going for," he said.

Janeshia's voice gushed. "This room is the most romantic place I've ever seen. It does something to me."

"You are the most beautiful part of this room my dear," Walker thought to himself. "Would you like a drink? I make the best rum and coke. It's guaranteed to warm you and quench your thirst," he smiled holding the glass.

She sat down on the sofa and leaned back sipping her drink. She looked out of the window, gazing at the stars.

A few minutes later Walker sat down on the sofa. He stretched out his arm and made himself comfortable. After a few minutes he put his arm around her.

She looked up at his handsome face and smiled softly. It seemed like a perfectly natural thing. Having Walker's arm around her felt good. She closed her eyes for a second and savored the moment.

The two of them sat in silence several minutes sipping their drinks.

As Walker sat with his arm around her his fingers gently caressed her shoulder.

Janeshia exhaled with a long sigh of contentment, before she broke the ice. "So whose house is this anyway?"

"I don't want to boast but the home belongs to my family."

"What do you mean your family?" She looked at him puzzled.

"This is my parent's home, Janeshia. Well, it's my mother's

home, since my father passed away a few years ago. But someday it will be mine."

Janeshia looked surprised, "You still live at home with your mother?"

"That's a firm no." He paused looking embarrassed. "I have my own condo in Los Altos. I......"He hesitated. "I ....I"

She smiled. "So is your mother here?"

"No, my mother is away in Monterey visiting friends."

"So you only brought me here to look at this view?"

He was so close she could feel the warmth of his breath and the smell of his male aroma. He turned to face her. "Yes and no," he said. "I...I brought you here so that you could be here beside me and look at this beautiful view together," his eyes held a sheen of purpose. "So that I would have a memory of us being here in this spot that I would cherish forever," he said squeezing her shoulder softly.

The gravity in his voice transfixed her. The heat of his skin touching hers sent her emotions reeling. She tilted her head and stared back at him.

His eyes held her piercingly gentle, caring and loving. Like the eyes of the mother for her child in the painting above the fireplace. "I care deeply about you Janeshia. I brought you here because I wanted you to see it, my family home. The place where I grew up and played as a child. I wanted you to see a different side of me as a man, and I hope you would maybe then feel something for me," he murmured low.

An intense emotion filled her. Janeshia felt over-whelmed. She struggled with what her letting go could do to their working relationship. Her thoughts raced. She thought about what her best friend Larissa had said about having sex with Walker. She shook her head and clumsily the hand shook holding the glass. Walker's strong hand steadied her. He took the glass from her hand.

His voice oozed sexual tension as his green eyes probed hers. "So do you like my view Janeshia?"

Her breath caught in her throat. She was hypnotized by the slow mellow sexual tone of his voice.

Janeshia steadied her gaze on his. She didn't want Walker to think his wealth interested her. She still worked for him. "None of this matters," she raised a brow and looked around. "The wealth thing, this view, I still work for..."

"Stop thinking Janeshia. Do you know how much I want you, I need you?"

She watched the desire rage in his green eyes. Her heart was lodged in her throat pounding. "I want you too. But sometimes wants needs and desires…." she found herself whispering.

He moved in close. His lips just inches from hers. "Don't think about this too much. Just let the desire take hold."

A feeling of intense pleasure leaped between them.

He pulled her close and let her feel his arousal. "Look at me Janeshia Aurore James. Do you feel how much I want you?"

His mouth lowered to hers, the kiss was soft, warm and electric. The taste of him felt like a drug and she had to have more.

Janeshia leaned in closer. Her arms encircling his neck as she kissed him harder. "You know I like the sound of hearing you say my full name like that," she said leaning in and kissing him harder. His kisses were addictive.

As Walker devoured her with kisses his hands traced her body. His hands went to remove her clothes.

She pulled out of his embrace and tugged out of her top. Walker reached over and pulled out her top and helped her with her jeans. She stood before him in her underwear.

Walker had to fight with all his restraints. He stared back at her black satin corset and matching thong. "God you're beautiful."

She helped him with his shirt. His torso was muscle-toned beautiful. His soft tone olive complexioned skin greeted her. His muscles were taunt and prominent. She could smell the scent of his body. It was intoxicating.

Then Walker moved forward and lowered his head and took her nipple into his mouth, sucking softly. He eased her down on the sofa. He'd wanted her so long. The touch of her flesh undid him. Tonight he was hungry for his release.

Janeshia moaned as her whole body tingled.

Walker pushed her legs apart as he levered himself down. She felt his body there. Hot, probing, pushing, penetrating, He drove himself into her.

She shuddered in the pleasure he was bringing. "Don't stop," she commanded wrapping her legs around him. The intensity of the union was so overwhelming she thought she might die.

His mouth found hers again. Their tongues matched the rhythm of the song of sex their bodies played.

Walker cried out as his orgasm blasted through him.

Janeshia shouted out. "If this is a dream I don't want to wake up.

They both trembled.

Janeshia relaxed and Walker pulled her close and held her tight. She felt safe with the heat of his body. She snuggled in close and fell asleep.

Hours later, the sound of heels clicking on the marble seemed so far away.

Janeshia nodded as if waking out of a dream. She was naked lying crushed against the hard strength of a muscular body. She wasn't cold and realized someone had thrown a warm thick blanket over her.

The man stirred and wrapped his arms securely around her. She snuggled in closer enjoying his warmth.

Slowly her eyes opened. She looked out of the huge picture window in front of her. She watched the silvery moon slide from behind a blanket of clouds. It made her sigh with contentment. Slowly she started to close her eyes.

There was that noise again. It sounded like heels clicking on a marble floor.

Instantly bright lights flooded the room.

"What in God's name is going on here?" A woman's shocked voice gasped and sliced the air.

"Mother!"

Embarrassed, Janeshia threw the blanket over her head as she buried her face into Walker's chest.

"Young lady your face looks familiar, she gently said. "The few seconds that I saw of it", the lady softly chuckled. "Well son, are you going to introduce us?"

Walker peeked under the blanket. "Janeshia this is my mother Claire Marie Edward-Perrault. Mother, this is Janeshia James, as I am sure you very well know."

"Janeshia, come from under that blanket and say hello," Claire Marie giggled warmly. "I got caught doing the same thing with Walker's father. My child there's nothing to be ashamed about."

Janeshia brought her head out and said hello. She stared back at Claire Marie Edward-Perrault in amazement. The gentle kind voice belonged to the face of the petite elderly woman she saw standing in front of her. Her almond shaped face held a pair of distinct sparkling deep green eyes.

Walker shot a glance at Janeshia.

"Mother," he said. "I thought you were spending the weekend in Half Moon Bay, at Lamina Symons."

"I was, but my good friend old Lamina Symons started cheating at cards. I told her the last time that the next time I caught her cheating I was not staying the night. And so I came home," she sighed. "Serves her right, it will teach her a lesson."

"You never stay mad at Lamina for long," Walker said. "Okay then mother don't you have something else to do?"

Claire Marie snorted with a giggle. "You're right Walker, I can't stay mad at Lamina for long," she sighed.

He cleared his throat loudly. "So mother don't you have something to do?"

She shrugged. "I'm doing something now Walker, I'm meeting Janeshia Aurore James, you know I've been hoping to finally meet you. You are a beauty," she said looking questioningly across at her.   "I've heard you've been doing a great job at the foundation since I left."

"Well, thank you for that compliment," Janeshia said tensely. "I've been trying to do my best," she said aware that beneath their banter was an awkward situation.

Claire Marie breathed out with emotion. "I don't know why we are stilling her hiding behind words. It is obvious to me that you are doing great things with my son too. I know this because you both went to such great lengths tonight to make sure that your wants, needs and greediness would cause this embarrassing situation."

The moment was silently awkward.

Janeshia's smile was tense. "Whew! I don't know what to say. I am so sorry this happened," her words nervously tumbled out. "I know you are probably wondering why I'm here….I mean in your home at this time of night, but Mrs. Edmond-Perreault this will never happen again," she said nervously.

Claire Marie held a calm authoritative stare. "Most folks address me as just Mrs. Perreault. Though I do love my maiden name Edmond, there is no need to use it. In fact my friends call me Claire Marie," she smiled warmly. "Don't worry my dear. I'm not wondering why you're here. In fact I'm glad you are here. Did you know my son talks about you a great deal?"

"No....I didn't know that," Janeshia shook her head.

Claire Marie laughed softly. "You two should get properly dressed. Walker please show Janeshia to the bathroom down the hall. I'm sure she wants to freshen up."

"Sure," he replied.

"Oh and Walker when she is finished, bring her to the great room," Claire Marie commandingly said. "There's a gas fireplace there. The room heats up in no time. We can have some tea and talk."

Then she turned and walked out of the room.

In a knowing instant Janeshia stared back at Walker. She leaned over and whispered. "Walker, my middle name is never ever to be said in a sentence with my first name."

"Never?" He asked.

"Never!" Janeshia breathed under her breath.

"So does that look mean you're staying to have tea with my mother?"

"I don't think I have a choice," she huffed out.

Two hours later Janeshia discovered that Claire Marie Edmond-Perreault was a sincere person who extended a warm hearted welcome to visitors to her home. She also discovered she was a most enthusiastic conservationist.

Their group had been joined by Mae Frances Marquez. She was Claire Marie's assistant, but seemed more like an old friend.

The four of them enjoyed a pot of tea.

Janeshia sat next to Walker on the sofa. She cautiously

glanced toward him. His attention was elsewhere. He was responding to a text message. She studied his face. The outline of his profile against the room's soft light entranced her. She loved his chiseled jaw line. She wondered what it would feel like if she ran her finger alongside of it. She licked her lips without realizing it.

Someone giggled. Janeshia's spine stiffened. It was Mae Frances and she was looking straight at her. Nervously she turned away.

Mae Frances eyes her unflinchingly. She made sure Janeshia caught the hint she was sending as she stared between her and Walker. "So you two were having sex?" she winked. "Don't be ashamed. Sex was around doing biblical days you know."

Startled by her directness, Janeshia's mouth dropped open in indignation. "Excuse me?"

"Janeshia," she murmured leaning in close. "Young lady we are living in modern times. Don't you know we've all been greatly affected by the sexual liberation movement of the 1960's? It's a fact," she said with great emotion. "And I believe good sex is a must in any relationship. So how did you find Walker after giving him a try?"

"Mae Frances is just joking Janeshia," Walker leaned over and whispered. "Aren't you Mae Frances?"

Mae Frances leaned forward and picked up Walker's cup and saucer. "If you say so Walker?"

"Yes I do say so," Walker said leaning back.

Mae Frances shrugged as she turned to neatly stack the empty cups and saucers on the cart.

Walker cleared his throat and quickly changed the subject. "By the way Janeshia, didn't you say you would like the recipe for the *N'Awlin's* Spice hot tea? Well Mae Frances could write it down for you. She makes the tea often enough."

Mae Frances shook her head. "If you want the recipe Janeshia, then ask Walker. He'd give it to you, as well as his heart, the shirt off of his back and probably all of the money in his pocket, in a heartbeat, especially if the two of you are doing the.....Oh what is that new term for having sex?"

"Knocking boots," Claire Marie added *with* a sudden amusement.

"I like the term boning," Mae Frances said shaking her head. Janeshia was mortified.

Walker laughed nervously and took her hands. "Janeshia just ignore the two of them, please?"

Her eyes held his. Something flashed behind his and it spoke volumes to her. He kissed her hand. It made everything right and she smiled.

A sudden look of amusement flashed on Claire Marie's face as she watched from across the room. The truth was staring her in the face. She had seen the look Janeshia had given Walker earlier. It was becoming more and more apparent that the girl had feelings for him. Even though she could tell Janeshia spent a great deal of time trying to hide it. She eyed Janeshia with a speculative look and cleared her throat. "Did I hear you say you wanted the recipe for *N'Awlin's* Spice tea Janeshia?"

Startled by her name being called, Janeshia answered quickly. "Yes."

"Well you're in luck my dear. I believe I can provide you with a copy," Claire Marie said proudly.

Janeshia blinked back in surprise. "That's very kind of you."

Claire Marie walked in closer. "Janeshia, did I mention that when my Walker was a boy I always put Red Hots in his tea? It made it extra sweet and spicy. Walker loves things sweet and spicy," she hesitated. "Just the way he liked it. You always did like things sweet and spicy didn't you Walker?"

"Mother," he scolded softly.

"Oh Walker, I did promise Janeshia her recipe. Would you do me a big favor?" Claire Marie asked without waiting for a response. "Please go and fetch that extra *N'Awlin's* recipe book I have in the kitchen on the book shelf, for Janeshia. I think it would make a great gift for her. And it does have the recipe for the *N'Awlin's* Spice Hot Tea,'" she said.

"Mother, if you just wanted me to leave the room, you had only to say so," Walker said.

"Well, if I must be blunt with you Walker, then yes. I would like for you to leave the room. I need to speak to Janeshia in private. Don't you have to check your messages or text somebody?"

Walker tilted his head and forced a smile. He knew when he wasn't wanted. "Mother you really do want me out of the room. Okay, I'm leaving for now. But mother, don't go telling all our family secrets while I'm gone. You and Marie Frances don't want to frighten Janeshia off now do you?"

Claire Marie and Walker looked at each other

"Don't worry Walker. Janeshia is in good hands. You go off for a while and keep yourself busy," she said giving her son a look that dismissed him.

From out of the corner of her eye Janeshia watched as Walker left the room. It quickly dawned on her she wished he didn't leave so easily. She felt strangely alone. She could sense someone staring. She lifted her gaze and her eyes met Claire Marie's. Suddenly she felt like Sabrina Fairchild when Linus Larrabee was sent to deal with her.

The clinking of crystal startled Janeshia and broke her gaze.

Mae Frances held her head high as she walked across the room. Her blue white hair looked like a crown framing her face. Her steady petite frame easily lifted and carried over a tray holding a beautiful vintage crystal decanter.

Janeshia's eyes caught sight of the pinwheel motif on the side of the crystal decanter. It was like nothing she'd ever seen.

Mae Frances put the tray down on the table in front of her. She filled three glasses with a deep golden brown liquid.

"Would you please have a glass of sweet rum with orange liqueur with us Janeshia?" Claire Marie asked. "It's an old favorite of mine."

Janeshia nodded her agreement as Mae Frances handed her a glass.

Claire Marie studied her. Even from where she sat it seemed like an invisible light showed on Janeshia's face. She was amazed at how much she looked like her mother. She smiled, warmly lost in her thoughts. She thought about that long ago promise made. She left the foundation just to make way for Janeshia. She wondered if she ever knew that. A word flashed in her mind. It rolled off her tongue before she knew it.

"Proposition."

Janeshia looked up puzzled. "What was that?"

Claire Marie's voice rasped out. "Oh, excuse me I was just thinking out loud about something I did once when I was young and beautiful like you. You know I made a promise to someone, after they made me an offer I couldn't refuse," she said with a matter of fact waive of her hand. "But I'm getting off the subject. You do know my dear, you are very beautiful, Janeshia."

"Thank you for the compliment," Janeshia shrugged. She

glanced at Mae Frances. She wondered why she hadn't engaged in their conversation. She watched and remained silent and kept sipping her drink.

"Are you seeing anyone special my dear?"

Janeshia's brain clicked, wondering what she was thinking. "You mean dating?"

"Yes," Claire Marie didn't wait for an answer. "But first I would like to drink a toast to you Janeshia for all the hard work and dedication that you do for the foundation."

Janeshia watched as Claire Marie took a sip of her drink. She took a sip too.

Claire Marie smiled at Janeshia and raised her glass a second time. Silently she took another sip.

Anxious to please, Janeshia did the same.

"Now Janeshia I would like to make another toast to your accepting my proposition."

On impulse Janeshia looked up and hesitated. "Proposition? What proposition?"

Claire Marie fought back a smile. "Ahhhh the one you and I shall discuss, tonight."

Mae Frances finally spoke up. "Well ladies, I guess that's my clue to refresh our drinks."

Chapter 16

The Proposition

Claire Marie Edward-Perrault didn't blink as she gulped down her last of sweet rum. She took a deep breath and put the glass back on the table. "Janeshia, you have the bone structure I want for my future grandchildren."

"Oh?" Janeshia asked reaching for her glass. Her hand was unsteady.

Claire Marie rose and advanced toward her. "Do you have a boyfriend? Oh no of course you don't. Or you wouldn't have been...."

"What?" Frustrated Janeshia threw her an irritated look. She hadn't expected to be asked this. What did she expect after the way she had just been caught in a compromising situation with her son? She wondered if Claire Marie expected her to turn in her resignation. She tried to be polite. "Ah....I...I...Why are you asking?"

Claire Marie shrugged her shoulders. Her expression

softened and looked strangely protective. "I was just asking," she shrugged. "Only you know your heart my dear, but I've found that many young smart women sometimes make foolish choices. Or spend their lives fantasizing about Mister Wonderful while they watch the years go by."

Janeshia watched Claire Marie's back as she walked past. Her thoughts raged. Why hadn't she just resigned the first day Walker showed up out of the blue and started micro-managing her at the office? She knew why, she'd been instantly attracted to him.

"You are very good at your job with the foundation, Janeshia," Claire Marie said, sitting back in her seat like a regal Queen taking her thrown. "You handle it well, very well. I am grateful to you for your great work," she hesitated. "Being the director of the foundation has its advantages, wouldn't you say Janeshia?"

"Yes, of course it does," Janeshia said.

"I'm sure you enjoy the prestige and recognition it brings. And I believe you love the money you make?"

Janeshia nodded agreement. She quietly studied Claire Marie's mesmerizing deep green eyes.

Claire Marie's serious expression was hypnotic. "I consider you a wise woman and what I have to say is for your benefit too," she took a sip of her drink. "Let me explain. I consider my son Walker to be an honest and generous man," she said. "But I'll be honest. He's the most talkative Geek I ever saw. But," she said with a paused. "Every Geek needs his Angel. I'm afraid if I don't step in with a mother's understanding and a matchmaker's heart, my son is doomed to lose you forever," she said tapping a manicured fingernail against her empty glass high.

Mae Frances rose instantly, strolled over and refilled her glass.

Janeshia's eyes flickered with a cool reserve as Mae Frances stepped closer to refill her drink.

Mae Frances slid a glance at Janeshia. "Good men are hard to find, especially ones with no medical history of heart problems, mental issues, or an STD" she whispered in her ear leaning over to fill her glass.

Mae Frances spoke so softly Janeshia thought she had misunderstood her. Janeshia looked into her eyes. "I beg your pardon."

"I think you should take Claire Marie's proposition and marry that Geeky son of hers," she said staring boldly. "Most girls are looking for a rich husband, aren't you?"

"That's not what she said," Janeshia utter with a puzzled look.

Mae Frances nodded. "Ah Hm. That old lady is matchmaking you up with her son," she said then turn and walked back to her seat.

At last understanding rose up and greeted Janesha. She stared back at her. Then she looked in the direction of Claire Marie. This was some kind of marriage proposition. "Mrs. Perrault. I mean Claire Marie. I agree with you on the part about Walker being a geek," she said. "Let me put it bluntly. I can't imagine what you mean by the matchmaker part. These are modern times. Match making is a thing of the past."

"Sometimes a mother has things she must do," Claire Marie lifted her chin in an imperial gesture. "I would again like to say my son is a fine man, a very fine man. Such a man would make a woman a good husband, a very good husband."

All three of them took a sip their drinks.

Mae Frances cleared her throat. "I'll say it again. Good men are hard to find, especially ones with no history of an STD," she chuckled lightly.

All at once Janeshia tossed back her head and laugh out. "You can't be for real!"

Claire Marie's eyes widen in surprise. "This proposition I make to you right now is real because I have a mother's understanding. And I can tell by your eyes you don't find my son revolting. In fact I believe that there is something there or you wouldn't have been sleeping with him."

Janeshia could feel the blood drawing from her face. Her throat felt uncomfortably tight. She wondered what kind of game she was playing. The sooner this was over the sooner she could get out of there. She cleared her throat determined to set the record straight. She was just fine being single.

"I'm sorry but I just can't take any of this seriously. You see what would be the benefit for me. I have a great job that I love....I...I make an excellent salary......"

Claire Marie interrupted. "My proposition is for your benefit too. I believe you love your position as director of the foundation. And well my proposition would allow you to keep your position as director of the foundation for as long as you like."

Janeshia was taken by surprise. "Are you talking about my keeping my job?" The reality of what Claire Marie was saying was starting to set in. "Let me understand. You are making me a proposition about keeping my position as director of the foundation? Were you considering firing me?"

Mae Frances stared shrewdly at her. "Janeshia, I do have to say it again, good men are hard to find, especially ones with no history of an STD. And their mother has lots and lots of money," she took a sip of her drink.

Frustrated Janeshia stared between the two women. She thought of leaving the room. But remembered she barely remembered how to get back to the front of the house. Then she didn't have her car. She slowly relaxed and wished their conversation would end.

Mae Frances came to her defense. "But you know Claire Marie I have to agree with Janeshia," Mae Frances said. "She made a good point. You should make it clear if you are considering firing Janeshia if she doesn't accept your proposition."

Claire Marie's eyes flashed. Her mouth opened and then closed.

"Let me just say this," Mae Frances barreled on. "If I were in Janeshia place, sitting at this time of night, with a strange looking old woman laying out a proposition of marriage on me? I would be afraid to say yes too," she said unflinchingly. "Of course Janeshia wants to know if she would be fired. Wouldn't you?"

Claire Marie's face turned pale. "For goodness sake, I never said anything of the kind. What I meant was that life is not like some pages in a romance book," she said. "No one can live happily ever-after without some compromise."

Mae Frances nodded. "Okay, I get it. You're talking about a proposition as a compromise."

Janeshia was silent.

Claire Marie's expression was polite but stern. Her eyes sharpened. "Yes, we could come to a compromise. I do love my son." She shrugged. "And you know I've carefully considered Janeshia's strengths and ah….wants too," she faintly said.

"Thank you, I think that was a compliment. Or the rum is starting to numb my rage," Janeshia condescendingly said.

"Yes, you bring much to the table, my child," she said

excitedly. "You have excellent bone structure, that I know will be passed down to any children you have. Your lovely parents hale from Louisiana and are fine and upstanding and any man would be lucky to be their son in law. And well, I love my son. But I know I said that before. And together we can both have what we want," she hesitated and then reached for her glass of sweet rum.

"Claire Marie you are rattling on. Get to the point of your proposition or compromise," Mae Frances egged her on.

"Janeshia, if you do not believe in compromise you will learn that life can be hard and brutal. You can keep your position on the condition that you seriously date my son Walker for the sole purpose of marriage," Claire Marie studied her empty glass.

"Whew!" Mae Frances giggled, rose and refilled her glass. "Claire Marie I didn't see that one coming!"

"Oh my God! Janeshia said with shock and dismay. "I can't believe I am hearing this." Her mind could not take hold of what she was hearing. She took a deep breath and composed herself. "You can't be serious?"

"I am serious. For life is serious and I feel that you should date Walker for at least the next six months," she said eagerly. "After which you will marry him, God I pray you will marry him. And as his wife you will remain in your post as director. Yes I think that is a good idea if you start dating Walker right away. In six months you should know him well, if not better. The details of this compromise proposition can be worked out in length later."

"Christ I didn't see that one coming," Mae Frances interrupted. "But Claire Marie, it's only a good proposition if Janeshia isn't seeing anyone. If the girl is dating someone else, how can you impose your proposition on her?"

The two women looked at each other. Then they both looked at Janeshia.

Claire Marie turned her full attention back to Mae Frances. "But the girl was just having sex with my son. Anyway Mae Frances I do believe I did ask her earlier. You heard me ask her earlier."

Janeshia was thunderstruck as she stared between them. It was truly amazing how the two of them could hold a conversation as if she wasn't in the room.

"Really now Claire Marie," Mae Frances said. "Yes, you asked her, but Janeshia never answered. And having sex is different nowadays. Don't you watch the reality shows? Young folks have sex just to be having sex these days. It doesn't mean a thing."

Janeshia maintained her show of cool composure. "She didn't want to involve herself in Mae Frances' conversation. She took the moment to get the conversation back on track. "Yes Claire Marie you never let me answer about whether or not I was dating someone else," she said. "Just so you know. I am currently dating someone and I wouldn't know how to tell him that in order for me to keep my job I must date and marry my boss's son."

A shocked expression seeped across Claire Marie's face.

"Well, now I believe this is what they call the tide changing," Mae Frances said.

Janeshia's brow creased slightly. She felt her forehead perspiring. Awkwardly she smiled.

"Oh my. My son has a rival," Claire Marie said with a wild light in her eye. She was acutely curious about who could be her son's rival.

"I suppose this now changes everything. I don't see you as a woman who would force her will on another," Janeshia said curtly.

Mae Frances awkward laughter filled the room. "You don't know Claire Marie very well. But then, most folks think that fragile, old, sweet lady and kind looking face is true weakness. It ain't. It's a mask for the strongest warrior queen I've ever seen."

Claire Marie cleared her throat discreetly. "Huh, Janeshia let me tell you what a wise woman once told to me. Every woman is a selfish woman, a selfish woman with selfish reasons all of her own. And I too am one."

"All the same, this should change everything, right?" Janeshia looked for understanding.

Marie Frances chuckled. "She's got you Claire Marie."

"Yes, you are right my dear." Claire Marie sipped her sweet rum. She entertained her own thoughts. She concluded that at the present time Janeshia had no reason to know she was an egotistical and calculating woman, especially when it comes to her son Walker, or to her. She smiled softly when she spoke again. "Again Janeshia, I had no idea you were in a relationship. Please accept my deepest apologizes for any misunderstanding. Of course I wouldn't hold you to that silly proposition I made. But just for thoughts sake, keep it in the back of your mind. Marriage propositions have been around for hundreds of years. They are as o, marriage was the institution created by wealthy people to preserve their wealth. Sort of like I want to do today. Just remember, you will be well taken care of and I'm speaking in the millions. Both in dollars and in property," she cautiously said.

Mae Frances picked up the bottle of sweet rum. "Ladies let me refill your glasses."

Janeshia breathed in deeply and took a deep swallow of her sweet rum. The rum calmed her. She felt the worse was over.

Silence hung between them.

All at once Claire Marie's eyes flashed. "So tell me Janeshia, what is your young man's name. That is, if you don't mind my asking." She shot a glance at Janeshia. "And I must be invited to the wedding. Of course we must have a press release done on your nuptials."

"His name….." She hesitated. "I'm not sure you know him…..I mean we are not planning on being married anytime soon," nervously Janeshia played with a loose strand of her hair.

For an insane moment Janeshia could have sworn she saw Claire Marie's eyes twinkling with mischief.

"It's getting late Janeshia I can tell you're getting tired. I'll get my Walker to take you home," she smiled. "Oh by the way, do you like the theater Janeshia?"

"Why yes I do very much, she answered."

"Good, then I have someone to go with me my next visit to the San Francisco. It'll be my way of showing you how truly sorry I am for any misunderstanding," she answered. "Oh and Janeshia, please keep what we discussed tonight in your strictest confidence. Walker has no idea you and I are having this conversation."

Janeshia nodded.

A few minutes later, Walker eased his car off highway 92 onto highway 101 heading towards San Jose California.

"Thank you," Walker said.

"For what?"

"For the kindness you showed my mother. She enjoyed your visit. You know rich people get lonely too."

The quiet of the night filled the air and the soft humming of the car slowly lured her asleep.

Walker watched her sleep, a very content man, as the highway loomed before him.

Chapter 17

Phone calls, a gossiper and an eavesdropper

Across town, Aurore Allen-James dialed the number quickly. It was high time she had a private chat with her daughter.

It had been nearly two o'clock in the morning before Janeshia got home. Now, four hours later, she ran her tub full of warm water and slid into it. The water felt like heaven. She sighed, leaning her head back to relax.

The piercing sound of the telephone shattered Janeshia's quiet moment. She flung her arms out furiously and reached for the cordless phone.

"Where have you been Janeshia?"

"Hello Mother? I'm in the tub."

"Being in the tub hasn't stopped you from talking to your mother before," Aurore Allen-James said with urgency. "Unless you're not alone?"

"No mother….I mean yes mother I am alone." Janeshia stammered. "Why are you calling?"

"Can't a mother call to check up on her only child?" Aurore

asked with concern in her voice. "Janeshia, you know I'm not one of those mothers' who try to run her child life."

"I know you're not," Janeshia replied. She could tell her mother was worked up about something.

Surprise was apparent in her mother's voice. "Janeshia, I heard about your dating," she paused. "Why didn't you tell me you were dating Walker Edmond-Perreault?"

"Because Mom I'm not dating Walker. We had a business dinner. That was all. Anyway, who told you about it?"

"I heard it from your cousin Greystone's mother, Julie."

Julie James was a gossiper and an eavesdropper for as long as Janeshia could remember. She smiled knowing her cousin Greystone James would never betray her trust.

"Mom, you know Julie listened in to one of Greystone's conversations. As usual she got the story all wrong."

"I know that Janeshia baby," Aurore said. "I was just upset that she made a big thing out of knowing about it before me." She paused. "Besides, I figured I needed to tell you something before big mouth Julie James let the cat out of the bag," she breathed deeply. "Janeshia, all of our families know each other," she said with urgency. "The Edmond-Perrault's, the James', the Allen's all of our families go way back. You know that all of us old ones were born way back in Louisiana."

Janeshia shivered. Her bath water was starting to turn cold. Sighing she looked up at the ceiling and laughed. "Yeah, I didn't know they all knew each other. Look mother why haven't you told me this before? Never mind. My bath is getting cold."

"You know I wouldn't mind if you were dating Walker. His family is good people."

Janeshia was glad her mother couldn't see her rolling her eyes. "That's good to know mother, but I can't date Walker. I'm dating someone else."

"Oh!" Aurore grunted.

Janeshia was lost in her memories. She closed her eyes. "He's a really great guy."

Irritability quivered in her voice. "What's his name?" Aurore muttered.

Her question woke Janeshia out of her fantasy. Her eyes opened wide. She bit her bottom lip. "Look mother I really don't want to tell you his name right now. And don't go asking Larissa or

Greystone or his mother Julie," she commanded.

Aurore's voice sounded heavily into the phone. "Look baby girl, all mother really wants to know is if he is a real person or a figment of your imagination? Janeshia, you know how you can get heavily infatuated with someone who doesn't even know you are alive."

Janeshia stuttered in shock response. "Mother isn't it Sunday? Shouldn't you be at church or something?"

"You know I should. But I didn't go," Aurore's voice bauble through the phone. "Can I help it if a mother needs to make sure her only child is safe and sound? And actually dating a real live person?"

Janeshia sat up in the tub. "Mom I'm sorry. I promise I'll call you more often."

Aurore's voice was tense. "What about visiting your mother and father more often?"

The question threw her. She realized it had been over a month since she'd been by to visit. Thinking hard she said. "Okay Mother, I promise I'll visit you just as soon as I can. That is if I don't catch my death from sitting in this cold bath water."

"Good! You do that and I'll tell your father you're dropping by today for a quick visit. Bye now," Aurore said, abruptly hanging up the phone.

Chapter 18

That old feeling again...

A few days later, For once Ramsey had no coherent plan as he walked patiently to his car and loaded his suit case.

He quickly dialed the number. "Hi Tamara," he said urgently into the phone. "It's me Ramsey again. I'm leaving the airport now. Are you sure Ms. James will be in her office?"

"Yes, are you sure you don't want me to tell her the flowers are from you?" Tamara asked.

"Yes I'm sure. I want to see the look of surprise on her face. I should be there shortly, see you then," he assured her before hanging up.

Tamara was nervous and strangely affected by Ramsey's voice. He sounded like a hunk over the phone. The man had called the office several times before. Now he was coming over.

Tamara walked over to Janeshia's office and quickly knocked and entered. As was beginning to be her style lately, she didn't wait for a response. She walked over to Janeshia's desk and waited quietly studying her boss.

"Well what?"

Tamara giggled before speaking. "Some guy named Ramsey Montgomery keeps calling for you. He said he wants to take you out and for me to keep you here until he gets here," she commented excitedly. "Whew! His voice sounds so….So sexy. I hope it's not the only thing sexy about him. Oh by the way, he's the guy that sent you the flowers earlier."

Janeshia looked up at her from the files on her desk. Calmly she asked. "How long did he say it would be before he comes over?"

Tamara was amazed at her calmness. "He should be here any minute now. Maybe you should change or something before he gets here. Don't you have a dinner dress in your office closet or a sparkling glittering evening blouse? Janeshia you should spruce up before he gets here."

"Calm down for Christ's sakes Tamara. He's just a man."

Tamara's eyes brightly stared back at her boss. "But this is like your first date. And since Walker Perrault is no longer coming around showing you any interest, you've got to make the best of this first date, first impression thing," she said.

Tamara's words hit a nerve. She turned her attention back to the file on her desk. She needed to analyze the figures. She could at least have part of it done before Ramsey arrived.

"Tamara, don't you have some work to do?"

A short time later, Ramsey waited quietly as Tamara marched purposefully and opened Janeshia's office door.

"Janeshia there is a breathtakingly handsome and very charming man who wants to see you and no, he does not have an appointment," she said out of breath.

"Who is it?"

"He said his name is Ramsey Montgomery," Tamara said grinning from ear to ear. "The Ramsey Montgomery, the multi-millionaire venture capitalist."

"Show him in!" Instantly Janeshia rose to her feet. A shocked smile blazed across her face.

For a split second Ramsey stood in the doorway and couldn't move. He swallowed hard. "Janeshia you look beautiful, like a gift from the God's," he said walking over to give her a hug. "I've just arrived back in town. And the only thing I could think of was to see you again."

Shock surprise and something else registered on Janeshia's face as she caught sight of Ramsey Montgomery again. She smiled wide embracing him. She was amazed at how his mysterious eyes could weave their magical spell on her again.

His charming smile disarmed her. "Janeshia I was hoping you would have dinner with me tonight."

"After those beautiful flowers you sent, I can't say no," she said.

Ramsey grinned wide. "So where do you want to go?"

"Do I have time to change my clothes first?"

Hours later, Ramsey held her hand tight as they walked into the restaurant.

The old building had a retro elegance that reminded Janeshia of an old night club right out of the 1950's. Lively modern music met them as they entered. They were shown to a round table with two chairs. The elegance and charm far exceeded Janeshia's expectations.

Ramsey ordered champagne.

They conversed easily over dinner and talked about their likes and dislikes about everything from art right down to their favorite subject in college. Finally Ramsey asked how Janeshia's day went and she filled him in.

Ramsey's eyes gazed over. He smiled softly and inclined his head and studied her. He watched her finish her dinner.

"I'm sorry, was I muttering? I must be boring you to death with my stories about work."

"Oh no," he smiled. "I enjoy hearing you talk. I talk about business all the time. Talking with you is such a wonderful diversion. It's like talking with a long lost friend."

A glimmer of appreciation appeared in Janeshia's green eyes.

"So Janeshia, how did you like the lobster dinner I ordered? I hope I didn't go too far imposing my love for hollandaise sauce? You could have ordered something different if you wanted."

His smile told her how much he appreciated her. It made her feel special. "The lobster was excellent. I too enjoy a great hollandaise sauce," she said her long fingers playing with her champagne glass. She took another sip.

"Wow! I'm dining with a girl that loves the same food that I do. It gets better and better."

All throughout dinner she caught Ramsey gazing at her. Each time she caught him staring he shifted his gaze.

Janeshia felt herself relax.

"You're growing on me Janeshia!" He said abruptly. "You are easy to get along with and you're beautiful and you're smart," he smiled. "I can't believe you're not married. You would think some guy would have realized you were a prize and scooped you up by now."

Janeshia felt herself blush.

His eyes were warm and amusing. "Well since I chose the main course, you should choose dessert," he smiled.

"No dessert for me thanks," she smiled.

"A woman that doesn't want dessert, you are a great catch. I'm so glad you went out with me tonight. This is the beginning of a wonderful relationship," he nodded. "I knew my being determined to go out with you had sound reasoning. I'm glad you made me earn every minute of it."

He gestured a toast with his glass.

Janeshia's heart raced from his warm compliments.

There was a moment of silence and then Ramsey leaned over and touched her hand.

"You're so charming. You know that? I want to make everything perfect for you."

Janeshia almost lost her breath at the sound of his words. She reached for her champagne and took another sip. Ramsey was watchful and attentive to every detail. She liked that about him.

"I've never had a man say so many sweet words to me, Ramsey. I don't know what to say."

"Just say the night isn't over and you'll dance with me.

Believe it or not they do have a great dance floor in the basement of this place."

Ramsey looked around for the waiter. "Waiter is their dancing tonight?"

"Yes sir there is, downstairs its ballroom night. They've got everything from Big Bands to the Foxtrot. Why the DJ will even take requests."

Janeshia lifted her glass and toasted. "Great! The end to a prefect evening," she said. "Oh, and Ramsey if we miss a step or two dancing, no one has to know it but us."

"That's my girl," Ramsey agreed. "Care to dance?" he asked holding out his hand.

She took two breathes and stared at him and gave him her hand. She liked that about him, she thought.

Chapter 19

Lawyers and retainers oh my....

A few days later, Larissa London closed the door of her office. She wanted to drown out the sounds of the noise coming from just outside her door. She sat at her desk and played back the message. Her eyes glistened with wonder as she lifted her phone and quickly dialed the number.

"Hello, I'd like to speak with Mrs. Edmond-Perreault, please," Larissa politely said into the phone.

"This is she speaking. This is my private line. Is this Larissa London?"

"Yes, I was returning your call."

"Thank you Miss London for calling me back," Claire Marie's voice was crisp and friendly. "I'll cut to the chase," she said quickly. "I read an article about you in the *San Jose Valley Times*. And in it you stated Janeshia James was your best friend."

"Yes Mrs. Perrault.......Yes Janeshia is my best friend. Why do you want to know?"

"Yes, well I know you are a very busy young woman and your time is valuable but well, since you returned my call I will assume you are available to have lunch with me today?"

"Yes, I am," Larissa said.

"Good then meet me at Scotts at one o'clock. I have reservations."

Later that morning, Larissa got off the elevator and made her way to the lobby of Scotts. She had agreed to have lunch with Walker's mother Claire Marie Edmond-Perreault.

She gave the hostess her name and was amazed at how fast she took her to her table.

Claire Marie Edmond-Perreault wore jewelry that looked as regal and noble as she did. She sat patiently looking around the room. She looked like a queen sitting on a throne.

Larissa reached her table and held out her hand. "I hope you haven't been waiting long."

Claire Marie's manner was like an old world aristocrat. She smiled and nodded. "Larissa, it is so good to see you. You are right on time my dear," her gold bracelet caught the sunlight.

Larissa smiled warmly and admired her jewelry.

Claire Marie wore only a couple of pieces of jewelry. The pieces were unique. Her wide gold bracelet had a deep rose design that looked expensive.

Larissa's eyes caught hold of the vintage brooch and she couldn't stop staring.

Claire Marie reached into her black patent leather Gucci purse and pulled out a matching eye glass case. She put on a pair of small gold wire-rimmed glasses and studied her menu.

Larissa enviously sighed and shook her head and looked again at the brooch.

"I see you like my Vintage Gold, Diamond, and purple Pearl brooch. There is one just like it in the American Museum of Natural History."

Larissa shook her head and thought maybe she misunderstood what she'd just heard. She cleared her throat and said. "It's very beautiful. I'm afraid to ask if it's real."

Claire Marie leaned forward with interest and gazed back over the rim of her glasses. "All my jewelry is real," she looked at her over the rim of her glasses.

Larissa blinked. "I can't believe you're not afraid to wear that in public."

"Why not, it's insured," Claire Marie said firmly. "Larissa, aren't you more curious about the real reason I called you here?"

"Yes, I am," Larissa said cautiously.

Claire Marie lifted her water and lightly took a sip. "Well I need to retain you as my lawyer again. Only this time it is for my own personal use and not the foundation. However, it's maybe that it involves both," she nodded her head. "But first let me buy you lunch," she said looking over the menu. "I'm not watching my calories and I must have something that tastes good on my tongue and very satisfying to my tummy. I'll start with the Boston Clam chowder, and then I'm having the Prawns, Scallops, Chicken, and Sausage Jambalaya with Dirty Rice," she said smiling sheepishly. "So Larissa, I suppose a young woman like you, watches what she eats?"

Larissa picked up on Claire Marie's playful sense of humor. "No, in fact I think I will order what you're having."

Claire Marie waived her hand. "Good, I'll have the waiter take our orders."

A few minutes later steaming hot coffee sat in front of them.

Larissa reached for the cream and wondered where a lady as petite as Claire Marie put all that food she'd just watched her eat.

Claire Marie leaned over and smiled. "You and I have done business in the past that was, shall I say satisfying for the both of us, correct?"

Larissa raised a brow and nodded. "Of course we have."

"Good. Good," Claire Marie's words dripped with approval. "So tell me what you know about the financial books for the foundation."

"Not much really, just what you showed me six months ago. You explained to me then something about a decrease in profits, but when you checked again, there had been no change. Then it was decided to increase security. So you had several advance security safeguards at the foundation." She paused. "From what I was told, the higher security monitors the computer system every day, checks inventory regularly and monitors all of the programs budgets and financial records."

Claire Marie shook her head. "That is correct. But I've come to believe our security is an illusion."

Larissa gazed up with a stunned expression.

"You see Larissa, I feel I need you to take a look at the security system, you can do this off site of course. I will show you the latest financial report so that you can see my suspicion. Let me assure you, your expenses will be covered," she hesitated and looked around. "And Oh, I will be paying you extra for this job because I also have a very delicate job for you to handle. Sad to say, I must insist upon having you adhere to your strictest confidentiality policy regarding the matter."

"Yes, of course," Larissa nervously smiled staring back at her. She looked around the restaurant. To anyone walking by, Claire Marie Perrault looked like a sweet, extremely well dressed youthful looking matriarch, but looks were deceiving. Claire Marie was a confident, shrewd business woman who was skillful at letting everyone around her think that they were in complete control. She kept a sharp eye on the family's business using her years of bookkeeping experience.

"So Claire Marie, what else is it you need me to look into this time?"

Claire Marie pulled a large oversized envelope from out of thin air and laid it on the table. She slowly tapped a well lacquered fingernail against it. "Here, take this envelope with you when you leave. And don't share the contents in side with anyone. You'll see what I need for you to do."

Chapter 20
Dates & Nothing to speak of...

That Saturday morning sky was cloudless blue, as Ramsey and Janeshia made the drive on Highway 101 from San Jose to Monterey California.

Ramsey smiled softly as he glanced at her from time to time while driving. Earlier he'd set his GPS system to sound out their progress every ten minutes. "Per my GPS system we should reach Monterey within the next half hour."

Ramsey hummed along as his CD player played a soft jazz tune.

Confined in the long car ride with Ramsey Montgomery gave her many moments to think. For the first time she realized Ramsey Montgomery was just like any other man confined to a small car space with a woman. He ran out of things to say. She noticed he'd take a glance at her a couple of times, but he didn't say a word. She sensed too that he was sort of a loner.

Janeshia slid a sideways glance and studied him. Ramsey didn't fault his sexuality. It just seemed to ooze out of him without effort. He was cool and in command as he sat behind the steering wheel.

She tried to remain cool and aloof as she studied him.

His eyes stayed on the road.

"Can I tell you something?" His words feel into the silent air between them.

"Sure."

"You look real good in those jeans," he said trying to hide his smile. "In case I forgot to mention it." He swallowed hard hoping she didn't see the proof of just how much he liked seeing her in her jeans.

Ramsey's flirtatious smile caught her off guard.

"You don't say?" Janeshia looked out of the window, suddenly bashful.

He watched her glancing out of the window. "I bet I'm missing some really great scenery passing by," he said. He cleared his throat. "Someone once told me the drive to Monterey will steal your heart away, just like a beautiful woman. Just like I know you could."

Janeshia flushed. She realized she should say something nice back. She studied him out of the corner of her eye. She was glad he didn't wear his suit and tie today. With an embarrassed expression she said, "You look pretty good yourself in those jeans you're wearing. In case I forgot to mention it before."

The two laughed together. Slowly the laughter faded.

Janeshia realized she would have to struggle to keep their conversation going. For the first time she realized Ramsey Montgomery was sort of a loner. She shook her head trying to think of something else to say. "It's hard to believe you are a Venture Capitalist," she said eagerly. "I always thought them to be shrewd gray haired old men with a dry sense of humor."

"Your description is outdated. Times have changed," he blurted rudely.

Janeshia disliked his abruptness. The moment was tense between them. Neither one said a word.

He stole a glance at her. "Okay, I guess now it's my turn to say something to break the ice. Did you know Janeshia that California has a warm, sunny Mediterranean climate very similar to France? It allows California to produce some of the superior wines?"

"Oh really," she said with amusement in her voice. "What are they?"

"What?"

"I want to know which wines are superior," she said.

Ramsey's lips curled up into a grin. His voice was

effortlessly charming. "Oh, California has a slew of originals; but the one I was referring to is the Cabernet Sauvignons. Now they are far superior to the Best Bordeaux produced in the southwestern region of France."

"Hmmmm interesting," Janeshia said wistfully. She stared at his eyes. They blazed strangely as he poured out that tidbit about wines. His eyes looked like a used car salesman about to close a deal. She turned and stared out of the window.

"So now it's official, we've both said something to get the other person's attention. And we have broken the ice."

Janeshia laughed softly. "You are so right."

A half hour later, the ocean view crescent over the highways edge. Cascading waves made the shoreline entering Monterey breathtakingly beautiful.

A few minutes later Ramsey made a right turn and parked his car in a parking lot under a sign that pointed Fisherman's Wharf straight ahead.

"Wait, I want to get the door for you," Ramsey said.

The ocean air was cool and crisp and instantly flushed Janeshia cheeks as she stepped from the car. She was glad that she wore the pink cable knit scarf her mother made for her. She pulled it closer from the chill. She traced her hand over the scarf. It made her feel warm like her mother's embrace against the chilly air.

"Thanks. Where are we going?"

"We are going to have lunch at *the* Old Fisherman's Grotto Restaurant. It's been a favorite of mine for years. Not to mention it's been a landmark here in Monterey over 50 years. The Clam Chowder is the best I've ever tasted."

Their hostess sat them at a window table overlooking the breathtaking harbor view.

Over lunch she told him about her position as director of the foundation.

Ramsey looked at Janeshia. "I must say you really do like helping people. I like that about you. You give back to the community."

"Thank you," she said.

His eyes were amused. "I bet when you love someone you love hard," he said watching her. "I believe that love is the only thing that is pure that we carry with us until the end."

She looked him in the eye. "I read a quote almost like that." She bit her lip trying to remember. "I think it was Louise May Alcott who said, *"Love is the only thing we can carry with us when we go, and it makes the end so easy."*

"Then I must say, I agree with her," he smiled. "I'm amazed. No I want to say, I'm impressed with you Janeshia. Not many people nowadays can recite Louis May Alcott. I like that about you. I like it a lot."

Janeshia blushed. She took another spoon full of clam chowder. "You were right Ramsey. This clam chowder is the best I ever tasted. I would say I've found a new love."

Ramsey nodded agreement.

"So what did you do on your business trip Ramsey, if you don't mind my asking?"

"Nothing to speak of. First I went to Manhattan to look over a bunch of accounting records, a few business plans and a few stock portfolios. I had meetings every day for almost two weeks and none of them resulted in a final decision on any of the business plans," He chuckled softly and put down his spoon. "The third week I went to London to visit an old college professor of mine. His name is Professor Higgins. Now I enjoyed every minute I visited with him. But enough about that," he said. "I'm dying to know more about you"

Janeshia flushed. "What do you want to know about me?"

"Do you have any family?"

"Well yes, of course I do." She breathed out with a puzzled expression, wondering where their conversation was going.

Realizing the confusion on her face he added, "I was just wondering. I have a mother you see," he hesitated. "But my father died when I was young," he lied." My mother never remarried after my father died."

"Oh I'm sorry to hear that. Both my parents are alive. And they are still very married."

"Any brothers are sisters?" he asked.

"No," she said.

"Not even a step sister or brother?"

Janeshia hesitated from his probing. "Ah. Is there something else you want to know?"

"I'll be honest you have such a giving helping nature that I just assumed you were from a large family," he let out a slow breath and licked his lips nervously. Unwanted memories tried to surface in his mind. He tamped them down in his mind and then the lie flowed easily off of his tongue. "I wished for a brother or sister," he sadly said, with a long sigh. "Anyway as I told you before I've lived a lot of different places, but only with my mother of course. It was a kind of lonely childhood."

The sadness in his voice shook her. The questions he asked now made sense. "Oh I'm so sorry," she said with a shake of her head.

"Don't be," he smiled. "Now that I'm an adult I resolved myself that I will be happy. I seek happiness. I will work on it until I have it and I am certain that I will have it because I believe in working hard."

The two talked easily for well over an hour.

Ramsey paid their waiter and they left the restaurant. He took her hand and led the way down the wharf.

"Come on Janeshia you've got to see the view at the end of the pier."

A seagull took flight just as Janeshia leaned against the pier's railing. A smile lit up her face as she looked out on the vast ocean and sky before her. "Ramsey if I haven't told you yet, I am so enjoying this place."

Ramsey moved in closer and stood directly behind her. "I'm glad. When you are with me Janeshia I'll do whatever it takes to make you happy."

The wind blew suddenly.

He looked down at her as the wind whipped loose a strand of her hair. Her face beamed radiantly against soft rays of sunshine.

All at once she tilted her head and stared up at him.

Janeshia wondered why Ramsey was staring at her that way. The man puzzled her.

"I could get used to having you in my life like this Janeshia," he smiled. "Really easily," his arms closed around her as he pulled her close.

Janeshia's heart jumped.

She leaned her head back against his shoulders. Suddenly she smelled a strong floral scent that was strangely familiar to her. The air felt cold and changed around her. She felt strange being in his arms, like someone was watching her. She he pulled out of his embrace. Her breath caught in her throat, as she stood there and stared.

A woman stood directly in her eyes view and watched them. She was tall and regal looking. She had a round face with cool blue eyes as blue as the sky. Her silver colored hair was braided with gold ribbons and hang down her shoulder. The end of her hair was left loose and blew softly against the wind.

"Ramsey Montgomery, I thought that was you!" A man's voice sliced the air. "Christ I haven't seen you in years."

The woman began to fade at the sound of the man's voice.

Without a glance in her direction Janeshia watched as Ramsey clasped the man's hand tightly and pulled him out of hearing distance.

Puzzled Janeshia steady herself, stunned by Ramsey's deliberate rude snub. He didn't even attempt to make introductions.

In an instant the woman reappeared in front of her. "It's a good thing you didn't let him kiss you. He really wanted to kiss you badly though," the woman she saw earlier smiled softly. "But he was rude, don't you think?"

Janeshia didn't jolt as she stared straight through the woman's crystal clear blue eyes. She knew she wasn't hallucinating. "Yes he was rude," Janeshia agreed.

"You remember me don't you Janeshia?"

She nodded and nibbled on her lower lip. "I haven't seen you for years."

"Hmmm I'm glad you remember me. You know I'm not one for making small talk Janeshia," the woman sighed. "She looked in the direction of Ramsey.

Janeshia followed her gaze.

"Are you sure he's the right one?" The woman's smile never wavered.

"He's nice," Janeshia said.

"Nice you say, I hope so." The woman said softly. The woman's voice grew faint like the wind. "Well I guess you know your own mind. I guess you know what kind of man you're attracted to. But don't forget to follow your heart. Most times the heart knows what's best," the old woman's voice said softly."

Janeshia sighed, "Do you know if he is an honorable man, or a dishonorable man?"

"Janeshia, you can be so stubborn sometimes. True things of the heart between a man and a woman do not need interpretation from others."

"What did you say?" Janeshia couldn't make out what she said at the end. Suddenly the wind blew hard in front of the woman. "Remember Janeshia men lie."

The hairs on the back of Janeshia's neck itched.

"Who are you talking too?" Ramsey asked.

Janeshia straightened and turned her head around to stare at him.

She turned around to double check if the woman was still there. The space in front of her was empty. "Oh, no one," she lied.

She tilted her head and gave him an odd look. "Ramsey, that was rude of you. Who was that guy you were talking with earlier?"

"Who? Oh, that was Van Palmer. He's a notorious liar and probably a thief."

"Ramsey, I was talking about your rudeness not introducing me," she said starting to lose patience.

Ramsey had no intention of upsetting her. "Look Janeshia, I'm afraid you don't understand. Your privacy would have been lost if I introduced you," his gaze on her face never wavered. Her eyes were her best feature he thought as he studied them. Her eyes hid something valuable behind them. Something unattainable, something he knew he had to own. He loved beautiful objects. She was beautiful. He was mesmerized. He cleared his throat. "He would have made our being together today something ugly. Or worst yet he would have tried to flirt with you and I would not know how I would have controlled myself," the pain in his voice was real. "Look Janeshia let me apologize."

"Excuse me," the woman said bumping into the couple. "Please sir….Buy some flowers for your pretty lady. She is a very beautiful woman and a beautiful woman needs beautiful flowers. And beautiful flowers can fix any situation."

Janeshia held her breath. She wanted to get a better look at the woman's face. She locked eyes with the woman. She didn't recognize the grayish brown eyes that stared back at her.

The woman smiled again.

It wasn't her Janeshia thought.

"I guess I'd better pay for the flowers," Ramsey said reaching for his wallet.

Chapter 21

Someone Got a New Love

The next day Janeshia was still angry at herself for letting Ramsey buy her forgiveness with a bunch of flowers. She stood at her sink and filled the tea kettle with water.

Before she could beat up on herself another minute her telephone rang. Startled, the water splashed all over the place as she almost dropped the kettle.

"Hello," she said, reaching for a towel to dry up the spill.

The voice on the other end threw her for a loop.

"You are where?" she asked.

Suddenly her doorbell rang.

Janeshia walked to her front door and opened it.

"These are for you Janeshia, how are you? Are you okay?"

"Mother!" Janeshia exclaimed with a look of surprise before giving her mother a quick hug. "What are you doing here? And why are you giving me flowers?"

Aurore Allen-James pushed back her prefect curled mass of glossy coco brown hair with auburn red streaks. She was a very pretty, petite, trim woman and flawlessly dressed. "So baby, do you like mama's new hairdo?"

"Mother, I see you'll still let Brooke work her magic? So you are into frosting now?" Janeshia asked. "Why are you bringing me flowers?"

"Oh baby, Brooke's Beauty Nook is the only place I trust to do my hair. And it's no longer called frosting. It's called highlighting," Aurore Allen-James said with pride. "The flowers are from your father. He figured maybe if he sent over a bribe you'll come and visit him more often. Me, I prefer to do things the old fashion way. Just show up unannounced at my only daughter's door bright and early on a Sunday morning and see if I can catch a man in her bed," she chuckled. "From the way you're looking right now though, I pretty sure if there was a man you would have scared him off in that faded out robe."

"Really mother," Janeshia smiled.

"Oh, go and put some clothes on Janeshia and take me to the grocery store. Afterwards we can go back home and surprise your father and make him breakfast."

Going to the grocery store with her mother had seemed like a good thing three hours ago. Now she was not so sure anymore. One thing she was sure of was that her father had already fixed his own breakfast by now. Another thing she was sure of. Buying groceries was not what her mother had in mind when she asked her to accompany her.

Janeshia walked over to a rack of clothes that her mother was flipping through. "Mom, I thought you wanted to fix Dad some breakfast?"

Her mother gazed up at her and gave her a strange look. "Your dad knows how to fix his own meals if he gets hungry. Besides, we're spending quality time together," Aurora smiled and grasped her daughter's hand in hers. "Come on baby girl, act like you like shopping with your mother."

"Oh my goodness!" announced a lifting demanding voice. "Mother and daughter together. Why Aurore, you and Janeshia simply look adorable. You two could grace the cover of Mother Daughter magazine," the woman with the squeaky voice said. "My....my, I haven't seen you two together in ages."

Aurore leaned in close to Janeshia's ear and whispered. "Hmmmm baby girl, don't look now but here comes the family's drama queen. It looks like you were right. We should have gone home and fixed your father something to eat. Now we'll have to stay and consort with the family's gossiper and an eavesdropper."

"Shhhhh Mom, Cousin Julie might hear you."

Janeshia knew the voice. It belonged to Julie James.

Julie James gripped her black leather hobo handbag tightly as she walked over. Her fingernails were painted a brilliant red. They matched the red silk blouse she wore. Her dark colored hair was blunt cut and longer on one side. It distinctively framed her face.

Julie strutted over and gave Aurore a hug first. "Oh Cousin Aurore, I see you're still letting Brooke do your hair. That's just so sad. Brooke doesn't know a thing about doing hair."

"A word of advice Julie dear, everyone loves a compliment but no one loves another person's opinion," Aurore said putting her arms around Julie in a hug. She leaned close to her ear. "You know what they say about opinions? *Opinions are like assholes*, everyone's got one and everyone thinks the other guys stinks!"

"Yuck!" Julie muttered stepping away from Aurore.

Julie recovered quickly. She glanced over at Janeshia. She pulled her close in a hug and said, "Oh you poor child how on earth did you come out so well with a mother like Aurore?"

Janeshia pulled away and pretended to be interested in the rack of clothes in front of her.

"Julie James, you'd better look out there! I heard you. I'm standing right over here," Aurore warned sarcastically. It was obvious Aurore wasn't happy about Julie being there.

Aurore's eyes arched. "Look Julie, I over look a lot of things you say and do because we're family. Why don't you put all that energy you've got for putting your nose in other people's business back into your own marriage?"

Julie James chuckled lightly. "Oh Aurore, you are forever the family charmer. Now you know I just love toying with you."

Aurore managed a smile. "Yes, I'm sure you were."

Julie glanced around and raised a manicured nail and pointed. "Oh Aurore I was in here earlier. And I found something you'll just love. I know how much you love *Royal Silk*, well there's a whole rack of them out there by the fitting rooms in the back and they are on sale."

Janeshia glanced up at her mother's face. Her eyes were glowing. Her mother did love *Royal Silk*. "Mom, it is your favorite."

"Yes, it is." Aurore smiled softly. "You know Julie, you are good for something. I'll just go and take a look."

"You do that," Julie said.

Janeshia nodded.

Aurore stopped abruptly. "Janeshia if you need me you know where to find me."

Janeshia watched her mother stroll to the back of the store.

Janeshia stood there and gazed back at her Cousin Julie. "That was nice of you Cousin Julie."

"You know Janeshia you should really try to get your mother to give me her baked salmon recipe," Julie said making small talk.

Janeshia looked up. "What's on your mind Cousin Julie? I can tell you're really not interested in Mom's salmon recipe."

"You know I've been dying to talk to you alone. I hear that Walker Perrault has moved on, he's dating someone else now dear," Julie said with a mischievous smile.

"Oh really," Janeshia shrugged. "I don't know why you think I should care?"

"Oh, I just thought you'd want to know that he was dating a much younger woman and I hear she is very beautiful," she shrugged. "I bet that makes you jealous?"

A chill ran through her. Janeshia arched a brow and laughed out nervously. "I never told anyone I was dating Walker Perrault. Why should I be jealous?"

"Oh yes that's right, I'm so sorry I forgot, I did only overhear that you were dating him. I never saw it firsthand."

Silence fell between them.

Janeshia returned to the search through the rack of clothes in front of her. She hoped her Cousin Julie would take the hint and walk away.

Luck for her Julie did walk a short distance away from her. She was glad. It gave her a moment with her thoughts. She didn't want to admit it but she was upset by the news about Walker and another woman. She couldn't shake the chill she felt earlier. She didn't know why. She never gave him any encouragement. But still Cousin Julie's revelation had made her feel humiliated.

Julie finally made it to the rack of clothes Janeshia was fingering through.

"Wow, you must have missed this one. Look at this top Janeshia. The color would look great on you. Not to mention you can wear it with that gold Cleopatra necklace your father and mother gave you for Christmas."

Janeshia half took an interest in the top and reached for it. Julie was right. It would play up her necklace.

Oh my Lord!" Julie screamed and put her hand over her mouth. She stiffened and held her breath. She grasped Janeshia by the elbow to steady her. "Don't look now but it's the man himself. The man we were just talking about and it looks like he's got a new love."

"Walker?" Janeshia couldn't believe his name fell from her lips. She looked up. Her gaze caught his. Her green eyes took in the young woman standing by his side.

Janeshia couldn't believe it. The young woman was beautiful. Her amber eyes glittered brightly against flawless skin that didn't require much makeup. Her Brunette hair hung long and lush against her shoulders. But though she wasn't that tall it was her jaw dropping figure that you knew men were attracted to.

Walker and the young woman came over and halted in front of them.

The moment was awkward.

Janeshia gave him a steely smile.

"Phoebe, why don't you go ahead and get started shopping," Walker said. The manner in which he manipulated the young woman out of distance showed he was not going to make introductions.

"Walker Perrault, this is a surprise. You remember me I hope. I'm Julie James."

"Yes, you're Greystone James' mother," he said. "It's so good to see you again.

His eyes watched Janeshia's and nodded.

"So who's the young lady?" Julie asked. "What's her last name?"

"Oh Phoebe Wright, she's just a friend I promised to take shopping. Phoebe loves to shop."

Of course she does. What young woman doesn't?" Julie said.

Janeshia opened her mouth to say something.

Just then Phoebe Wright marched purposely over towards them. Her arms were heavily laden with several items of clothes.

Phoebe gazed up in awe. "Walker look, I found some great

things to try on. What do you think of this negligee? Hot pink is my color huh?"

Janeshia's eyes locked on the young woman. She had a moment of jealousy.

Walker cleared his throat. "Look, we really must be going."

Janeshia stood there thunderstruck.

Julie waited until Walker was out of earshot. "So Janeshia honey, did you pick up that Phoebe didn't go very far in school? She's what the old folks used to call a boom, boom girl," she breathed out slowly. "You know the kind men like to take a ride on. I guess we know what ride Walker's now riding on."

Janeshia was silent. Her day couldn't get any worse.

Julie glanced at Janeshia. "You okay?" she reached out and put her hand on her shoulder.

Janeshia gave a small nervous laugh. She didn't want her true feelings to come out. "I guess by the way she was built, men weren't going out with her for her brain."

"No honey, men aren't interested in that girl's brain, for sure." Julie nodded. "Now that I've seen Walker and that Phoebe creature, I'm glad you're not interested in him. In fact, I'm glad to hear you've taken an interest in that guy Ramsey what's his name," she said waiving her hand. "You know, years ago it was rumored that he went through a nasty divorce. But I don't remember all of the details."

"Hmmm" Janeshia blinked back startled by the revelation. She should have supposed Ramsey Montgomery had a life before her.

"Oh, but you wouldn't care about the details. You're just grateful you've finally found someone else who wants to date you. That ought to show Walker," Julie's mouth spread into a thin lip. "But I'll tell you what, if I hear any sordid details about either Walker or Ramsey what's his name, I promise you'll be the first to know."

Chapter 22

Our Secrete Town

Three weeks later, after Janeshia's encounter with Walker and Phoebe Wright she dated Ramsey Montgomery exclusively. For the past two weeks they'd been inseparable.

Traffic breezed alone highway eighty that early Saturday morning. The sun was slowly going down over the mountains.

"How long have you been planning on our making this trip together Ramsey?"

His hands griped the steering wheel tighter. "I was hoping since we first meet, but seriously, once you agreed to come with me last week I've worked on putting this weekend together day and night," he secretively grinned.

"I'm sorry but what was the name of this town again?"

Ramsey's smile broadened. "Secret Town and a secret place where the two of us can be alone."

She gasped in surprise. "That's a real name. I just saw the sign back there. I thought you were joking."

Butterflies swirled in her stomach as she watched the mountain range go by.

A few minutes later, Ramsey turned on Wild Irish Road. He pulled up in front of a cabin nestled between a beautiful pine forest.

Quickly Ramsey got out of the car walked around and opened her car door. He stood like a chauffeur with his arm behind him. "Welcome to our Secret Town love cabin my dear. I hope that you enjoy your stay and the fun that is to come," he teased.

"Thank you and I'm sure I will," she smiled.

Ramsey unloaded the car. He took the bags and escorted her into the cabin.

The cabin was romantic and cozy with two master bedrooms that shared a huge large bathroom complete with an oversized Jacuzzi tub.

Janeshia looked at the shared bathroom.

"We share the bathroom but you get your own room. I'll put your bags in this room here, Janeshia. You relax, have a hot bath and have a moment to yourself."

Janeshia walked into the room and noticed the fresh red roses.

Ramsey smiled. "You like? I had the flowers delivered and set up before we got here. In fact, the food that I catered in from the restaurant should be here shortly. I'll make sure everything is set up perfectly for our first night alone together."

He walked to the door. "Oh there's a bottle of *Grand Reserve* Merlot on the table. Enjoy," he said. "But don't drink too much, I want you to enjoy the dinner I've got planned for us."

Almost three hours later, their intimate dinner had been delicious and every bit as perfect as Ramsey had said it would be.

Janeshia fidgeted as Ramsey poured her another glass of wine. She took another sip and sat her glass back on the table.

Ramsey looked at her from across the table, as he finished his glass of wine. He was just watching her. His mind seemed to be contemplating her. He reached for the bottle of wine it was empty.

He got up and turned up the music.

His eyes widened in admiration. "God you look great in that dress Janeshia," Ramsey said taking her hand and pulling her away from the table. His hand lingered and caressed the nakedness of her shoulder.

"You look great too," she said. "I especially like that cologne you're wearing. It's citrusy and very masculine." Her eyes lingered and looked at the open collar of his shirt. His chest was distinctly hairy but not unusual. It reminded her of someone.

"I want to make love to you Janeshia," he said pulling her close. He leaned over and nibbled her ear lobe. His hands slid down and cupped her breast. He let his hands slide lower to her hips. He cupped her cheeks.

She felt her body grow warm at his touch.

"Janeshia?"

All at once Janeshia tensed up. The tone of his saying her name sounded strangely familiar. She drew in a deep breath. She thought she was hearing voices. Her thoughts were elsewhere far away. All at once she felt guilty thinking about Walker. She blinked rapidly wondering where that thought came from. She pushed the thought from her mind. Walker had Phoebe. Why shouldn't she have Ramsey?

Ramsey moaned.

Walker's face burned in Janeshia's mind. She shook her head to clear her thoughts.

"Janeshia, now all we have to decide is which room do we go to? Yours are mine?"

He didn't wait for her to answer.

"Let's go to mine. I just remembered there's something I want to show you," he said pulling her along to his bedroom.

Minutes later, with her hands on her hips, Janeshia stood at the door of Ramsey's room mesmerized by the size of it. The room was neat and tidy.

"Go on in Janeshia," he said gently giving her a push, as he watched her walked further into his room.

Hot desire roared through his body as his thoughts raced. She was the sexiest woman he'd ever met, who hadn't expected him to pay to have sex with him. His thoughts cautioned him, he wasn't paying to have sex with this one so he needed to be nice and gentle. He threw back his drink and put down his empty glass before closing the door.

Janeshia slowly explored the room. "Wow, she said.

Ramsey closed the distance between them. He stood behind her and thought the room felt warmer.

She stood still when she felt his hand unzip her dress.

"Now it's my time to say wow," he said standing there mesmerized by her beautiful face, full breasts and long legs. "That corset and thong looks very becoming on you."

He turned abruptly with her dress. He walked over and neatly folded it before laying it on his dresser.

She stood there watching him with a perplexed look on her face.

"That's a little pet peeve of mine. I don't like clothes thrown on the floor."

"Come follow me," he said taking her hand as he walked back. He led her to the bed. "Have a seat."

Janeshia sat down quietly and watched as Ramsey turned his attention to the tray beside the bed.

He turned over the two glasses and poured. "I know you sort of like an after dinner sherry," he smiled pouring her a glass and handing it too her. "I prefer something a lot stronger, bourbon," he said pouring the brown liquid into the glass. He tossed back the bourbon and swallowed hard. Almost as if he had taken some kind of drug and was making sure he washed it down.

She watched as he poured another.

He held up the glass in a toast. "Here's to a night you won't forget. Drink up. Neither one of us have to be anywhere tomorrow or tonight for that matter."

Janeshia watched as he gulped down his glass. She followed his lead.

Ramsey filled his glass again and downed it. That was his third one if she was counting. Not to mention the two bottles of wine he put away at dinner.

He leaned down and captured Janeshia's lips in a hard kiss. His mouth plundered hers. "I'm going to make you feel good all over," he said easing her back.

For the next few minutes they sat together on the side of the bed holding each other and kissing.

They both enjoyed the sensation of each other.

Then abruptly Ramsey pulled away. He got up and began removing his shirt and pant. "It's about time I removed my clothes."

He sighed as he reached for her again. His hands drew her close. His lips roamed her neck and shoulders.

"Mmmm," he purred.

His hands wandered to her breast, cupping, squeezing her. He pinched her nipple.

"Oh!" Janeshia moaned from the pleasure of the sensation.

They stayed like that several minutes simply tasting and kissing each other. And then his hands pushed her back against the bed.

Janeshia clutched the sheets as she went down.

He lay down beside her and he placed a rush of hot kisses on her face and her neck.

She shivered when he stopped abruptly and pulled away and reached for a small remote. He pressed a button.

She couldn't believe the massive television that popped up out of nowhere at the foot of the bed.

The television came on.

She watched as the picture came into view. A girl was lying on her back a man was laying between her legs. She could hear the distinct voices of their moans.

Ramsey laughed again and kept laughing like an inexperienced teenage boy. His face was glued to the television. He reached out and grabbed her breast hard. He flicked her nipples with his thumb.

She winched.

He reached out and pulled her hand and guided it across his body.

"Look how you aroused me Janeshia You deserve the best me. I'm going to give you the best part of me," he moaned softly. Janeshia couldn't believe this was happening.

He kissed her hard as he panted, his leg straddling her. "You know this will be the best ride you ever had. Give me a few minutes and I promise I'll take care of your clitoris and do that thing you women like done. Just as long as you promise to let me take you on an even better ride."

Janeshia wrenched back in pain. "Stop!"

His jaw dropped open. "What's the matter?"

"Get off of me Ramsey!" she demanded. "I need to go to the bathroom. I've had too much to drink, she lied."

Without another word he rolled off of her.

With as much dignity as she could muster. Janeshia slipped out of the bed and made her way to the bathroom. She stayed in the bathroom as long as possible. She sat down on the side of the

Jacuzzi tub trying to think.

Janeshia looked up and her eyes caught sight of several tiny bottles sitting on the sink. Curiously she walked over and examined a bottle. The label was from an herbalist shop in San Francisco. The street name was located in the heart of Chinatown. She read one bottle. The label said it was for sexual enhancement. Another bottle had the name *Zolpidem;* it was the generic name for a powerful sleep aid.

She pressed her hand to her mouth to smother her laughter. If Ramsey took these with all the wine they had at dinner, he would sleep for hours.

Janeshia could still hear the loud noise from the sound of the television. She tiptoed over to the bathroom door and looked into the bedroom. Ramsey lay awkwardly on the bed. He was sound asleep.

She turned her attention back to the tub and filled it with water. At least she could have a hot bath before she went to bed.

Hours later, Janeshia didn't know how long she slept. Suddenly she felt her body shiver. She thought she was dreaming. "Yes" she moaned and gasped. The sensual pleasure felt like an orgasm coming on.

"What are you dreaming about?" Ramsey murmured.

Janeshia opened her eyes and looked back at him. He was fully dressed. The morning sun slowly crept upon the window.

Ramsey leaned back on the bed and looked back at her.

"Damn Ramsey you woke me from a wonderful dream," she whispered.

He grinned wolfishly. "I hope your dream made you happy."

"Yes it did," she tensely replied fluffing her pillow.

"Good," he paused busying himself. "Look Janeshia I know I let you down when it came to the sexual intercourse thing last night," he nervously hesitated. "I'm sorry. Let's just say I had too much to drink," he said quietly. "Please accept my apologies for the....Mishap."

"Oh that? Yes sure," she said with a perplexed expression.

"I promise to make last night up to you another time. But right now, I have to leave," he said giving her his hand to help her up.

Instantly she felt relief. "Leave?" she asked scooting off the bed clutching the sheet.

"Yeah, I had an urgent call; I need to get back to town right away. So go on get your shower and pack. I want to be out of here in the next half hour."

A half hour later, Janeshia stared out of the car window as they drove away. She exhaled deeply, relief flooding her whole body. She watched the landscape go by wondering how a man like Ramey could look like the real deal but be totally lacking in the sex department. She smiled softly with her thoughts. She remembered hearing her best friend Larissa say. *"Some men who looked like the complete package couldn't make love worth a damn."*

Chapter 23

An arrogant smooth criminal...

Adam St. Charles left work just before eleven o'clock. He made sure he was there when his boss, Janeshia James called and checked in. He'd assured her everything was well. How convenient it was for him that Janeshia was out of town. It made him angry that she wouldn't tell him where she was at.

He smiled and ran his hand through his hair and leaned by the door. Everything was going just as they planned.

Adam kept his expression bland as he stood for a moment and watched the mystery man. The rented office space inside the Mandarin Office buildings in Hayward California was most convenient. Here office space could be rented by the hour, day or month.

Lately he started calling the mystery man, Mr. Clean, because of the way he made sure none of the accounts or the money could ever be traced back to them.

Adam glanced at the clock on the office wall. It was just past four o'clock. If he left now he could arrive back in San Jose within the next hour. That is if traffic was good. He hoped she'd be waiting.

"Things are working great Adam. This deal allowed us to charge a higher fee for our services. The two of us netted just over a hundred and fifty thousand. You're cut this time is seventy grand. Don't forget we split the expenses in half. It's what we agreed upon. Great job, by the way on setting up those off shore accounts in the Cayman Islands. They were a perfect idea. Are you sure no one will be able to trace them back to us?" he asked. He glanced up at the noticeable silence. His fingers drummed the envelope on the table. His fingers gripped the envelope and then slid it across the table forcibly.

Adam just stood there leaning against the wall daydreaming.

Adam looked up startled. "I'm sorry, did you say something?"

The Mystery man got up and walked over to the edge of the table and retrieved the envelope. He held it out. "Your mind is not on business today Adam. There's your money. Count it."

"I guess my mind is elsewhere," he said as he slowly walked over.

On a woman no doubt," the mystery man said and grasped the envelope tighter. "Take my advice, Janeshia James won't screw you. She's not the type of woman who needs a man to buy her things. Not that you've got enough money, not yet anyway," he chuckled softly.

Adam's chin came up in defiance of the insult. He clenched his teeth as he reached for the envelope. "I'm not interested in Ms. James in that way."

The mystery man's eyes were cold as he stared back at him. "Look here, you arrogant smooth criminal. What we're doing here is illegal. We don't need you messing things up. So don't lie to me!" His eyes sparkled dangerously. "I've seen the way you look at her. But this is business. So don't you do anything to mess up our business arrangement, you hear me?" he asked with a trace of malice and anger in his voice.

Adam replied sullenly. "I don't know what you mean?"

"Don't think that I'm stupid Adam. That scar under your eye looks like a tear from a woman's finger nail. I would bet money you've had some cosmetic surgery? The doctor that did the job was good. But he couldn't cover all of your scars, now could he?"

Adam stood frozen in the spot and bit his lower lip feeling his anger rising.

All at once the mystery man laughed out. "You're dismissed Adam. I'll see you next time. Go and work off some of that anger. And make sure the woman is willing!" he laughed, heading for the door. "Oh and Adam make sure you lock up the room."

Adam waited until the door closed completely.

"You bastard, I'm just using you until I get what I want," he muttered viciously beneath his breath.

Almost two hours later, Adam St. Charles paced the hotel room. He walked over to the window and looked out again.

A soft knock sounded on the door.

He quickly walked over and opened it. "Damn Phoebe where have you been? I've been ringing your cell phone ever since I left Oakland," abruptly he closed the door. "What did you do to your hair?" he demanded.

She took a deep breath and spun around in a circle. "I had it done, you like?" she cooed.

"I like a lot!"

"It's the same shade as Janeshia's," she giggled softly. "I thought it might help Walker like me. And look I got contacts the same color as Janeshia's eyes. This ought to stop Walker from ignoring me. He treats me like I was rotten meat left on the stove."

Adam stood there staring. The resemblance to Janeshia was freaking uncanny. "Say, who did your make-up? It's a true likeness."

"Thanks, I had it done at House of Channel's over on First Street. I showed their makeup artist a photo of Janeshia. He made me up to look just like her."

"Has Walker seen the make-up yet?"

"No, he's only seen the hair color. Say, how about a hug?" she asks extending her arms.

Adam leaned in and gave her a hug. "Well, don't show him the full look with the make-up just yet. We don't want him getting suspicious," he said. "So why did you do the make-up anyway?"

"I figured it would put Walker in the mood to scratch an itch I've got. You know that Walker fellow isn't interested in giving me a workout in the having sex education department. If you catch my drift."

"I catch it. You keep working on him baby. But in the mean time I'll enjoy your makeover," he smiled.

Phoebe hesitated and then smiled as she felt bulge in his pants grow large. "From the feel of things Adam I'd say I've interested you?"

"Yes you can. Come here!" he demanded. "You poor baby let me see if I can reach that itch you've got," he said kissing her hard. His tongue filled her mouth.

She moaned.

Quickly Adam pulled away and led her to the bedroom.

Chapter 24

Heart matters, let's get together......

A few days later, at work Janeshia played the weekend with Ramsey over in her mind. No matter how she looked at it, Ramsey's behavior was strange.

The sunlight filtered through the window and its rays danced on the crystal vase of red roses sitting on her desk.

Her eyes glanced curiously at the unforgettable large crystal vase of red roses. The design on the vase was distinctive and unusual. The card attached to the vase made mention of an undying love. Her emotions were still raw when she thought about their time together at the cabin. He never said the words *I love you*, nor did his actions ever display the same. There was no show of tenderness in his caress. His actions gave her pause and made her fearful. In the end what someone felt for you and how they express that feeling to you through touch and emotion was an expression from the heart. And one thing was clear, expressions from the heart, did matter.

Lately she felt a little depressed feeling like she was all alone in their relationship. She gazed bleakly out of the window. Since they had returned, her calls to him had gone unanswered. Abruptly she looked at the telephone sitting on her desk. All of a sudden the telephone rang, and she jumped.

She prayed it would be Ramsey.

"Hello Janeshia?"

"Hello Ramsey," she said briskly. She swiveled her chair around to stare out of the window.

"Janeshia, darling I've been meaning to give you a call," Ramsey said with a deep concern in his voice. "Did you get the flowers?"

"Yes, she said with a smile in her voice. "They are beautiful. Did you really mean what you wrote on the card?" she asked but didn't wait for a response. "When can we get together? So I can thank you for them in person?"

"Look Janeshia I can get away to see you tonight," his voice was rigid. "Let's have dinner at the Fairmont. I'll meet you there say at eight o'clock?"

Janeshia was a bit surprised. "Okay, sure I'll be there," she paused only for a second. Her voice squeaked out in a faint whisper. "Hey could I ask......"

Ramsey interrupted abruptly. His voice was urgent. "Good....Good. I.....Look I've got to go."

He hung up.

Slowly Janeshia hung up the receiver slowly. She turned and stared out of the window.

Adam St. Charles walked towards Janeshia's office door. It was closed.

Tamara Bell, her assistant, looked up at him.

The two of them glared at each other.

"What do you want Adam? I think Janeshia is still on the phone."

"Then I'll just knock on her door and see if she's available. That is if you don't mind Tamara?"

Tamara slanted her eyes in protest.

Adam walked quickly past her and knocked softly then swung the door open without waiting for an answer.

Janeshia turned around abruptly. Her face frowned when she

saw Adam.

He glanced down at her. She was staring out of her window again. He noticed a pile of reports spread out on her desk.

"Excuse me Janeshia but I need a moment of your time."

Janeshia swiveled her chair around to her desk.

Adam took in the dark circles under her eyes. He watched her with intent eyes. She looked exhausted. He gave her a contemptuous look. "I see you've been letting your work pile up on your desk?"

Janeshia's confidence was shaken. She hated the way Adam could make her feel inadequate. "Oh…Yeah well," she shuddered. "Is there something you wanted?"

Adam raised his brow in concern. "I don't wish to upset you. I was just offering to help. However not today," he hesitated. "Today I wanted to ask you for two favors. The first one being if I could leave early and the second if you could recommend a good restaurant."

Janeshia breathed out slowly. "Your leaving early is a reasonable request. In fact I'm leaving early too," she nodded. "Oh yeah, about that restaurant, of course Morton is one of the best restaurant's in town."

At nine thirty that night, Janeshia sat quietly in the lounge area of the Fairmont Hotel looking around the room. Ramsey was over an hour and a half late. She'd called her cell phone for the past half hour with no answer.

Clank, clank! The hard clanking noise of a man's shoe hitting the marble floor came from the corridor. A pair of black men's shoes came into view. She glanced up.

The man wearing the shoes glanced at her as he walked quietly by. He smiled softly. Quickly Janeshia turned her attention away.

All at once a familiar voice sliced the air.

"Janeshia! Is that you?" Adam asked smugly as he closed the gap between them.

Stunned, Janeshia looked up suddenly.

With a wise guy expression he said. "Don't tell me you're waiting on your date?"

The corner of Janeshia's mouth twitched nervously. "I am," she announced rudely. "Or I was." She stood up. "I was just leaving."

Instantly Adam stood beside her motionless. A terrible sadness came over him. He looked back at her with a lost expression. As if someone had knocked the wind out of his sail. His shoulders slumped. He took a deep breath. His voice shook, as he turned to walk away. "I'm sorry if I'm brothering you."

Janeshia's heart went out to him. Her hand reached out and touched his shoulder. "No, I'm sorry Adam. I didn't mean to be rude. Is everything okay Adam? You look a little down."

The two stood in silence several seconds.

Adam glanced back at her. A deep sadness creased his brow.

Janeshia thought Adam was about to cry. She tugged at his sleeve. "Here Adam, let's sit down."

"Thanks," he choked out in a low sob.

Janeshia quickly glanced at her watch. She wondered how long she should stay and try to console Adam. If she left now she could stop off and grab a burrito before the taco shack closed.

Adam glanced back at her with a look of gratitude.

She felt guilty for wanting to ditch Adam while he was feeling so down.

A few minutes later Adam faintly smiled and said, "Thanks for being so nice, Janeshia. I guess you can tell I was kind of at a loss. I've never been any good at the dating thing," he whispered in a sad voice.

"Oh Adam," she said softly patting his hand.

"Ah Janeshia, do you think I could tell you what happened?"

She nodded with a deep concern.

He stared into the distance and spoke slowly. "When I was thirteen, I liked this girl named Annabel Dawson. I asked her to go out with me and she agreed," he shook his head admiringly remembering. "It was the best Saturday of my life. I took her to see a movie. We did the corny kids' stuff and shared popcorn together. I took her to the movies every Saturday for the rest of that summer too," he paused. His eyes glazed over. "Then school started back. And I thought everything was fine. I thought that she was just busy all the time, because we were back doing the school thing. I had a best friend named Danny Webber. He was the coolest kid I ever knew," he choked out. "One day I stopped by to visit Danny because he'd stayed home sick from school. His sister let me in. I went up to his room and caught him screwing Annabel's brains out. Then later I found out Annabel was only going out with me hoping she could be close to my best friend Danny Webber. I guess I haven't had any luck with girls since."

She reached out and touched his hand.

He sighed heavily and kept his eyes on the table. "I'm sorry Janeshia for letting my emotions show like that. I guess I was just fooling myself about my date. I was attracted to her and thought she was attracted to me. But as you can see I was wrong."

Janeshia glanced up with a caringly expression. She patted his hand comfortingly. "We've all picked the wrong people at times. Look at me. I've just been stood up tonight too."

Adam's lips slowly bent into a faint smile. "I guess we both have something in common," his eyes slightly glazed over with a pleading expression. He leaned over and took her hand. "Janeshia if you don't mind," he hesitated. "Could I ask you to please have dinner with me?"

Janeshia pulled her hand away from his. She waived her hand so that he wouldn't feel slighted. "I'm not sure if the main restaurant is still serving. Its ten o'clock."

Adam said with a smile in his voice. "But you'll have dinner with me, right?"

"Sure, I've got to eat too…."

He interrupted. "Good and I know an even better restaurant than this one." He said not waiting for her response. His hand motioned for the waitress, "Here let me pick up your check."

Adam's eyes gleamed as he paid the waitress and took Janeshia's arm. "Ready? Let's get going."

They strolled through the lobby of the hotel.

An hour later, they ate angel hair pasta with chicken breast, in a white sauce with mushrooms.

Adam was opening another bottle of Chardonnay. "I guess you really were hungry," he smiled. "I'm so glad you took me up on my offer for dinner."

"Wow Adam, I didn't know you could cook so well. What you did with that frozen chicken breast was amazing." She took a sip of her wine. "By the way your home is absolutely wonderful."

"Well, you've only seen the kitchen and the garage, please let me show you around. I insist," he insisted.

She hesitated and smiled softly.

Adam refilled their glasses. "We're friends now. Now that we've spent this time together you can see that I'm human just like everyone else."

"Yes of course we're friends Adam. But it's getting late. You need to take me back to my car," she said abruptly. She reached for her jacket and remembered she took it off. She hugged her shoulders.

"Janeshia, you're not getting cold. I have the thermostat on 79," he smiled somberly. "You're not thinking of leaving without seeing my place. I know what you're thinking. You're a woman alone and we work together. So I promise I'll only show you the first level, it's my living space. No bedrooms. Look I would feel hurt if you didn't. But I would feel honored if you'd let me show you around."

"Okay but then I have to leave. You must take me back to my car," she insisted.

Several minutes later, Janeshia followed Adam from room to room and drank in the furnishing.

Adam led her into a huge room with a high ceiling. The room could only be described as a great room. Walking through Janeshia was in awe of two huge windows, covered completely with plantation shudders. Hardwood floors gleamed lending a masterful entertainment flow to the room. An extra-large fireplace was flanked by two large lion statues. Hanging above the fireplace was a huge modern art painting. A plush long dark brown leather sofa sat away from the fireplace.

Janeshia walked over and stood in front of the fireplace marveling at the lion statues. She glanced up. Her eyes caught sight of a darkened wall. Once her eyes focused, she shuddered with a cold shiver. A vast array of hand guns and knives meet her gaze.

Adam's eyes caught her gaze. He cleared his throat. "I see you noticed my collection. Don't worry none of the guns are loaded. They are only for display," he assured her. "They are only to add to the feel of the room and make it a true man cave décor."

Nervously she paused. "Yes, it is a man cave," she agreed. She thought quickly about something nice to say.

Adam walked over by the fireplace and pressed a button. The modern art painting gave way to a seventy inch flat screen television.

A thought struck her. "Wow Adam, this room show's you've obviously been busy decorating. Did you pick the colors yourself?"

"Yeah, the walls are the best features. I love rich neutral browns. You can tell this is where all my extra money goes."

Thinking quickly Janeshia turned and faced Adam. She chose her words carefully. "Your home is exquisite and exceptional." She paused. "I love your use of colors. I can't say enough. And now that I've seen your beautiful home I really should be going."

"Have a drink with me," he said walking to the bar. "We must toast your liking my home. You know I value a great compliment."

Quickly Adam poured two brandies and walked back and handed her a glass.

Janeshia lifted the drink. She eyed him over the rim of her glass.

"Thank you Janeshia for having dinner with me. And allowing me to show you my exquisite home"

Janeshia drank from her glass. The Brandy tasted good.

Adam studied her. "Janeshia.......Janeshia....I...I want to...." His hands gripped his drink awkwardly. He quickly gulped down his brandy.

He closed the distance between them and reached out his hand to touch her shoulder. He paused a moment and looked into her deep green eyes.

"Janeshia, this isn't easy for me," he said his voice low. "I have wanted to talk to you privately like this for a long time. I need for you to know something.....Our working together," he hesitated.

She interrupted holding her glass tight like a shield. She

glared up at him. "It's getting late Adam, I really must get going."

Adam's hand traveled lowered. He touched her hand. "Please let me say what I have to say."

Janeshia could sense the change in the atmosphere. The air was warm and tense.

"We spend a lot of time together. I …….."

The doorbell rang out loudly.

A nervous twitch moved in Adam's left eye. "Who the hell is that at this time of night?"

Abruptly Janeshia put down her drink. She was glad for the interruption. She tossed Adam a cautious smile. "You have company Adam. And I really must be going. I'll call a taxi to take me to my car."

Adam's left eye twitched again. It made his expression look sinister.

Janeshia's eyes caught his expression at that precise moment.

He caught her staring and lowered his head embarrassed.

The doorbell rang again followed by a sharp knocking.

Janeshia pushed past Adam and strutted to the door. "I'll call a taxi and wait for it on your front porch," she repeated, this time with a determined sternness.

Adam quickly followed her.

Amazingly he beat her opening the door.

"Adam! Adam my old friend I know I didn't call. But you said I could impose on your good nature anytime." Walker Perrault said sternly strolling into the room.

Adam shifted uneasily and cleared his throat loudly. "Walker I wasn't expecting you. But as always it's good to see you."

"It's good to see you too Adam," Walker replied.

Janeshia staggered nervously back at the sound of his voice.

Walker reached out and steadied her. "Janeshia, I hadn't expected to see you here."

"I…I..," she whispered.

Walker's eyes sought hers. He looked down on her with an inscrutable look as his arms securely locked around her.

A film of confusion over-took Janeshia as she looked up at Walker. Something called out to her in the primitive. Seeing him stirred her emotions. That old mysterious attraction she had for him grew fierce within her and made her heart beat wildly. "I was just leaving. In fact I was just calling a taxi," she uttered nervous and embarrassed.

Janeshia didn't know why but all of a sudden she felt the need to explain. "Walker, I was stood up by my dinner date tonight. And Adam rescued me from sitting alone at the Fairmont. He graciously invited me over and prepared a wonderful dinner," she said in one breath. "I don't know why I'm explaining. But anyway I really need to be getting home. Look, I'm going to wait out front until my taxi comes."

"Well of course you will do no such thing. Look Adam and I can talk later," he said attentively.

All at once Walker turned his head and looked back at Adam. Janeshia thought she had imagined it. Walker was deliberately pretending to be pleasant. But a rage was boiling behind his eyes.

Adam walked closer. "Of course Walker and I can talk later," he cleared his throat loudly.

Janeshia glared back at Walker's face. Finally she realized Walker was still holding her. She pulled out of his arms and looked away nervously. "I don't want to interrupt whatever important thing you came over to talk to Adam about," she said apprehensively.

"Oh, it wasn't important," Walker's expression was so convincing.

Adam glanced at Janeshia unsuspectingly. "Walker is right Janeshia." He swallowed hard knowing he might be in a precarious situation. He still had his wits about him. He realized Janeshia hadn't been aware he had been in the process of seducing her. He studied them. His stomach churned knowing he'd been so close to having her. He couldn't understand it. He was twice the man Walker was. With a calm expression he said, "Janeshia it is too cold outside for you to wait for a taxi. We don't want you to catch a cold. You must take Walker up on his offer to drive you to pick up your car."

Janeshia heard the care and concern in Adam's voice. It made it easy for her to nod her head yes.

A few minutes later, Adam watched them leave and closed the door. He was seething with rage. He was angry at himself. Just a few more minutes and she was supposed to be naked on the leather sofa panting for him. Walker would have come in and found him fucking her brains out. Now he was standing there with a hard on. His plans went wrong. He quickly walked over to the phone and dialed the number.

The telephone line clicked rapidly in his ear. After two rings, he heard a little static and then her voice echo over the telephone line.

"Hello?"

"Hello Phoebe, it's me Adam. What the hell happened? You were supposed to keep Walker busy until I made the call."

Phoebe cleared her throat. "I'm sorry Adam. I know that was the plan. But there was nothing I could do to change Walker's mind. I told you before the man is trust worthy and has an innocent streak a mile long. Innocent is hard to beat. And Walker is one the most innocent and trusting men I've ever known," her voice shook nervously.

"Don't lie to me Phoebe!" Adam screamed into the phone.

"Look Adam I swear to you. In fact, you can check the caller ID on my cell phone. Walker has not picked up a single one of my calls today."

"Where are you?"

"I'm almost at your door. I knew you'd be mad. So I'm hurrying over," she hesitated. "As a matter of fact, I am about to ring your door bell right now."

"Good," his tone was brisk as he opened the door. "Get in here; I need you to earn the money I've been paying you."

As quickly as he could Adam put his arm around Phoebe's waist and pulled her toward the great room.

Phoebe made no protest and started unfastening her coat as they walked.

She hurriedly took off her coat.

Adam walked over and sat down on the sofa. "Take off your sweater.

Phoebe did as she was told. She then released her bra. Her soft full round breast burst into view. She nudged closer to Adam.

Quickly Adam's hands threaded his hands through her hair and pulled her close. His mouth captured one of her breast. He sucked gently.

Phoebe moaned.

Adam pulled away. "You're beautiful," he murmured. "Do you need me?"

"You know I need you Adam," she moaned.

"Then show me how much you need me Phoebe," he said

reaching down and unzipping his pants.

Phoebe lowered her head.

"That's my girl," Adam growled.

She worked her lips and then her magic fingers stroked him, as she performed the magic that Adam loved.

Adam moaned and growled loudly as he felt her tongue slick and hot slid across his groin.

Suddenly Phoebe abruptly stopped and looked up at him. "What?"

"Adam if you scream out Janeshia's name again. I want my money, all of it now," she paused. "And if you don't give it to me. I'm not coming back. You understand?"

He looked back at his erection and knew he would have promised her anything. "I won't.....I won't. I promise," he murmured.

Phoebe started back at him for just a moment longer. "You'd better not, you asshole," she whispered under her breath, before she resumed what she had been doing.

Deep in her heart, she didn't believe him.

Chapter 25

Larissa, Mrs. Olsten & the perfect one for you...

It was the first time in weeks Larissa had seen Janeshia. She studied her face. "Janeshia you look so tired. And you sounded so strange over the telephone. I had to come over and check on you. Goodness, we've both been so busy lately we never get to see each other," she said reaching to help herself to a second serving of orange chicken.

"Don't you think this *Garlic Shrimp* tastes funny?" Janeshia asked spitting it out of her mouth into a napkin.

Larissa grabbed the box of Garlic Shrimp. "I'll eat that too if you don't like it," she said. "Goodness Janeshia, if I knew you'd lost your appetite, I would never had stopped off and picked up so much food. I've never seen you eat so little before. Anyway, I don't have a date tonight, my having garlic breath won't matter."

Janeshia ran her hands through her hair as she walked over and purposely sat down by her best friend. "Larissa, I don't know what's wrong with me lately. I can't sleep. I can't eat. I think my blood pressure is high," she sighed feeling her forehead.

Larissa shrugged. "Do you want me to call an ambulance, or a shrink or would you just like to talk to me?"

Janeshia sighed. "First I've got to know what you have been

up too."

"Whatever do you mean?"

"I mean that when I talked to my cousin Greystone, he mentioned that he thought you were back to believing you still had a knack for doing investigation work."

Larissa shrugged. "I don't just have a knack, I'm gifted. I can spot a fraud a mile away," she sighed. "Well, I'm good at doing the investigation thing. In fact I have a client."

"Names please?"

"Janeshia you know I can't give out a client's name. Anyway weren't we talking about you and Ramsey? Weren't you upset with him about something?"

"Yes I was and just for the record. I want you to know I know you are changing the subject." Janeshia breathed out. "Anyway, at first I thought I was upset because Ramsey hadn't tried to call me or contact me or anything. But the more I think about it, I'm more upset that Walker saw me at Adam's house. And then the whole time during the drive when he took me back to my car, he didn't say a word to me. Not a single word. It was the loneliest drive of my life. Oh what must he think of me?"

Larissa watched her friend intently. "Janeshia, what's gotten into you lately? You've been madly in love with Ramsey for weeks. Now you are worried about what Walker thinks?"

Janeshia shook her head and choked back a sob. "Oh Larissa I'm so down in the dumps lately. I feel so unhappy lately. I just don't know how to explain it. When I look at it, I really don't have a lot in common with Ramsey. And then there's Walker. When I saw him the other night," she paused. "We are the same. We like so many of the same things. I don't know. I'm just so miserable…." Her voice tapered off. She looked off into the distance with her thoughts.

Larissa took another bite of food and peered back at her friend. "So do you just want a good listener or do you want me to tell you what to do?"

"What did you say?" Janeshia asked anxiously.

"Oh never mind, I know you're not paying attention," Larissa said but didn't wait for an answer. "Anyway who cares if Walker saw you at Adam's place? You're in a romantic relationship with Ramsey. And as you will recall, Walker was going out with Phoebe Wright. And the girl does have assets men seem to love and women envy."

Janeshia looked back at her friend, her well arched eyebrows raised in surprise. "Well I'll admit, when I saw Walker with Phoebe I was a little jealous. She's not Walker's type. I mean, I'm more of Walker's type than she is," she blurted out without thinking.

Larissa looked thoughtfully at her best friend. "Oh and you think you are all right for Walker?" It was an outrageously personal thing to ask. She hoped it would encourage her friend to tell her true feelings.

Janeshia laughed and shook her head and hoped her friend didn't see the truth. "Ha! No......That is so not true," she turned away. "Larissa, I didn't say that I was right for Walker. I don't know what I'm feeling about Walker. Sometimes I just miss some of the nice things he used to do. He used to say," she said with a deep searching look. "Did you know he used to put a little array of Blue Violets with a small heart shaped card on the windshield of my car? Gosh I miss that," she said with a deep sigh and murmured hoping she didn't hear. "He did so many unexpected things that I just took for granted."

Larissa's eyes brightened. "Hmmmm let me see if I can keep everything straight. You admit you are annoyed that Walker is seeing Phoebe? Yet you say you only miss him. Next you tell me you miss the guy but you say it's not true that you really think you and Walker would be better for each other. And finally you are in a romantic relationship with Ramsey"

Janeshia rubbed her brow. Her voice rambled and she changed the subject. "You're over analyzing everything as usual Larissa. Anyway, who said I was in a romantic relationship with Ramsey?"

"Okay, then next I'll have to get the facts straight on just what Janeshia Arizona James believes is a romantic relationship. So answer me this question. It's about Ramsey. Have the two of you had sex yet?" she probed.

"Oh my goodness! I should have known you were going to ask that! And in that high society attorney voice you always use when you want to make someone feel like they are on trial," she said amused. "You know I bet there is a shrink somewhere who would just love to analyze you to find out why you always talk like that when you talk about s-e-x."

"No there isn't, because I only talk like that when it's proper to do so. When I am actually screwing some guy, I say the word fuck. Now don't change the subject," Larissa demanded. "Anyway I can tell what you did with Ramsey just by looking at you.

"Okay go ahead, tell me. I want to hear this," Janeshia said gazing at her friend as if she was a loony.

"My lawyer instincts tell me there's been a lot of heavy petting between the two of you. That you wanted more. But no true sexual intercourse has happened between you and Ramsey."

"Your lawyer instincts," Janeshia sputtered in disbelief. "Really Larissa, my sexual relationship with Ramsey……," she hesitated and swallowed hard. "Well, it is a little bit complicated," she sputtered out. "Oh how do you always know?"

"Okay, I figured out as much. Now spill it. I want all the details!" Larissa shrilled.

"I guess I may as well tell you the truth. Ramsey was lousy in bed. In fact we never had intercourse. He got way too drunk that night and he acted like a teenager the whole time. I was glad when he passed out. But the next morning the guy did this *it's time we left* thing and cut our trip short. We left within the hour."

Larissa shifted uncomfortably. Like an old observer in a courtroom. "Whew, that must have been a huge let down for you. I really don't know what to say. Next time if something like that ever happens again you call me. I'll come and get you. God knows what could have happened. "

"Yeah you're right," Janeshia shrugged. "You were right when you said some men look like the complete package but they are inadequate in doing normal stuff in normal ways."

Larissa's smile widened. "What I really said was…..Some men who looked like the complete package can't fuck worth a damn."

Both friends laughed out.

"Come on, let me help you clear away this food,' Larissa said making her way to the kitchen.

The two friends chatted easily, catching up on old times and Janeshia's recent dates with Ramsey Montgomery.

Twenty minutes later the dishes were cleaned dried and put away. Janeshia grabbed a paper towel to dry her hands.

Finally Larissa spoke up. "Whew! You and your men problems," she said indifferently shaking her head. "I knew Ramsey was strange from the beginning."

"Okay, on wise woman with ten degrees from the University

of the minds of men. What do you mean?"

The two of them strolled leisurely from the kitchen back into the living room.

Janeshia sat down in one of her two Ascot chairs and kicked her shoes off. She nestled in cozily.

Larissa took the other Ascot chair and grabbed the pearl gold color pillow. She clutched it in her hands choking it. "I can't put my finger on what it was exactly, but when I saw Ramsey, I just knew there was something sinister and shifty about him. I just wished I pushed the issue with you more to stay away from that man."

Janeshia glanced at her friend. "Oh come off of it Larissa, you don't mean that. The man is exceptionally handsome how can you say he looks sinister?"

Larissa glanced at Janeshia sharply. "Honestly, it was like a sinister animal was lurking within. He had such a negative look in his eyes, like something was incomplete, like he was hiding something. Maybe it was just from his years of being a CEO and always having to hide behind a poker face," she said shrewdly. "And then he's always off on one of those business trips, claiming he's doing CEO stuff, yeah right?"

"Yes well that is true. The man is a CEO."

Larissa regarded her with a quizzical eye. "Janeshia haven't you realized that Ramsey never brings you around any of the local places where there's a chance he might run into some of your friends or family?"

Janeshia leaned back in her chair deep in thought as she studied her best friend. Larissa did have a point. "But...."

Larissa looked back at her best friend with a deep concern. "But what? Janeshia I know you, Ramsey's not being around much really does bother you. You need a man who's available and exclusively yours," she said touching her friend's arm. "I know you tried so hard to get him and it's none of my business. But is Ramsey really right for you? Does he make you happy?"

The smile in Janeshia's eyes vanished. She glanced up with a puzzled expression. *Sometimes Larissa could make so much sense,* she thought.

The two friend's eyes locked, understanding each other perfectly.

A few moments later the doorbell rang.

"I'll get it," Larissa said. "You don't have any shoes on

Janeshia," she quickly grabbed a napkin to wipe her hands.

"Ding! Dong! Ding!" The bell rang out again.

"I'm coming, hold your horses," she yelped.

Larissa peeked through the key hold and shrieked. "Mrs. Olsten?" She slowly opened the door.

"Hello Larissa, my I come in? Where's Janeshia?" Mrs. Olsten asked but didn't wait for an answer. She strutted into the living room. "Oh Janeshia there you are."

"Mrs. Olsten is everything alright? My, you're dressed up," Janeshia inquired.

Mrs. Olsten frowned and sniffed the air. "It smells like Chinese food in here," she said folding her hands in front of her. "Look Janeshia, I was on my way out to the dance at the Senior Citizen center when I happened to notice that young man of yours looking awfully sad waiting by the elevators," she said pausing. "So I invited him in," Mrs. Olsten said. "But he's been over at my place for over a half hour waiting for your friend Larissa to leave and I'm afraid if he stays any longer, he's going to make me late for my dance," she shrugged her shoulders. "Janeshia I must beg you to please take your boyfriend off of my hands and get him off of my sofa before he leaves a permanent crease."

Janeshia swallowed hard. "Excuse me? My boyfriend?"

"Yes you know the one you had over here before. That Walker fellow, the one I think is perfect for you," she paused. "Stay right here I'll go and fetch him for you."

Larissa stifled a laugh. "Janeshia has a boyfriend. Janeshia has a boyfriend. Boy is this going to be interesting. Should I stay or should I go," she laughed. "You know Janeshia I could just go and eavesdrop in the other room?"

"Oh shut up!" Janeshia ordered.

A few moments later Mrs. Olsten appeared at the door with Walker in tow.

Walker darted into the living room and uttered quick greetings. He pushed his hands nervously into his pockets.

"Janeshia here he is. I really must get going," Mrs. Olsten said with dignity. "Now you two enjoy your evening. I know I certainly will enjoy mine. The dances at the center are so much fun."

Mrs. Olsten stopped talking abruptly and fixed her attention on Larissa. "Oh Larissa, I almost forgot that you were here," she said sternly. "Shouldn't you be somewhere else? I mean don't lawyers have clients to meet or something to do? I don't mean to be rude but you should give Janeshia and Walker a little privacy. Don't you think?"

"Yes, Mrs. Olsten you are completely right. I'll just grab my purse and follow you out," Larissa said, she loved that Mrs. Olsten was being the matchmaker.

Larissa grabbed her purse and gave best friend a glance and pinched her as she walked by. "Janeshia, I'll give you a call," she said closing the door after them.

Seconds later, Walker cleared his throat softly. He tentatively asked. "You maybe, were wondering why I was over at Mrs. Olsten's?"

Janeshia stood there staring silently.

Slowly Walker walked further into the room. He was wearing a classic black men's two button suit with a cream colored shirt. The combination made Walker look incredibly handsome.

Walker brushed past her as he walked by strolling over to look out of the window.

Janeshia closed her eyes and breathe in deeply. She loved the primitive sensual quality Walker always radiated. She felt the heat rising in her body. She wanted him badly. She smiled softly realizing that those feelings only happened with Walker. She shook her head remembering Ramsey could never make her feel as hungry for him as Walker did.

Walker's voice interrupted. "Janeshia are you alright?"

Janeshia opened her eyes. Her mouth dropped open in wordless surprise when she found Walker staring.

Her deep green eyes watched him like a hawk stalking its prey. She felt like she was walking through a dream. Her thoughts raced back to the last time he was here at her home. Desire shot through her. Burning and intense she could feel her body starving and burning for the lovemaking that only Walker could give. She spoke without realizing it.

"God Walker, I never noticed how terribly handsome and sexy you are," she softly said off of the top of her head. "It must be that suit. It's torturing me, screaming out that you must really look good naked underneath," she said boldly looking down at his crotch.

"You look rock hard and standing at attention."

Walker gave her a quick glance. His body tensed. "What did you say?" he asked as he walked closer.

Janeshia looked back at him. She was surprised to see a crooked grin tug at his mouth. Then she realized what she had just said. She clapped her hand over her mouth and blushed embarrassed.

"Please excuse me. I don't seem to be able to control the words that come off of my tongue. What I meant to say was would you like something to drink?"

Walker looked deep into her eyes and his fiery gaze held her, refusing to release her. He closed the gap between them

Janeshia stood there and couldn't move.

"Yes I'd love a drink."

"I'm so sorry Walker. I have no clue why I said."

They stood facing each other.

Walker looked at her questionably. "I don't want you to apologize. I like the compliment," he leaned down and clasped her chin with his fingers.

She looked up at him.

He saw her pulse, beating in her throat. He knew what he wanted. He murmured. "In fact, if the truth be told, I love the compliment and the woman that gave it. And I'd like nothing better than to make love to you, if you want me to."

The kiss was warm, soft and gentle as he lightly brushed her lips. Slowly he teased her.

Impatiently she nipped at his lips wanting more. She groaned.

He kissed her harder, licking and nibbling at her mouth until she gasped. He swept his tongue between her parted lips he caressed her tongue with his own.

Abruptly she pulled away.

He froze his heart stopping. "What's wrong?" he protested.

She pulled off her shirt. "I want to feel your hands touching my body," she said as her hands reached out and started unbuttoning his shirt. She looked back at him.

Walker looked back at her tenderly. He drew in the scent of her. Hurriedly he eased off his pants.

He froze again and looked around. They were still in her living room.

"What's the matter?"

"Janeshia are you sure you want to do this here in the living room?"

"Yes!" She exclaimed exultantly. "We can do it again later in the bedroom. Right now I feel like the cork of a champagne bottle about to explode," her lips curved into a sensual invitation.

Walker's hand eased her back on the sofa. His hands slide down and found her breast them. "Your breasts are like ripe fruit," he said as his mouth covered one of them.

Janeshia didn't have a chance to respond before a shock of pleasure pierced her body. She drew in a deep breath and moaned.

His mouth moved from her breast back to her mouth, smothering her moans as his hands slid down lower and lower, touching and possessing her.

Her legs opened eagerly for him. Her body arched against his.

She let her body surrender completely to the passion Walker's touch ignited. She felt him there as his body probed, then pushed and then thrust against hers. She felt the hot pleasure of delight grow as she lost herself in the mindless pleasure of loving and being loved. Her hips moved frantically to the rhythmic contact of his body.

She cried out with delight at the pleasure he gave. She felt the swift intake of breath when she shuddered with desire as she felt him release the physical delights of his body.

Afterwards they laid still. Walker's body imprisoning hers, slowly and quietly he rose up and looked down at her. "Look at me Janeshia," he commanded. "I love you. Do you know that?"

She swallowed hard. "But what you don't know is that I love you too."

"Then that's great, we should talk ……."

She reached out and pressed her fingers to his lips. "Shhhhh. No more talking about love okay?"

Walker nodded pulling her close.

Chapter 26

Claire Marie Perrault & her memories....

Two weeks later, Janeshia finally made up her mind. She had to break things off with Ramsey.

Although she had spoken to him on several occasions, she had still not seen him in person. When he'd called her at work earlier that Friday morning she told him things were over. It was time to move on. But Ramsey had proven to be unbelieving that things could be over between them. He persuaded her to meet him for dinner. She had agreed with the promise that if he didn't show up for dinner, nothing else needed to be said.

She checked her watch. It was well after eight thirty. She had been waiting for him for almost an hour. What a lonely way to spend a Friday night she thought. But this was her last time being stood up by Ramsey. Now he had to understand things were over between them.

For several minutes she was caught up in her own thoughts and she forgot where she was. She slowly reached for her cocktail, finished it and smiled. Now more than ever she was sure she wanted to be with Walker. Quickly she waved her hand for her waiter to bring her check. She was about to pay her check and leave when she looked up and stared at the man walking her way.

"Ready to order some dinner?" he asked leaning over to kiss her check.

The question was ordinary enough but coming from Ramsey Montgomery whom she hadn't seen for weeks, made her angry. How dare he walk in here saying nothing more than are you ready to order dinner when she hadn't seen him for weeks?

Janeshia could feel her body tense. Her voice was seething. "I don't think I'm hungry. In fact I was just about to leave." She rose.

"None sense," Ramsey laughed softly. "Calm down Janeshia and please sit down. You agreed to talk to me. And I agreed to meet you here in town. Right here in front of any local reporters that maybe sitting right here, at this very moment."

"Why would our personal lives be of interest to a local reporter?"

Ramsey felt overwhelmed by his own ego and boasted. "Janeshia you forget that I am Ramsey Montgomery, a CEO and a man with the best venture capitalist connections this valley has ever seen. Hell, I'm the most well connected man in this valley period, if I do say so myself. Any reporter with a thought of his own could easily connect the dots and figure out who I am. Then I'm sure they'd make up a scandal so huge that it could make our lives at the very least uncomfortable or at the worst destroy both of our lives."

She knew he was right. But she kept her guard up. She leaned back in her chair.

"Okay let's have dinner then we'll talk."

Ramsey pinned her with his gaze. He smiled. "I'm so glad to hear that," he said as he quickly waved their waiter over to take their dinner order.

An hour and a half later, Janeshia sat her fork down. The remnants of her dinner sat before her as she slowly sipped her wine.

Ramsey held up his glass and studied the wine. "You know Janeshia I bet you don't know that the Pinot Grigio is an Italian light bodied wine that is the most popular one produced out of Pinot Gris grape variety. Did you know that?

"No, but I figured it was your favorite. Since you've drank two bottles all by yourself," she said.

He chuckled softly. "Wine gives a man courage to hear the things he fears most. You know what I fear most, Janeshia?"

Janeshia merely nodded. She looked back at him questionably. "No, but I'm sure you are going to tell me."

The lines around Ramsey's mouth tightened. "I fear losing you. I don't want you to break up with me. I need you Janeshia. In fact, I am a man who is willing to make sure you are available for me exclusively, I'll pay any price you name," he hesitated.

Janeshia gasped. "Pay any price; you talk like I'm for sale Ramsey."

Ramsey's jaw clenched. "Who said that? I never said that. That's not what I meant and you know it Janeshia," he leaned over and whispered. "What I meant was that I want to make you a proposal. Let me be clear I mean a business proposal of sorts."

Janeshia crossed her arms over her chest. "You know Ramsey, you really should stop talking. I'm starting to dislike you more and more."

"Don't break up with me. I couldn't stand it if anyone found out you broke up with me."

"Oh, so that's what this is all about," she shook her head. "The great CEO Ramsey Montgomery doesn't like to be dumped?"

"No!" He doesn't like it when a woman doesn't find him irresistible. Why can't things just go on the way they have been Janeshia. What will it take to make it continue? I'll give you anything you want; a car, a house, money for you, money for your foundation. You name it!"

Janeshia raised her voice. "What don't you get Ramsey? Don't you get it? Don't you understand? Ramsey a relationship has to be built on something more. On the quality of time two people spend together, on love. Not on things! That's why I'm breaking up with you!"

"Janeshia! Is this man bothering you? Do you want me to call for help?" The question was politely asked but with a stern tone.

The sound of a familiar voice sliced through the air.

Janeshia whipped her head around. "Oh my God Mrs. Perrault?"

Janeshia took two deep breaths and rose to greet her. She was amazed at how pale and shaken she looked. "What are you doing here?"

Claire Marie Perrault walked closer with her head held high

with a dignity that would have made any queen envious.

"Janeshia, I asked you before, please call me Claire Marie," she said taking her hand to steady herself.

Claire Marie turned and looked Ramsey straight in the eye. There was something familiar about him. "Mmmm, who is this young man you're having dinner with?"

"Ramsey Montgomery this is Mrs. Claire Marie Perrault," Janeshia quickly made introductions.

Claire Marie greeted Ramsey with a courteous smile. Her gaze never left his. "May I call you Ramsey, Mr. Montgomery?" she asked but didn't wait for an answer. "And may I please be allowed to join the two of you?"

Ramsey gazed back at her. "Mrs. Perrault, I don't see you as taking no for an answer. By all means have a seat."

The next few minutes were intense as the three of them sat together.

Janeshia sat and noticed how it appeared that Mrs. Perrault stared at Ramsey as if in a trance.

Even Ramsey seemed to notice. He leaned over and whispered "Janeshia, do you think Mrs. Perrault fell asleep with her eyes opened? What do you think she finds so interesting about me?"

Janeshia shook her head. She leaned over and touched Mrs. Perrault's hand. She didn't winch.

'Mrs. Perrault! I mean Claire Marie," Janeshia said shaking her hand. "Are you alright?"

Slowly Mrs. Perrault turned her head blinking. "I'm fine...I'm fine. I'm just lost in my memories. Memories don't leave like people do."

Ramsey cleared his throat. "Mrs. Perrault I hope you don't mind my saying this. But you've got one of the most intense stares I've ever seen. It seems like you can look straight through a person," he hesitated. "If you don't mind my asking, why were you staring at me so intently?"

Claire Marie Perrault took her time answering. She seemed to be choosing her words carefully. Her eyes looked so sad. "I'm so sorry to be making a pest of myself," she took a deep breath. "But all that I can say in my defense is that you look so familiar to me Ramsey. You remind me of a boy I once knew."

"What happened to the boy?" Janeshia caringly asked.

"I was told he died in his youth," Mrs. Perrault hung her head sadly.

Ramsey rubbed his chin nervously. "I'm so sorry for your loss. I bet that must have been hard on you," he said. "I can see the loss still greatly affects you. Goodness I don't know what to say."

Both Ramsey and Janeshia looked at each other in silence. Janeshia handed Mrs. Perrault a tissue.

"Thank you for your kindness Ramsey and you too Janeshia," she said blowing her nose.

"How did he die, your young man," Janeshia touched her hand. "If you don't mind my asking."

Mrs. Perrault cleared her throat. "Oh, I was told he died in a plane crash," she said closing her eyes fighting back tears. "For years I was haunted by my memories of losing him."

She took a deep breath. "I loved him so much. Now seeing you Ramsey makes me sad for the loss of him…"

She openly sobbed.

"God Janeshia, can't you do something to calm Mrs. Perrault. I hate to see a woman cry," Ramsey said.

"Oh don't mind me Ramsey. I don't wish to upset you. In fact I have a favor to ask. Would you indulge an old woman and give her a hug?"

For a moment Ramsey looked at her in silence. Then he slowly rose and held out his arms.

Claire Marie Perrault rose quickly and walked into his embrace. She clutched Ramsey hard around the waist firm as if holding on for dear life. Her trembling slender hand reached up until it touched the top of his head. Then her nibble fingers ran down the back of his head feeling the bump on the back of the head. Her fingers continued their descent moving swiftly down to the base of his neck. She felt the ridges.

After a few seconds, Claire Marie Perrault said. "Thank you so much for indulging in an old woman Ramsey," she said releasing him. "First love lost is the saddest love of them all."

Ramsey pulled away looking baffled.

He turned his attention to Janeshia.

"Janeshia, I really should be going. I'm pretty sure you wouldn't mind agreeing to finish our conversation some other time, please?"

Claire Marie held up her hand in protest. "Oh, I don't want to appear to be a bothersome old lady but Janeshia broke up with you for real. I believe Janeshia is seeing my son Walker exclusively."

Suddenly Ramsey and Janeshia stared at each other.

Claire Marie turned quickly and eyed Janeshia. "I mean Janeshia?" she said softly. "Do you think you should be meeting Ramsey Pharaoh Montgomery alone again? What would Walker think?"

Ramsey snorted out a laugh shaking his head. "Not many people call me Ramsey Pharaoh Montgomery. How did you know my middle name?"

"Oh," Claire Marie shook her head. "Well now your reputation precedes you. I must have read it somewhere in the newspapers. You are a well-known CEO."

"Ah, yes of course," he said.

Quickly Ramsey turned and focused his gaze at Janeshia and said softly. "Well now Janeshia, it seems you and I don't want to be causing any problems. I guess I'd better get going."

Claire Marie and Janeshia watched Ramsey walk away.

"I'm from a very old French family that hold grudges," Claire Marie said faintly.

Janeshia breathed out slowly. "Mrs. Perrault let me apologize for any misunderstanding about this evening."

"Oh, Janeshia I wasn't talking to you when I said that," she softly laughed. "And don't forget I told you to call me Claire Marie."

Janeshia studied her puzzled.

Chapter 27

Blackmail & holding a winning hand...

Later that same night, the night air was chilled as Janeshia left the hotel. She sighed with a deep sense of despair.

A man walked out of the restaurant and stepped right in front of her and yelled for a cab. "Taxi!"

His distinctly familiar voice made her jump out of her reverie. She gasped out loud.

At that precise moment the man turned and looked in her direction. He stared at her in wonder. "Janeshia? What are you doing here?"

A yellow and black taxi cab hurled to the curb.

"Adam, I was just going to get my car. I see you are catching a cab. I won't keep you," she said.

"No...No. It wouldn't be right if I let you walk to your car alone. The cab driver can get another fare," he said closing the distance between them. He hooked her arm in his. "Please let me walk you to your car. It'll give us a chance to talk."

Against her better judgment Janeshia relented. "Alright."

Twenty minutes later she shook her head wondering how she ever let Adam talk her into giving him a ride home.

"Well Adam it was good talking to you. It looks like we've reached your place. You can get out now," she said anxiously parking the car.

Adam smiled. "By the way I wanted to tell you. You did a nice job handling the board the other morning."

"What?" She smiled Adam was giving her a compliment.

Adam turned and stared at her. "Good, now that I have your attention maybe you can hear me out Janeshia. Why don't you come inside and let me offer you a drink."

"No!"

She could see where this was leading. Nervously she replied. "Okay what is it this time Adam?"

Adam's eyes narrowed immediately. He rubbed his face. "I see I will have to persuade you a little bit," he sighed. "Okay I think you will want to hear what I have to say. In fact I know you will want to hear what I have said, especially since it has to do with work you're continuing to receive, shall we say, the great admiration for the things that you do."

Janeshia breathed out slowly. "What do you want Adam? Is it some recognition or is it a new position at work?"

Adam leaned forward and made sure he had eye contact. He smiled sweetly. "I want you to sleep with me. You know have sex with me," he shrugged. "If you sleep with me I won't tell Walker that's what you and I were doing the night that you were over to my place," he said with a smug smile. "Walker thinks nothing happened between us the other night when you were at my place. And I'm sure you want to keep it that way?"

Janeshia closed her eyes tight. She couldn't believe this was happening to her. All at once she blurted. "What if I told you I don't give a damn about what you tell Walker?"

Adam could see she needed to be convinced. His thoughts raced. He needed more ammunition to persuade her. "Ah you don't mean that." He paused. "Because I'm sure that maybe you would care about what Walker's mother Mrs. Claire Marie Edmond-Perreault thought if she knew about you and me. And then there's the board of directors. I wonder what they would think about their director sleeping with one of the employees."

Adam watched her face fall. He laughed softly.

"What?" she asked. She gripped the steering wheel and stared straight ahead.

Janeshia's anger fumed as she tried to ignore his laughter. She thought quickly. "So what, tell your lies, I don't care! I still say no!"

"Well then I guess I will just have to use my Ramsey Montgomery card," he said grinning wide. "You know Janeshia with my Ramsey card it looks like I'm holding a winning hand."

"Mrs. Perrault saw me with Ramsey, Adam," she said staring him straight in the eye.

"Yes I saw the three of you together," he sneered. "Janeshia, Janeshia! I guess you didn't think this thing through, now did you?"

Her anger fumed as she tried to ignore his laughter. She locked eyes with him trying to outstare him. "Are you trying to blackmail me?"

"No…..No…I can see you don't understand," his eyes never left hers. "You see I know you love your career more than anything," he murmured.

Adam waited a second or two and smiled. His teeth looked huge like the Wolf in Red Riding Hood. "So I've saved the best piece of news for last," he paused to letting his words register. "And it's all about you and Ramsey Montgomery."

Janeshia heart beat harder and harder. The suspense was making her tense.

"How would it look to the board of directors that their precious super woman Janeshia James was being a harlot in the community? How would they feel knowing you are dating a married man? Especially when you never could figure out why he kept standing you up"

Janeshia was rooted to her seat.

"Hmmmm, I wonder if Mrs. Perrault knows that Ramsey Montgomery is married," Adam laughed out.

He slowly reached over. His fingers softly caressed her face. Then his hand traveled lower and cupped her breast before moving lower edging closer to the inside of her thigh.

"Stop it Adam," she said pushing his hand away. She choked back a sob.

"Ah I'm sorry," his thoughts raged. "I want you calm and willing," the voice inside his head said.

He cleared his throat. "In fact, I'll tell you what, I'll make this easy for you. I'll give you a couple days to think it through," he said getting out of her car. "Then, I expect to see you here at my place. You give me a call when you're ready," he said sternly before closing the door. "And Janeshia don't make me wait too long."

After an hour of driving aimlessly, Janeshia found herself walking across the front porch and banging loudly on the door.

The hollow sound of footsteps echoed. The front porch light instantly came on.

Janeshia started crying loudly as soon as the front door opened. "Oh Larissa, can I please spend the night with you?"

"Janeshia, what's wrong? Get in here quick. Is somebody after you?"

"No," she said heading into the hall way.

With a choke in her voice Janeshia said. "Oh Larissa, I've been having a real rotten day!"

"Come inside kiddo and tell old Larissa all about it," she grasped her best friends arm and pulled her down the hall.

Janeshia signed. "Oh, it's just that things at work have been so crazy and with my crazy relationship with Ramsey, I just get so lonely sometimes," she hesitated. "In fact I've been so lonely lately I've been almost tempted to take up with Adam."

"What?" Larissa paused abruptly and looked at her friend. She went to open her mouth then realized Janeshia was staring.

"Babe who's at the door?" A male voice sliced the air.

"Who's that?" Janeshia pointed.

"Oh him, "Larissa shrugged and smiled wide. "Well my best friend forever, may I introduce to you Mr. Forcier Devereaux, better known as Force. Now my BFF and my boyfriend have met, isn't this great!"

Janeshia felt nauseous. "Oh God, I'm feeling sick!" she put her hand to her head. "Oh no I didn't mean because of you Forcier...I mean….. Oh God I've got to go to the bathroom."

A half hour later, the last thing Janeshia remembered before falling off to sleep was adjusting the nightgown Larissa had given her to sleep in. This was right before Larissa pulled the comforter up over her and told her all would be well in the morning.

Chapter 28
Shameful episodes that didn't stay hidden.....

At nine thirty the next morning, Larissa London slowed her car and turned into the rustic charming elegant drive way with a wrought iron locked gate with thick pillars of stone sitting on either side of it.

She let down her window and pressed the button on the voice monitoring system. "Hello, Larissa London to see Mrs. Perrault."

"Yes, she's waiting to meet with you in the library," a male voice called out to her. The wrought iron gate opened slowly.

A few minutes later, Larissa breathed out slowly as her heels clicked loudly on the marble floor. She knocked at the library door.

"Come in," Claire Marie Perrault called out. She was perched behind a massive desk in a winged back chair. The room looked like it had been decorated for a man.

Larissa looked around the room. She never tired of looking at the elegant walls with their old world charm. The crown moldings in the vaulted ceiling would always fascinate her she thought.

For a moment she almost had forgotten why she came. She turned and gazed at the woman sitting behind the desk.

Tendrils of softly graying hair framed Claire Marie's almond shaped face with a natural grace.

"Larissa, please sit down. I almost called you to cancel."

"Oh, why?"

A flicker of concerned emotions showed on Claire Marie face. ""Walker is here. I'm afraid we may be interrupted," she nodded. "Quick please tell me is Janeshia alright?"

"Yes," Larissa said. "She was still sleeping when I left the house."

Claire Marie's sharp gaze speared her. "That is good. She needs her rest. I think it's best if she isn't exposed to Adam. See if you can think of something to keep her from work for a few days, if you can."

"Okay, I will," Larissa replied.

A grimace of concern etched across the old woman's face. "I've tried and tried to think of where to find the answers. I guess you know, every family has secrets. Shameful episodes that they wish would stay hidden."

A heavy silence fell between them while Larissa digested what she heard. She finally spoke up, hoping it would help the conversation keep moving. "Yes, all families do."

"I grew up in Alexandria Louisiana. In fact, I was born there. So was Walker's father. In the South, children are the ultimate gift that a wife gives her husband. After I married Walker's father, Edward Walker Perrault, I discovered I couldn't conceive. We tried everything," she paused. "Walker's father didn't blame me and he even told me it didn't matter. But do you know how humiliated and frustrated I felt?"

Larissa blinked at her sudden revelation. She kept her mouth shut and listened attentively.

Claire Marie's voice quivered. "I did something back then. I think the answers can be found back in Alexandria Louisiana."

Startled by her words Larissa asked, "You want me to go there?"

The sound of feet shuffling at the door interrupted them.

Claire Marie nodded and pressed her finger to her lips, commanding secrecy.

Suddenly the door of the library opened.

"Hello Larissa, I didn't know you were here," Walker said entering the room and shutting the door.

He walked over and perched on top of his mother's desk.

"So Larissa, how is Janeshia doing?"

"Oh Walker Janeshia is fine. She was a little nauseated when she arrived last night."

"Nauseated? Last night? What's wrong with her?" He asked with a look of deep concern.

"Ah," Larissa and Mrs. Perrault looked at each other.

"Oh, Janeshia is fine," Mrs. Perrault assured Walker. "She's just a little tired from all the stress she's been under lately. I'm sure Larissa is taking good care of her best friend."

Larissa nodded. "Yes, I am taking very good care of Janeshia. In fact, I persuaded her to take a few days off from work. She and I have plans to do the Girl Friends Getaway in Carmel, California, for a couple days."

The two women looked between each other.

"Good," Walker said standing to pace. "Mother, perhaps Janeshia is overworked. Maybe she needs help. May be I should go into the office for a few days."

Mrs. Perrault's shoulders stiffened. "Calm down "Walker. You've been given everything Larissa and I both know, Janeshia is fine," she said eyeing Larissa to be silent.

Larissa gazed between mother and son and felt like she was watching the opening of a possible battlefield. She cleared her throat. "Claire Marie, I believe we were talking about Alexandria Louisiana. Would you like to discuss it further or is our meeting concluded?"

"Yes, I think we should. In fact, I think my son should handle this delicate family situation," Claire Marie gave a small smile. "Walker, I need from you is for you to go to Alexandria Louisiana and find Mama Moue Redbones for me. She's the one with all the answers, "her eyes pleaded. "Look my son, I can only trust you to handle this for me, please."

"But what about the foundation?" he asked continuing to pace.

"Walker," Mrs. Perrault sighed heavily. "Larissa will be with me if anything comes up. But nothing will. You go and get packed. I want you on a plane for Alexandria today,"

"Okay Mother," he strode toward the door.

The door closed soundly.

A play of emotion crossed Claire Marie's face. "Oh Larissa?"

"Don't worry I know what you want. You want me to go and keep an eye on him, right?"

"Yes, he is my only son," she said. "But don't let him know."

"I understand," Larissa nodded.

Chapter 29

Las Vegas, Nevada & Yvonne Celeste...

As the yellow streaks of sun light signaled the start of a new day and filtered through the open curtain, the abruptly ringing of the phone forced the man's eyes wide opened.

The telephone rang again.

"Hello"

"Mr. Montgomery?"

"Yeah."

"Look Mr. Montgomery, this is the manager of the hotel, there is a car and driver refusing to move from our front entry way unless you come down. They've been waiting for you for over an hour," the manager said. "I sorry...."

"Tell them to go away," Ramsey gruff out.

The manager's calm voice escalated. "Look this woman was threatening to call the police and make a scene. This hotel has accommodated you as much as we can. But....."

"Okay, I'm coming down."

"No, you don't understand. I'm calling to apologize we

couldn't stall her any longer, we had no choice the woman is on her way up."

"Okay don't worry," he said sitting up on the side of the bed. Something stirred in the bed next to him. Then he remembered he'd stopped off at a burlesque style lounge and picked up a woman.

He reached for his wallet.

"Hey you…..Miss…..Whatever your name. Wake up! You need to go….N-O-W. Here's something extra for your trouble."

The lady was pretty; her long legs were lean. Her jet black hair seemed even longer. She quickly reached out slender long fingers and took the money before rolling out of bed and grabbing her dress. She was used to getting dressed quickly. She made her way to the door. Turned and titled her head coquettishly. "By the way you made my pussy sing." Her green eyes softened. "Oh yeah, you know that little problem I helped you with? Remember all you have to do is focus and concentrate when you do the lessons. It helps."

Ramsey stared at her unbelieving. He watched her close the door. Who knew I'd run into a sex therapist when I needed one, he thought.

He walked to the shower and closed the door.

Instantly a sharp knock sounded loudly on the bathroom door.

"Open the door Ramsey!" A woman yelled.

"Shit! How did you get in?"

"Your whore was leaving. I took advantage of her stupidity. Well aren't you glad to see me?" The woman scolded.

Ramsey looked up at the sound of the voice.

A Majestic framed woman with high cheekbones, a good chin, heavily painted sultry red lips and eyes like Yvonne De Carlo pushed past him.

She was quickly followed by a very large muscle bound broken nose man with a too close crew cut. He walked through the door like he owned the place.

"Hello Ramsey," the big man said. "I must perform my job. Yvonne Celeste would like for me to announce that she would like to pay you a visit," the big man chuckled.

Ramsey stared back at the man's blank dull eyes. He knew the big man wasn't big on brains. But he took his job seriously. He didn't want to piss the big man off. He gazed back at the woman standing in front of him.

All at once Yvonne Celeste reached out and slapped his face twice. "Ramsey you could greet your mother more enthusiastically," she scolded testily. "I also slapped you for being a cad and not returning my telephone calls."

The huge man laughed softly.

Ramsey grabbed his face. "Yvonne Celeste, don't come in here hitting me!"

"Mommy is sorry baby," her voice softens. She kissed her hand and rubbed where she'd slapped his face.

"Don't do that," Ramsey said pulling away.

"Look Ramsey, I don't think I like for you to call me Yvonne Celeste anymore. Plain mommy will be fine from now on. Anyway, I've missed you darling. I was just telling the Big Kona I don't see enough of you."

Ramsey stared back at his mother. Born Yvonne Celeste Anne Baptiste, she had been Mrs. Montgomery, Mrs. Cohen and Mrs. Singh. Each husband was married for his money. Each man left once she had enough of his money to satisfy her appetite for the green pieces of paper.

Ramsey cleared his throat. "Now what is it you want, Mother?"

"Mommy has to go out of the country for a while. I think a cruise will do me some good."

"You came all the way to Vegas to tell me that?"

She shrugged and her mouth turned into a frown. "No I came to Vegas to tell you tag, you're it?"

"What?"

His mother smiled big. "You're present is waiting for you just outside in the hallway."

He shrugged as recognition hit him. "Look, can't we discuss this? I'm sure we can work something out."

"No, Ramsey. We can't. You are the one who decided to divorce Carina. Carina Montgomery was the best thing you ever did in your life Ramsey and she took care of that kid."

Ramsey looked solemnly at her. The former Carina Jordan-Montgomery was a shy petite woman with a flawless complexion. She was a jet-black long haired beauty with deep green eyes. He thought he'd been in love with her. But she was in love with someone else.

"You and I both know Carina and I had an arrangement. She wasn't fulfilling her end of things and we ended the arrangement," he said bluntly.

"You were never home. How can you build a marriage when you are never at home?"

"Carina and I didn't have that kind of marriage."

His mother looked at him. "I know," a painful expression crossed her face.

"Look, I caught Carina in bed with another man, in my home. She knew the rules. I told her to never sleep with anyone in my home."

His mother stared back at him. "Carina was a young healthy woman with a healthy appetite for sex. I know you weren't servicing her needs. I've known for years you can't service a woman in bed. Why didn't you take my advice and see a doctor. You could have saved your marriage."

Ramsey's voice softened. "Mother, please stop. My marriage to Carina is over."

"Yes, but your responsibilities aren't and since Carina is no longer here to take care of your responsibilities. When I leave I'm leaving you a small gift," she hesitated. "Maybe I'll leave you two gifts just so you know I'm serious. I want you to be responsible."

As if on cue Big Kona closed the distance between them.

"Make it count Big Kona – I want him to feel it so that he doesn't smirch his responsibilities but don't hurt him too bad," his mother said.

"All right," the Big Kona said landing a blow.

Ramsey grimaced. "Damn, mother why?" he slouched over in pain.

His mother opened up her purse and took out a gold cigarette case. She put a cigarette between her lips and started to light it. She stopped abruptly.

"Kona go get our little gift and bring her in," she commanded. "Give the maid another hundred dollars for watching her."

His mother stared back at him. "Gosh Ramsey, I've been waiting to light up this cigarette for weeks. You see how responsible I am Ramsey? I didn't light it up. It's not healthy to smoke around a child," she paused letting her words sink in. "Now that is how responsible I want you to be. Because you're my oldest child and I know you can. Besides, you have always been more responsible than your brother."

Chapter 30

February an old friend ....

Two days later, Walker Perrault made his way out of Alexandria International Airport and slowly drove his rent-a-car through the city of Alexandria Louisiana.

The delightful city was located in the center of Longleaf Pine forest.   Walker drove past an old Dr. Pepper billboard and smiled, remembering that as a boy his father had driven him down Jackson Street. They were cruising and drinking ice cold Dr. Peppers together. The city held many fond memories for him.

He eased his rental car off of Highway 49 and took the Jackson Street exit. He was headed for PJ's to have a cup of their famous coffee and to meet someone.

He drove his car into the parking lot with high anticipation. Sure enough he spotted February Duvall's old beat-up 1962 Ford truck. It hadn't changed. Except now it looked like it had a few new dents.

Walker found a rear door just off the parking lot and went inside. He inhaled the rich aroma of freshly brewed coffee through his nostrils and thought he'd died and gone to heaven.

He spotted February sitting at a table in the back. He was thin, not more than five feet seven inches tall. He needed a shave. His stubble was gray and looked sharp enough to cut. His blue gray eyes held a beautiful twinkle.

His piping voice held a beautiful sound, like a musical note. "Hello Mr. Walker Edward Edmond Perrault Junior, it's me February Duvall, your father and mother's oldest friend. It's so good to see you again."

"Hello February, I guess I'll never get used to that Southern custom of calling people by their full given birth names."

"You just remind me so much of your dad. I feel like I have to say it at least once. How is your mother?"

Walker took a seat. "She's fine but she is anxious for some answers."

February nodded. "It's your dollar that you're paying me with. Shall we get down to business?"

Walker nodded thoughtfully, "So what have you got for me?"

"I've got a name for you and I know where the woman lives. But she won't give me any information. I've tried. I've been down to see her twice but she won't tell me anything," February said.

"Well did you offer her money like I suggested? I told you I would pay her for any information she provided," Walker said dryly.

February took a big gulp of his coffee. "She won't take any money, I tried. She said she wants to see you. She even said your name specifically. It was the strangest thing. I didn't tell a soul I was working for you. But this lady knew. Somehow she just knew."

Walker watched February take another gulp of coffee. The man must have had a tongue of steel. The coffee was hot. He watched the stream pour off of it.

"She just knew?" Walker asked.

"Yep, she said she saw your face in the swamp water. She said that she knew you were coming and she told me not to come back again unless I had you with me. Now I can't tell you your business, but you are a man that's worth too much money to be going down back up in the swamp and back woods to see some old woman who practices God knows what," February shuddered, his voice rattled on panicky. "I don't really want to go back that way myself. That woman owns a pack of fierce looking dogs'. He kept talking about the number of dogs the woman owned.

Walker interrupted. "What's her name?"

February looked around. Then leaned over and whispered, "Mama Moue Redbones."

Walker gazed at the February's eyes. He saw a hint of fear when he said her name. He watched his hand as he took a sip of his coffee. His hand was shaking.

February took out a silver flask. He poured it into his coffee cup. He took a big gulp then put the cup back down. "Walker's there's something you should know. This woman ain't some fake psychic playing around with a deck of cards or some old bag of bones. This woman is some kind of old fashioned conjure woman. The kind I really don't like to mess with."

He looked on amazed.

Walker's thought raced. He remembered the name, *Mama Moue Redbones*, was the name of a character in one of the stories his father used to tell him as a child.

"And how do we get there, the place where she lives?"

A fearful fidgeting shake took over February's hands as he went to lift his coffee. He placed the cup of coffee back on the table. "What? You still want to go?"

"You heard me, but I say it a little slower just in case you're heard of hearing…this time. How do we get to her house from here?"

"You have to take the back way in to the Kisatchie forest. Way back into the swamp land. There's nothing but wilderness back there and you have to travel by foot or horseback, until you reach her house."

"So when can we leave?" Walker asked.

"Look, well, I've already been up there two times already. That place is not a field trip full of fun," February said rubbing his face with his hand. "Look I'm not a man easily spooked, but that place has an eerie feeling. But let me make it clear, it's weird up there," he said looking off in a daze. "The wind makes a whispering sad and lonely song. It sounds like a dying love song or something. It does funny things to a man's heart. It can affect a man. I don't know if you want to go there. Look, I'm just trying to keep you from feeling that sort of crippling pain."

"Well, I thank you for looking out for me. But if it's the money you're worried about, I'm paying triple pay if you take me there and bring me back," Walker said assuring him.

February whistled. "For that kind of money of course I'll make another trip up there. I thought you wanted me to take you for free."

Walker finished his coffee. He come this far. He had to see Mama Moue Redbones, no matter what.

Chapter 31

Spa Day with Larissa the private eye…

Three days had passed, since Janeshia and Larissa had come to the Cypress Inn in Carmel California.

A bank of heavy clouds hang over the Pacific Ocean as Janeshia stared out of the huge window.

Janeshia turned her head and stared at her best friend in amazement. "Larissa, you were right. I needed this week off. This was the best spa experience I have ever had. It was just what I needed," she said yarning lazily.

Larissa sat up on her elbow as she watched their masseuse leave the room. "Thank God. I thought that woman was never going to leave."

"Larissa, you the only person I know that will spend money on a massage and then not take advantage and relax."

Larissa rubbed her temple. "This is not just a relaxing girlfriend trip Janeshia. For me it's business too. In fact it really puts me in a spot. With our friendship, I mean."

Janeshia propped her head on her elbows. "What do you mean? Larissa do you still see yourself as some kind of private eye?"

She raised a brow. "Yes, I do. But first I am always an attorney. You know I've done services for you and the foundation. But just so you know, like I said before I can't talk about a lot of stuff right now." Larissa looked back at her friend. "Look Janeshia, remember when we were kids and no matter what happened between us we were always friends. Well, now I need you to have that same confidence in me like you did when we were kids. It's real important right now because I need your help."

Janeshia sighed and propped up on her elbow. "You know I always will, no matter what."

"Good, because I know you are probably not going to understand why and I can't honestly tell you why right now, but I think you need to suspend Adam. In fact as an attorney, who at times in the past has represented you and done business for the foundation, I must insist that you suspend Adam," she said sternly.

"Larissa what are you talking about?"

"Mrs. Perrault insisted I make a few inquiries on Adam. I still have to check a few facts out. But Adam is a liability to the foundation and he may be a threat to you."

"What do you mean?"

"Let's just say you will be placing Adam on paid administrative leave until further notice. I've already had a courier service sent out to serve Adam with the notice."

Janeshia raised her hand and looked dumbfounded. "Looks like you've taken care of everything. I guess there's nothing that I can say or do," she sighed.

Larissa's expression relaxed. She smiled. "Now that we have the business part of this trip concluded. We can get back to having some fun."

"We've done everything fun that there was to do; shopping, girlfriend's spa day. Larissa I'm bored, what else is there to do now?"

"There is something else fun we can do. You and I can go and get dressed and go and see Miss Mary Mackeey."

Janeshia smiled. She wondered if Miss Mary Mackeey could clear her thoughts. At least help her determine who the best man for her was. Her thoughts raced. Maybe Larissa had something there.

Chapter 32

Miss Mary Mackeey sees all and then some...

In the glaring afternoon sun the little cottage painted in a deep purple color with a red front door looked mysterious.

A petite older woman peered at them. Her hair was braided into a crown around her round head. The braided crown was usual and so was the deep purple colored her hair had been dyed.

Janeshia stared at the woman's hair. She'd never seen such a deep shade of purple that vivid before.

"Hi, I'm Janeshia James and this is my best friend Larissa London."

The old lady grinned and her amethyst eyes sparkled. "I know who you are. I'm Mother Kahina, mother of Noita, whom you know as Miss Mary Mackeey. Ladies please follow me into the parlor," Miss Mary Mackeey is waiting for you."

Janeshia and Larissa followed Mother Kahina into a hallway tiled in black marble.

Larissa leaned over and whispered. "Janeshia this room looks strange. I don't remember this place looking like this."

Janeshia pointed and whispered. "Me neither."

"It's the wallpaper. It's a moving optical illusion," Mother Kahina said.

The three of them walked on.

Janeshia stopped and stared in amazement. "Hey look at that."

"It's some kind of design," Larissa murmured. "Interesting, it looks like a mask." She quickly studied the mask. "The thing has a whole where the tongue should be. And it's earless."

"You missed that arrow with a star going through it," Janeshia added. "Do you think it means something?"

"Don't know. It could," Larissa said with a puzzled expression.

Mother Kahina cleared her throat. "Ladies we are almost there." She waved them to follow her.

They turned a corner. Somber shadows on a wall stood in front of them. Several wall clocks hung on the walls. The clocks ticks loudly as they walked pass. They walked a short distance and stood in front of a door and a hallway. The hallway was painted jet black and seemed to go nowhere.

"Ladies please come in through the doorway. I'm afraid the black hallway is just an illusion," a rasped female voice called out to them.

Janeshia and Larissa looked at each other as they walked through the doorway.

The room they entered was round shaped with a vaulted ceiling. The room resembled a séance room of old, with heavy velvet curtains. A round table stood in the middle.

Seated at the table was a woman with beautiful gold earrings dangling from her earlobes, and from where they stood she wore all black. Around her neck was a beautiful solid gold necklace that resembled a Cleopatra collar.

Janeshia's green eyes glittered from the brilliance of the gold. She whistled softly. "Wow! I love that necklace you're wearing. I don't know which is more beautiful, your necklace or your eyes. They are an unusual shade of violent amethyst."

"Thank you. You are correct on the color," Miss Mackeey said. "I have some jewelry for you as well. Please put on this lavender and swamp moss bracelet. Wear it at all times while you're here. I'm Miss Mary Mackeey, by the way."

"Hi Miss Mackeey its Larissa London and my best friend Janeshia James. You remember us, right?"

Recognition dawned. "Oh yes you two came to see me years

ago wanting a love potion. But you were both too young for a love potion. Now I can see I don't have to worry about your being old enough," she laughed sounding as regal as a queen.

Janeshia flushed embarrassed remembering that time long ago.

Larissa gazed fascinated on her host. "Miss Mackeey if you don't mind my asking. How come it seems you never age?"

Miss Mary Mackeey hummed softly to herself. Her eyes narrowed as she cleared her throat and said. "Some people would be surprised to learn that immortals live among us. But I do sell my fountain of youth crème and I can see you need some Larissa," she said without blinking an eye. "But of course you really should stop burning the candle at both ends and get a good night's sleep."

Furious Larissa's mouth dropped open but no words came out.

Again Miss Mary Mackeey hummed softly to herself. "I do sell if you're interested. It only costs three hundred dollars a jar."

Janeshia turned slow and looked into Larissa's shocked face. But still no words came out of her mouth.

Miss Mackeey laughed and turned her gaze. "Miss Janeshia James you are here because you need some answers, right? So let's not waste out time. I believe this reading is for you?"

Janeshia grimaced. "Well I...."

Miss Mackeey interrupted her. "Larissa told me it was. So let me explain what I do. I use 24 carved symbols. Each symbol represents an extension of reality. You will hold the bag carrying them but just for a moment. I will then roll them out on the table before you and they will then help me see the truth by tapping into my psychic consciousness and then we will see what we can see," she said handing her a bag. "But first reach inside the bag and see what you can find."

Janeshia put her hand into the bag. Her fingers touched something. It felt like a thimble. She pulled it out and looked up at Miss Mackeey.

"Oh good, please put that on." Miss Mackeey commanded. "Now hand me back the bag."

Larissa interrupted. "So Miss Mackeey what's your source of power. I'm curious how you get your answers."

Again Miss Mary Mackeey hummed softly to herself as she threw the contents of the bag on the table. "Let's just say, not unlike how attorneys get their answers. Only our sources are more reliable," she laughed and fixed a fathomless gaze on Larissa. "Don't you know that everything in life has a spiritual dimension?"

For a second time that afternoon Larissa was speechless.

The atmosphere in the room grew suddenly still.

Sweet smelling scents over-took the room as the lights grew dimmer.

Janeshia closed her eyes. "I smell honeysuckle. My goodness, I haven't smelled that scent since I as a child."

The haunting music of a lone violin played a strange tune.

Janeshia tossed her head and threw back her hair as she gazed around the room. She couldn't figure out where the music was coming from. "Larissa do you hear that music?"

Larissa didn't answer.

"Larissa?"

She turned to look at her best friend.

Larissa's face looked like it had turned to stone. Janeshia stared in amazement. She glanced between Miss Mackeey and Larissa. Suddenly she realized Larissa was staring at Miss Mackeey, spellbound.

She felt an eerie sensation. As if she was alone in the room with just Miss Mackeey.

Miss Mackeey smiled as her amethyst eyes sparkled brilliantly. "Did you know Janeshia that in an instant, your life can change?"

"You put Larissa under. I mean in a spell or trance or something."

"Yes, the legal side of your best friend's brain can get in the way sometimes I think? Anyway, what may be said here today you may not want you best friend to know about just yet. I told her I only wanted to see you," she laughed softly. "My spell is harmless. This way she won't remember a thing."

"How did you do that?"

Miss Mackeey answered softly. "I have my ways."

"You are the real thing? Ain't you Miss Mackeey?"

Miss Mackeey nodded. "I am a pure psychic hand who recognizes both the male and female deity. I practice the oracle of old magical, so I can conjure or just tap into a person's psychic consciousness. You come to me and I see, what I see. I know what I know. I tell you what I see what I know."

Janeshia shrugged. "Then why am I here?"

Her gaze was keen as she stared back at Janeshia. "You see the runes symbols are chosen by your conscious mind. You are here to learn which one is good and which one is evil." She paused. "You see this stone here. It is the stone of protection."

Janeshia's heart raced with conflict. "I don't understand."

Miss Mackeey shook the bag out on the table. She spread the stones out and concentrated on them.

Time clicked by.

"The stones are clear. You are to be reminded you are safe in your own home, always." She paused. ." The stones tell me you know why you are here. Sometimes you have to lose yourself to find yourself. Always, it's about a man. Just like life and death are two forces in the universe; so is good and evil. One we say is magnificent while the other we call sinister. People can be that way too. And of course men are famous for being one or the other."

Janeshia felt strange. A surreal feeling embraced her.

Miss Mackeey spoke again. "The stones say a great queen has given you her protection. But you were frightened of her and did not understand her proposition. She seeks only to protect you and the child you carry."

Janeshia stared back at her. "Child? What child?"

Miss Mackeey looked back at her as if she was in a trance. "You had sex with your boss; this stone here represents the king. Your child belongs to him."

"What? How…..I mean are you sure? That can't be right. Shake that bag up again."

"Oh very well," Miss Mackeey said doing as she asked. She threw a bone out on the table.

Janeshia looked at the spot on the table where the figure rested. It was the same. "Do it over," she commanded.

"This is the last time young lady," Miss Mackeey sternly said. "You can't make the stones not tell the truth," she admonished.

Again Miss Mackeey shook the bag and threw the stones on the table. Out of the back the king stone flew across the table and landed face up directly in front of Janeshia.

"Yikes!" Janeshia breathed out slowly. She thought someone was standing behind her. She closed her eyes but only for a minute. The room felt powerfully charged. It felt strange and unusual like a physical dimension not of the earth's plane. When she opened her eyes her grandmother Lena Mae Allen sat at the table across from her. A nervous smile crossed her face. She knew her grandmother had to be an apparition. She'd been dead for several years.

"Grandma Lena Mae, what are you doing here?"

"Janeshia baby, I had to come. I need to tell you something. The past, the present and the future are one."

"What Grandma?"

"The future belongs to you. Use your instincts. You must. If you do not you will lose something you love very much. It will make you weep. If you let it you will weep for many years. Don't lose your way."

"Grandmother, I don't understand?"

"Remember you have the love of a man who truly loves you? Isn't that what you've always wanted?"

"But!" Janeshia blurted.

"The answers are there. All humans have limits on their wickedness. Look into your heart and seek out forgiveness, redemption and most importantly love. Think about what you will regret in life if you don't follow your heart. Seek out your true kinsman, your *Boaz*, for he is the only one that is pure in heart. He will redeem you."

Thunder sounded throughout the room. The apparition that was her grandmother seemed to grow faint.

"Janeshia hear me and remember. He who was once wicked is wicked no more. Seek them out for they have the answers you seek. Your baby will need its rightful father," she paused as a roar of thunder roared. "I must go. Miss Mackeey will tell you more. I can see the storm. It is fast approaching."

All at once thunder cracked and roared deeply and her grandmother vanished into thin air.

Janeshia wiped tears from her eyes as she stared back at Miss Mackeey. "My baby?"

"Now you see why I didn't want you friend to hear, yes Janeshia you are with child," she said. "She suspects but she knows nothing."

Wiping the tear from her cheek she realized Miss Mary was more than she seemed.

"I will awaken your best friend now. The two of you should be going back home to San Jose California tonight.

Suddenly a bright light in the room snapped on.

Chapter 33

The wing song, a voice as old as time...

In the early morning Walker stood beside his horse and looked out over the vast green landscape in front of him. The back way in to the Kisatchie forest was beautiful and mysterious.

"Dawn will break soon. We best get started," February said just before mounting his horse.

An hour later, Walker could have sworn he felt every bump as he made his way on horseback.

Wild grass grew lush and green around him. He noticed several strange bloom shrubs and flowers. He was glad they had left out early. He hoped to be soaking in a tub of hot water by the time the dark shadow of night made its way across the sky. The scenery was beautiful, containing some of the most beautiful natural beauty ever be held. From bald cypress groves and old growth pine to vast wild flat topped mesas and sandstone bluffs the Kisatchie National Forest offered some of the steepest and most rugged terrain you could ever see in Louisiana.

The old groves of bald cypress groves and old pine trees seemed to go on forever as they continued to ride up steep rugged terrains.

The horses just stopped as if someone commanded them to

and there she stood; Mama Moue Redbones, she wasn't as old as he thought she would be. But sometimes looks can be deceiving.

The wind sang like a voice as crystal clear sunshine rays streamed through an electric acoustic guitar. Her voice pierced the wind as she spoke in hush whispers; Walker looked at her and wondered if he ever saw her mouth move. But he heard her as clear as the day. The voice was old, and clung to his ears, ringing…..singing…..yes like singing….

She shook her head. A smile crept onto her lips as if a long lost son had found his way home…..“Well, well, well…..just look at you Walker all grownup… Looking straight at Walker she asked, “Have you come here to wake the dead?”

And then he heard her laughter
“Deeeee…..heeeeee….heeee…..” she laughed at him. “I'm only playing with you boy. Come on in why don't you?” she giggled. “It's good to see you again.”

Chapter 34

You underestimated me.....

A day later, Janeshia returned home and barely noticed her surroundings as she parked her car. She walked to the elevator, letting her mind roar on autopilot. She mulled over the past few days events.

There was so much to think about. She couldn't believe she really was really pregnant. But it would explain a lot of the fluttering her body had been having lately. But was it Walker's baby? She thought it over. He was the only person she'd had sexual intercourse with, and unprotected sex at that. What was she going to do? If Walker made her pregnant he needed to know.

She reached her condo door and fumbled with her purse, digging, fumbling for her keys. She was so frustrated with herself, she cried out loud admonishing herself. *"Damn Janeshia, no wonder you're pregnant. How could you be so stupid having unprotected sex with your boss?"* She found her key and opened the door struggling with her bag.

Suddenly she heard something behind her and looked over her shoulder. Her heart nearly jumped out of her chest as she jerked around. "What!" she blurted out. "Adam are you crazy? You nearly scared me to death!"

A desperate expression gleamed across Adam's face. With a touch of sadness in his voice he said, "I'm sorry I frightened you. Look I really need to talk. It seems everything has been going wrong in my life lately."

Thoughts raced through Janeshia's mind as she wondered what to do.

"Please," he pleaded. "I was just driving by when I saw your car pulling in to the parking garage. I figured maybe you wouldn't mind if I stopped by for a minute," a desperate plea escaped his lips. "Look, I can help you with that bag.

Janeshia stared at Adam and considered his request. "Okay put the bag in the hallway," she said. "Oh and Adam the kitchen is that way," she pointed. "There is some instant coffee in the cabinet by the stove. You'll find the tea kettle on the top of the stove, there's water in it just turn it on. Make us both a cup, and I'll join you in a minute."

"Thanks I'll do that," relief flooded Adam as he watched her turn and stroll down the hallway.

A few moments later Janeshia closed her bedroom door. A clean sweatshirt and pair of jeans lay on her bed just where she'd left them before she left on her trip to Monterey, California. She removed her sweater and pulled the sweat shirt over her head. She unfastened her jeans. A sudden strange sensation of cool air hit her all at once. She felt like she was being watched.

"I just love the sight of a beautiful woman removing her jeans," a familiar voice said. "Finally, I have you alone with no chance of escape," he chuckled softly. "Now all that's left is for you to remove those panties."

Janeshia's heart raced. "What the hell are you doing in my bedroom Adam? I told you to wait for me in the kitchen. Get out!" she said explosively.

"Funny but I didn't feel like a cup of coffee Janeshia. I brought my own drink with me. Would you care for some," he said removing a flask and taking a drink. "Ahhhh my drink is so refreshing. See for yourself," he said offering her the flask.

"No thank you Adam, please get out!"

Adam moved swiftly like an arrow release from a bow hitting its target. He closed the distance between them. "Now don't get all excited and I wouldn't scream if I were you. We can talk this out in a calm manner. Just you and me; all alone without the board of

directors or anybody else," his smile made his teeth look huge.
"Now sit down!" He pushed her down on the bed and sat beside her.

He took another drink from the flask.

Nervously she stammered. "Look Adam, we can talk
tomorrow at work. That way we'll both be refreshed and level
headed when we sort things out. Okay?"

He gruff out a menacing chuckled. "Sort things out? Oh
really Janeshia, you seem confused," he sarcastically said. "Funny.
That's why I'm here tonight, to sort things out."

She grimaced at the sound of his voice. "I don't know what
you mean?"

"Yes you do honey, I'm trying to give you a second chance.
Do you think you could get rid of me with a suspension notice? I'm
not going away that easy. I know too much."

"Look Adam, the suspension wasn't my idea."

"Yeah, I'm so sure you talked it over with the board. It
doesn't matter. I hold all the cards. This is your last chance."

"What?"

"You know, last chance to do the right thing," he said
sarcastically taking another swig from his flask. "In fact I was
hoping to change your mind so I wouldn't have to tell the Board of
Directors anything."

Janeshia stared back at Adam amazed. The scar under his eye
made him look sinister. She wondered why she never noticed it
before.

"Have a sip. It will relax you."

Janeshia shook her head.

"No? More for me," he said with a touch of impatience.
"Why didn't you come by my place like I told you too last
Saturday?"

"Look Adam I was busy on Saturday. I went out of town,"
she said.

Adam's eyes narrowed dangerously. "It doesn't matter. Like
I said, I hold all the cards. You underestimated me!"

She shrugged. "Look Adam, if this is about that suspension.
This isn't the way to go about having it removed."

"Then I take it that you haven't been paying attention to
details as normal," he said with a smug sophistication. His lips
pressed into a thin line as he studied her. "Yep, I can tell by the look
in your eyes you don't know what I'm talking about."

He could see the conflict on her face. She was distracted. He moved quick and grabbed her arm. With relentless force he pulled her closer to him.

Janeshia tried to rise. "How dare you Adam. Get your filthy hands off of me before I call the police?"

"What's the matter, my hands aren't good enough for you? Sit back down," he ordered.

Slowly she sat back down.

"Janeshia did you know that your poor management lately has led to some discrepancies? Some huge discrepancies, the big kind," he said, as a conning expression crossed his face. "The kind that can land a person in jail."

She breathed out slowly and stared back at him. Adam's eyes looked wild like a tiger about pounce on it prey. Uneasiness crept over her. She couldn't remember the last time she really checked the reports.

She swallowed hard and spoke. "If something is wrong with the books, it just means that you tampered with them."

His yes grew hard and cold. He spoke with an under tone of bitterness. "Me? I would never do such a thing."

"You are such a liar!"

His husky laughter mocked her. "Am I? Janeshia you should calm yourself. You look terrified. I know too much and you know I do," his voice was low.

"Call the police then," she said hastily. "I don't care!"

"You know what; maybe I should let you call the police. I can tell them I came over here to have it out with you, to reason with you to do the right thing. I'll say I even begged you but you refused." He paused. "Then I'll say that when I told you I was going to tell the board of directors that you've been tampering with the books. You became angry and upset and that's when you told me you were going to tell the police that I had broken in and attacked you." He took another drink and chuckled softly. "Does that sound like the right story that you were going to tell Janeshia? If you ask me, your story is not too convincing."

Janeshia was trembling.

Adam rubbed his chin confidently. Just a little more pushing and he'd have her right where he wanted her. He could tell Janeshia was thinking about what he said. Her emotions were written all over her face. He had a perfunctory smile as he leaned in closer. "You know Janeshia if I tell the board that the reason you suspended me was because I found out about what you were doing. Things could look real bad for you."

Waiting silence hung in the air between them.

Janeshia hang her head ranking her brain, trying to think what she should do. A deep despair came over her. This was all her fault. All her years of hard work were over now. She'd wrecked her own ship by not paying close attention.

"Oh Adam, why do you hate me so much?" her voice caught in her throat. Tears swelled up in her eyes. "I don't know what I did to you to make you hate me so much Adam." Tears rolled down her cheek. "Whatever it was, I'm sorry. I'm truly sorry....... I can't believe you would do all of this just to destroy me." She sobbed.

Tears rolled down her cheek.

The muscle in Adam's jaw tightened, as he tried not to look at her. She looked so sad and vulnerable. His passion grew.

The atmosphere in the room hummed with a very low unreal echoing sound.

Reaching out his fingers gently brushed away her tears. He hugged her close. "Janeshia don't be sad. I can't stand to see you this way, none of this has anything to do with you. It's about me. All of it's about me. I don't mean to hurt you," he said giving up the struggle and leaning down and brushing his lips lightly against hers.

Janeshia's mind was confused. She felt lonely. What was happening? Too much had happened to her lately. She couldn't think coherently. She didn't know why but she kissed him back.

Adam had been aroused since the moment he saw her removing her jeans. At the feel of her lips on his, he'd felt his body come alive with passion and desire. He had always wanted her. He thought back to the first time he met her. It had been his first day at work. He'd always desired to hold her this way. He needed to make love to her. He moaned as his mouth tugged and sucked on her bottom lip. He was tender and gentle with her. For some reason he knew he had to be. He took his time as he felt her mouth open to his and her tongue reached out to touch his. For several minutes, his talented tongue kissed her mouth.

A shock wave washed over her. Janeshia encouraged Adam with another moan.

The energy in the room was unreal.

All at once the bed shook violently.

Janeshia opened her eyes just as a chilled breeze wafted across her face and broke her from her trance. She could have sworn she heard weeping. A strong scent of lavender and sugar cookies filled the air.

She grimaced as the strong sense of fear engulfed her. She knew that scent. It was her dead grandmother's, Lena Mae Allen.

She pushed against his chest. "Get off of me Adam."

"Christ! What was that?" Adam asked, as he rose off the bed.

Janeshia groaned in frustration as her phone began ringing on the side of her bed. She shifted as the ringing of the telephone brought her back to reality. Like a shattering dream.

"Don't answer that," Adam ordered. "Let the machine answer it."

The answering machine bleeped loudly.

"Hello Janeshia this is Walker."

She sat up. She felt a chill of apprehension at the sound of Walker's voice.

Walker's voice strained out of the answering machine again. "I really need to talk to you. Please Janeshia pick up if you're there."

Frightened she felt like a child caught in the act of stealing cookies. She turned and stared at Adam. The feeling was overwhelming.

Deep sadness cooed out of Walker's voice as he continued. "Hey if you are there and you are listening," he hesitated. "What I wanted to tell you is that I'm sorry. I'm so sorry for everything. But mainly for being such a stupid jerk. All I've been thinking about is how empty my life is without you."

Janeshia sat up on the side of the bed and sighed. She bit her lip. She felt she knew that what she had just been doing with Adam was horribly wrong.

After a pause, Walker continued. "I've made a huge mistake. I let my pride get in the way of what's really important to me," his voice choked. "And you are the only thing that is really important to me. I don't care who you have dated or where you've been," he pleaded. "All I know is I want you back in my life, no matter what. You're the most important thing to me," he paused. "When you get this message please give me a call on my cell phone."

Abruptly the call ended.

"Oh Christ! What am I doing? Adam you need to leave

now!"

Adam's eyes swelled up in a jealous wage. "Like hell I do. You're not going to be throwing yourself at Walker ever again. You hear me?" he lunged pushing her back on the bed.

"Adam?" She protested. She realized quickly that she had made a huge mistake letting Adam touch her.

Adam's face twisted into a distorted inhuman mask. "You filthy slut, you're my whore now. I will not have you throwing yourself at Walker or any other man trying to seduce them, like you did to me!"

She froze to the spot. "Don't you talk to me like that? I didn't seduce you!"

His strong arms held her down. "Yes.....You seduced me," his breathing was strained. "Janeshia, must I remind you that your job is at stake? Not to mention your reputation in this community? Now let's get back to what we were doing."

His hands roamed her body.

"Adam are you insane? Get off of me you jerk!"

His dark eyes held a violent rage. "I am not insane you slut," his eyes watched her. "But I am going to make you feel insane. Insane with lust for me," he growled breathing hard against her flesh.

"No!" She pleaded. "Adam please!"

His grasp on her wrist tightened. "Nobody can hear you. It's just you and me," his mouth nuzzled her neck. "I like a woman with some fight in her."

Suddenly Janeshia realized Adam was enjoying her fighting him back the most. She took a moment to look around. Her eyes caught sight of his flask. Her thoughts raced. She knew what she had to do.

She stopped fighting him and relaxed into his embrace. She waited until Adam noticed.

He stared back at her and she held his gaze.

She licked her lips greedily and made sure he noticed. Then she purred, "Mmmm kiss me again Adam. I miss your lips on mine."

"Now that's more like it," he said leaning over. He did as he was told eagerly.

She let him kiss her harder.

"Kiss me again harder. I want to feel you tongue," she exhaled sexy and low.

Greedily Adam obeyed.

Her hands roamed his body. "You are such a sexy man Adam," she lied between her clenched teeth.

"I'm so glad you think so," he whispered into her ear. "See, I knew we were right for each other."

Janeshia realized that her ploy was working. She sucked on his tongue and moved her hand down and found his penis. She quickly stroked it and adjusted her leg.

"Ouch! You bit me!" Adam cried.

Quickly Janeshia brought her knee up and kicked Adam where it hurt. She kicked with her knew as hard as she could like she was kicking the devil himself. She wasted no time rolling off the bed.

"Damn! You little Bitch!" He screamed.

She reached and grabbed his flask and hit him right in the eye. Liquid spewed out onto his face.

"My eyes! My eyes," Adam screamed.

Panicked she ran quickly out of the bedroom and down the hall.

She heard Adam curse again as he tripped over his pants.

Once in the hall way she ran as fast as she could toward the front door. Suddenly her foot caught something and she went flying to the floor less than two feet from her front door. She tried to get up.

She struggled and cried out. "Let me go Adam!"

"No!" He blurted rolling on top of her.

The sudden jingling of keys startled both of them. Simultaneously they stopped struggling and looked up at the front door.

Slowly a key turned the lock. The front door opened slowly.

"Janeshia is everything okay? I heard a noise." Mrs. Olsten asked politely standing in the doorway.

She wiped her hair from her eyes as she caught her breath. She was so grateful the strange little old lady lived across the hall from her. "Thank God for you Mrs. Olsten, it's so great to see you again….."

Mrs. Olsten looked on bewildered. "I thought I heard something and I called and told Mr. Carlos Murphy to come quick and bring his machete." Her gaze settled on Adam sternly. "Young man if you don't let Janeshia up off of that floor I will have Mr.

Murphy slice you into a million pieces."

Adam frowned heavily as he got up off of the floor. "What is that old lady doing with a key to your apartment Janeshia?"

Mrs. Olsten grimaced. "Young man angels go where we are sure to find fools like you."

"Mrs. Olsten having a key to my condo is none of your damn business Adam," Janeshia said getting up off of the floor. "Adam, say hello to my neighbor, Mrs. Olsten and then get out!"

Adam growled at her under his breath as he buttoned his shirt.

"Janeshia don't you think we should call the police?" Mrs. Olsten said with deep concern. "I mean this young man was trespassing and he could have hurt you."

Adam's husky laughter filled the air. "I'm sure Janeshia doesn't want to call the cops, even on a foolish man like me." He turned and leaned in close.

She reached out and slapped him on the face. "Get out Adam!" Janeshia blurted. "Unless you'd like to stay and meet Mr. Carlos Murphy and his machete?"

Adam wiped his mouth and held her gaze as he walked through the door. "Janeshia this isn't over!"

Mrs. Olsten slammed the door as soon as Adam past. She latched the dead bolt and then jiggled her keys. She beamed back at Janeshia with pride. "You're safe in your own home always Janeshia. But really I still say we should have called the police." Her fingers clasped securely around the keys. "That character there is a madman running loose, he needs to be locked up in a cell with no key."

Exasperated Janeshia's voice shook. "Oh Mrs. Olsten!" Her beautiful features were marred by deep despair and shock with the thought of what could have happened if her neighbor hadn't thought to check on her. "I owe you one for rescuing me Mrs. Olsten. How can I ever repay you?"

"Calm down my dear," Mrs. Olsten said hugging her close. Her voice was soft when she spoke. "I saw that Geek Knight in shining amour fellow on TV today. I like him best you know."

"Who?"

"The one that look like the actor," Mrs. Olsten smiled softly, as she patted her back. "My dearest young friend, you don't understand. No problem, all is well. I'll tell you who one day soon.

You can treat me to lunch."

***

Hours later that same night, Adam St. Charles paced the center of his bedroom. He stopped and looked up at the mirror on the ceiling. He needed to get laid real bad. He checked the clock on the side of his bed. He'd called her over an hour ago. His cell phone rang.

"I'm on my way through the front door right now," she cooed. "Thanks for leaving the front door open. "I'm almost at your bedroom door."

"Phoebe you locked the front door behind you right?" Adam's gruff voice demanded.

She reached the bedroom door just at the moment he'd asked. "Yes, you know I'm a smart girl."

Phoebe Wright stood in the doorway and studied Adam. She knew that no matter what, this was the last time she was going to see him. In the beginning she thought Adam loved her. She wanted to believe it. That's why she did everything he asked her to do. She thought he'd take care of her. Maybe marry her. Now she realized Adam St. Charles was a selfish, greedy and sometimes cruel man.

Phoebe quickly walked over and closed the distance between them. She stood in front of Adam and crossed her arms. "Don't you have something you want to say to me lover? After Walker dumped me, you stopped taking my calls."

"Phoebe I'm sorry," his voice was less in control. "I swear I am. Didn't I give you the money I'd promised?

Her icy reserve started to melt. "Look Adam, I'm no longer the girl who runs to you and offers up her body at every opportunity. I've got plans of my own. Remember what we talked about?"

Adam took a deep breath. "Yes, like I said, before, I agree and accept your terms. This is the last time I ask you to do a favor for me."

For a moment Phoebe stood and looked at Adam. She wanted to believe him. She was glad Adam couldn't read her mind. She could tell it was all an act with Adam. For the last few weeks she dated Walker the monk for Adam. Her body was starved. Walker never touched her. If she took Adam back, it would be just a matter of time before he asked her to do him another favor with a different man. Then he'd ask her to do it again and again. One thing was sure. She didn't need a pimp. And Adam was just a well-educated pimp as far as she was concerned. She was sure of it. Adam was a user and a pimp. She knew that for certain now. Still she was horny and there was something about him that turned her on.

"I'm glad that you agreed. That's all I want to hear from you Adam. Show me a little respect. Okay lover I'll do this last thing for you," she purred. "I need a little servicing of my own from you," she said letting her hands glide over Adam's body stroking his needs.

"On baby, I'll agree to that."

"Now don't you want to kiss me Adam? Before I Ahhhh…..Get to work?"

Adam kissed her hard and long.

Phoebe let her hands stroke his penis. She could feel the flame had ignited into a raging fire. Her lover was hot and ready for her.

Adam's eyes grew wide with glassy excitement as Phoebe touched him. He was getting what he wanted. He took a deep breath and threw back his head feeling Phoebe working her magic. So what if he was lying to her. He was paying her good money to do his bidding and she was horny too.

Chapter 35

Mama Moue Redbones.....

Walker Perrault was lost in his thoughts as he stared at his cell phone. He looked up and a deep sense of loneliness overtook him as he looked out on the land first inhabited by early French settlers, his ancestors.

He breathed in deep. The smell of honeysuckle and flowering dogwood filled the air. The prairie floor of the Kisatchie National Forest was an eerie beauty of deathly quiet and beautiful wildflowers.

Again he checked his cell phone. No reception. He was sure now that his cell phone couldn't pick up a signal while he was in the forest. Now he was sure Janeshia wouldn't be able to return his call.

As he got closer to Mama Moue Redbones' home. The distinct smell of freshly cooking Boudin sausages whiffed threw the air. His thoughts drifted back to his childhood. And then he remembered the story he heard as a child about her. He smiled remembering it was really a poem.

> *Mama Moue Redbones...*
> *Pouty red face girl that's who you are*
> *Stone face, you came from another time and place*
> *Death you say is just another space*

To them who walked this earth before
To them who seek to know much more
They tell me once your last name was Jones
But no one now knows not for sho'
They only know you can take away their blues
And tell them who loves them ever true
You can combine two hearts together into one
But only if both hearts are sure
Yet awful pain each lover must endure
If their claim of love is not pure
For it is a sin to play love's heart game
When you know your lover's heart you cannot claim
Forever then your love heart flame must die

Walker shook out his thoughts and walked toward the back of the house. A black cast iron skillet was cooking outside on an open fire. He licked his lips. He could feel his mouth water just from the smell of the frying fish.

"Walker come on inside. The food is ready," Mama Moue Redbones said waiving him over. "We've got biscuits and gravy, grits, poached and scrambled eggs, Boudin sausages, fried catfish and fried gator."

"Woman you said you made me some grit cakes," February's voice called out. He was already seated at the table.

"I ain't lie, man," Mama Moue Redbones commandingly said. "You just sit back and enjoy my Bayou southern hospitality. Please eat up, enjoy yourself...."

February leaned over and whispered, "Walker should I eat? She was extremely rude to me the last couple times that I came up here. Now she's making nice. I don't know what to make of it."

"Man, you can't even whisper." Mama Moue Redbones laughter was like a roaring river. "I wasn't friendly with you February because you had a mission to complete. I needed you to bring Walker here. And now you have done so and I reward you with food prepared by my own hands."

Walker looked strangely at Mama Moue Redbones. "If you don't mind, could I ask you something?"

"Yes," she smiled.

"Can you tell me how you could help me?"

"Yes Walker, but I will not tell you right now. We must eat

and later we will gather the answers you seek. They must wait until the sun goes down. Then, and only then, can we call up those that walked this earth before. They will tell you the answers you seek."

Walker looked puzzled.

Mama Moue Redbones' mouth formed a thin line. "You have another question, don't you Walker?"

"Yes."

"Then ask me," she said.

"How do you know me?"

She smiled. "I've seen you before. Many years ago, though you won't remember me, I always will remember you." She rose and walked to a cabinet and retrieved a crystal decanter.

February squirmed in his seat.

Walker looked back at him.

Mama Moue Redbones sat down. "I am very happy to have company. Out here in the Bayou not many come to pay a visit. I like a little company to talk with every so often." She poured both men a glass of the amber liquid. "Having someone to share a fine meal and an even finer drink is what we live for. My preferred drink is Cognac. Would you both agree to have a glass with me gentlemen?"

February grinned wide and held up his glass. "Agreed Mama! Agreed"

Walker nodded and chuckled softly.

Hours later that same night, the midnight blue sky was clear overhead. Stars beamed bright as the full moon shone overhead.

Walker stood watching the fire he and February built following the instructions Mama Moue Redbones had given them.

The fire blazed brightly in front of him.

Mama Moue Redbones walked up to Walker. She offered him a small bag before moving on to offer the same to February.

"The gris-gris," February muttered reaching out his hand. "One thing I can say is Mama Moue Redbones is an old-fashioned soothsayer. If I hadn't been raised up by my grandmother who was gifted with second sight, I'd be terrified right now," he chuckled. "Whew! We gonna see some major conjuring now."

Quickly February reached into his pocket and removed a small flask. He took a big gulp.

"What's that?" Walker curiously asked.

"I call it courage. Do you want some?"

Walker shook his head no and kept his eyes on Mama Moue Redbones.

Slowly she reached in a bag that hung close to her side. She removed her hand from the bag and scattered a yellow substance on the ground around them.

Walker leaned over and examined the yellow substance. He looked close. It was cornmeal.

From out of nowhere the drums sounded.

February gazed up at Walker with a frantic expression. "Do you hear that? Its' that singing stuff I told you about. It's happening…it's eerie."

Mama Moue Redbones stopped her chanting. "The song is not eerie to anyone who has truly loved. It is a love song beyond time. Too bad February you have lived only for the yearnings of satisfying your body and not for the yearning to feed your heart's need to have an everlasting love."

February answered quickly. "I'm a Man, I have needs, I have rights, and this is the South. In the South a man can have a wife and a mistress so long as he can afford them."

"Afford them," Mama Moue Redbones chuckled. "We all do what we need to do. Sometimes in life, we forge debts that we can only see ourselves paying off when we see them clearly after death."

February took a deep breath. He smiled but said nothing.

"I am not judging you February. That is not my place to do," she said.

Mama Moue Redbones resumed walking around the fire chanting. "Walker, soon I will have the answers you seek."

Seconds later, Walker winched. "What?"

The fire blazed brighter. A sudden bright blue light flashed as Mama Moue Redbones seemed to change her appearance right before his eyes.

Her aura took on a shining hue. It was the most beautiful color he'd ever seen.

Walker rubbed his brow and wondered if he was just seeing things. He glanced up. February was mesmerized too. His eyes looked like they were going to pop out of his head.

Moving on instinct he turned and stole a glance at Mama Moue Redbones. She was caught in the snares of her chanting.

Mama Moue Redbones voice echoed with a trembling urgency. Her eyes slanted into slits. She looked like she had fallen into a trance. "Now Walker, now we will find the answers you seek." She chanted words softly in a voice that only she could understand.

As if an invisible power had been awakened, the fire roared loudly.

Mama Moue Redbones chanted louder.

Out of the mist of the fire a form took shape. The ghostly form flickered into human form.

Mama Moue Redbones' voice was hollow. "Welcome Sheba."

"Greetings Mama," Sheba said, her voice whispering like the wind.

Walker turned to look at the February. Both men's eyes held a puzzled gaze.

Sheba's voice emerged out over space and time. "Hello Walker, I've wanted for a long time to talk to you."

For reasons he couldn't understand, Walker stood gazing spellbound.

February muttered nervously, "Walker if you talk to that woman. You're talking with the dead."

Walker held his breath as he looked on. Sweat beaded on his forehead. The woman named Sheba looked like someone he knew. He muttered her name off of his lips before he knew it. "Sheba, for some reason you resemble someone I know."

Sheba's transparent image looked on approvingly. She smiled. Her voice was hoarse. "We are all but matter, particles and dust. Suspended in time and space, we are the ashes of the people we love today, yesterday and tomorrow."

He inclined his head and studied her presence. Colors swam and shimmered shiny around her.

"Hey Walker, are you okay?" The February nudged him. "Man I told you this place was strange."

"Yes, I'm fine," Walker rubbed his brow and swallowed hard. "I'm just a little confused by all of this. I can't even understand why my mother wanted me to come here."

Colors swam around Sheba. "You are here because your

mother asked you to come. A mother's love is a great love. A mother's wisdom is a great wisdom," she hoarsely whispered. Her voice echoed like the sadness of flowing tears. "As it was in the days of old, a woman's fertility affords her a higher status in society. Your mother Claire Marie tried hard to give your father Edward Senior a child. Before you were born they went to New York to help Claire Marie conceive. Your parents believed in the fertility clinic's treatments. Until they realized it was useless. They gave up and came back home. It was here at home that your mother sought the help of Mama Moue Redbones."

"What?" Walker stated unconsciously.

"Yes, you are a child brought forth to this land of the living from the land of dreams by the desire and love of your mother," she paused, "and father. They called your father Eddie the Warrior and your mother Claire Marie his lady love."

Walker took a deep breath. "Whew! Wait a second. You're telling me I'm here not because of a fertility clinic but because of …"

Sheba interrupted. "Yes Walker, you are here because you came to this earth by the means of God and the ancient spirits, and the calling of your own destiny."

"What?"

"You are your parents first born son," Sheba said.

"First born, I'm an only child," Walker spluttered.

Sheba's voice was tense. "No! You are not their only child!" The fire crackled loudly.

"You are their only child brought forth with the help of God, Mama Moue Redbones and the ancient spirits. However….You are not your father's only son."

Walker looked on dumbfounded. "What!"

Mama Moue Redbones crossed her arms and shot him an icy stare. "Walker you have a brother."

"No!"

Sheba's fiery flame burned brighter.

"Walker," February nudged him. "Don't go upsetting that Sheba spirit." He looked across to where Mama Moue Redbones stood. He pointed. "Nor do I think you should be upsetting her. She looks real mad."

"I'm not sure I should continue this," Walker said. "She's implying my father had a child by another woman?"

February leaned over and whispered. "Isn't it better that your father did rather than your mother?"

"Sheba, he must know the truth, all of it," Mama Moue Redbones pleaded. "Can't you see he is confused? He's thinking ill of his father. Next thing you know he will be thinking ill of his mother."

Reasoning dawned on Walker. He looked at Sheba. "You knew my mother couldn't come because she had to stay and look after the foundation? My father always felt she cared more about that place then she did about our family. Maybe my father did have another child. He was always gone."

Sheba smiled at him. "You are right Mama Moue Redbones, Walker is confused." The colors around her beamed and swirled. "His mother is why he is here. They have a strong bond. Yet he does not understand or suspect that something was wrong." She focused on him. "Your mother Claire Marie is an honorable woman. She takes her duties seriously. She took her oath to me seriously. I respect her for that. Please help to enlighten him Mama."

Walker was afraid of what he might say if he opened his mouth again. Abruptly he ran his hand over his mouth.

Mama Moue Redbones crossed her arms. "Walker, neither one of your parents had a child out of wedlock." Her face set into a frown. "You see, a terrible invasive injustice was done to both of them. Your mother's eggs and your father's sperm were stolen by an employee of the fertility clinic in New York."

The shining light of Sheba glowed. "The fertility clinic in was never successful in helping your parents conceive a child. But it was successful in helping one of its employees conceive a child. One of the employees stole your parent's egg and sperm and conceived a child. Your brother!"

Mama Moue Redbones inclined her head regally. "And you are needed to find your brother. Your mother promised an oath to Sheba and to me."

"What?" Walker asked puzzled. "Why can't Sheba just show you what he looks like in that cloud of dust and particles she has around here?"

"That is because the ancients will not permit it. Besides, even they know only the first born child always looks like the father. You look like your father Walker, but you brother does not."

Mama Moue Redbones laughed. "This is modern times

Walker, is it not? Do you want us to do all the work for you?" She huffed. "Don't you have a computer or some other gizmo with the internet on it?"

"So what if I do?"

The February chuckled. "Walker even I know you can look up almost anything on the internet. Think about it. You can find out who was working at that fertility clinic in New York?"

"Okay well enjoy a laugh on my account," Walker snorted. "Maybe I don't want to find my brother."

Mama Moue Redbones face creased with a deep frown. "You must find your brother. Your mother Claire Marie made a vow to Sheba for giving her you. In return she would keep Sheba's daughter safe." She paused. "Walker, Sheba's daughter is my niece. You know her as Janeshia," she hesitated. "Janeshia James."

At first Walker didn't understand. Then he swallowed hard and stared back at Sheba. A shiny white light glowed around her.

Silence filled the air.

A shocked expression took over Walker. Now he knew why Sheba looked so familiar.

"Oh my!" His eyes widened.

"Yes Walker, your mother stayed behind to keep Janeshia safe as she always promised she will do. She knows there maybe someone who wants to hurt Janeshia. And we believe it maybe your brother." She said reaching for his hand. "He wants to hurt her, because by hurting her. He can hurt you?"

Walker set his mouth into a rigid line. Now he understood.

Mama Moue Redbones walked over and took his hand. The warm touch of her hands encircled his. "Once you find your brother, look at his eyes. Look directly into them and behind them. You can see into his hidden place and then you will know who he truly is. And then you will have the answers you seek. And you will know what must be done."

Chapter 36

Ain't nothing like the real thing....

A day after the restless night he'd spent in the swamp with Sheba and Mama Moue Redbones, Walker awoke early, showered and dressed.

Larissa London, at the urging of his mother no doubt, had called him last night and told him she was booked into a room at the same hotel he was staying at.

He checked the clock by the side of his bed. It was nine o'clock in the morning. California has a two hour time difference. His mother would be out making her rounds by now. He wanted to call her and tell her what he had learned. He could do it later.

He reached for the phone beside his bed and dialed room service and ordered coffee. He hung up and headed for the shower. He was sure he could shower and change before room service made it there.

A half hour later, he watched the waiter finish putting the touches on the table. The white linen table cloth and fine bone china reminded him of the decadent high teas at the Fairmont Hotel in San Francisco, but with a Southern touch he found charming. He noted the waiter left an extra setting, but didn't question it.

The waiter strolled over signaling he was done. Walker

tipped him. From the look on the man's face the tip had been a generous one.

He caught a whiff of the freshly brewed coffee, walked over and poured himself a cup.

The coffee felt good going down.

The telephone beside his bed rang abruptly.

"Hello, Mother?" he asked assuming it was her.

"No Walker it's me Larissa London," her nasal California drawl sounded loud and clear.

"Oh, hi Larissa. I'd recognize your voice anywhere. I thought I caught a glimpse of you last night," he said.

"Yep, you did."

Walker sipped his coffee and listened.

"Look, your mother didn't want her only son getting lost in some swamp. She just asked me to come down and make sure you were okay. I was kind of like acting like your backup," her words tumbled out. "But I knew you could handle yourself out there in the swamp, Walker."

"Sure you did, Larissa. But I bet the real reason you didn't go back into the swamp was that you weren't interested in riding the whole way on horseback?"

Larissa's voice chuckled low into the phone. "Yeah, I always knew you were clever. So how are you this morning?"

"Surprisingly I feel pretty good after some sleep," he said. "Thanks for asking."

"Walker, I have a little problem. I need to ask you a favor."

"Sure, what is it?" he asked finishing his cup of coffee in one gulp, while holding the receiver in his other hand.

"I had intended to stay a few days longer," she hesitated. "But at the last minute something came up," she said anxiously. "Anyway, last night Janeshia flew in to meet me and she thinks I'm staying in your suite."

"My suite?"

"Not like your suite, like in our being together or something. Walker you nerd, this is Larissa you are talking too," she jokingly laughed softly. "Anyway what I meant to say was I gave her the wrong suite number when she arrived last night."

"Oh?"

"Look Walker, Janeshia's supposed to drop by this morning so that the two of us can have breakfast and spend the day together."

His caring voice sounded through the phone. "No problem, just give me your correct room number and I'll tell her."

"Walker I can't do that. That's why I'm calling you. I had to leave urgently. In fact I flew out very early this morning, before the crack of dawn. Can you please tell Janeshia that for me?"

"Sure," he tried to hide the smile in his voice. "That's not a problem."

"Walker," she hesitated. "Oh and please be nice to her, you see there's another reason I called. Something happened to Janeshia a few days ago. She's been under a lot of stress. She just needs to relax." Quickly she gave him a few of the details on what happen to Janeshia. She made sure not to tell him about the incident with Adam St. Charles. She didn't want Walker upset.

"Walker? Walker did you hear me?" Larissa asked.

"Sure, I will just tell her you had to leave," he said softly.

Walker was glad Larissa was on the other end of the phone and couldn't see how wide he was grinning. His thoughts raced, thinking of Janesha James. He focused his mind and saw her strikingly beautiful face, her deep green eyes, her smile full of white teeth and her superb figure. He could just feel his fingers running through her long sable hair. His smile widened, thinking of her big heart with love and kindness for everybody, including him. He smiled warmly remembering her.

"Walker, Walker did you hear me?" Larissa blurted.

"Sure," he collected his thoughts. "I can tell her that," he said warmly.

"Oh and Walker, I had intended to spend a few more days in Alexandria with Janeshia, we were supposed to do some sightseeing to give her a chance to relax."

"Relax?" He asked.

Caringly she continued, "Yeah, relax. Remember what we were talking about. Look she's been under a lot of stress lately. I knew you weren't listening to a word I said. Anyway well....A little relaxation would do her some good. I'm not telling you what to do, but take her sightseeing or to a spa or something. And you know a little relaxation would do you some good too."

"Okay Larissa, I guess I could do that."

"Thanks Walker and don't forget to tell her I promise I'll make it up to her."

"Sure," he said wondering in his thoughts.

There was a click at the other end of the line. He realized she'd hung up the phone.

Walker replaced the receiver. He thought about the past two years. Since he learned Janeshia was working for the foundation. He'd made it a point to be with her daily. He had positioned himself in her life for no other reason than to just be able to see her.

Walker knew Janeshia had no way of knowing his mother had conveniently vacated the position of director once she learned Janeshia had applied. He also now understood the special bond his mother had with Janeshia. He'd never understood it until now. It also explained why he knew her as a boy. Janeshia was the little girl at the Foundation's after school programs many years ago. Walker smiled with his memories. Now he could see why his mother had single-handedly made sure Janeshia had been hired for the position of director. It was the perfect place for her to protectively watch over her, just as the after school program had done when she was a child.

He shrugged as his thoughts raced. It also explained why his mother told him to let Janeshia have her space after she caught them having sex that night at the house. He had been torn about giving her some space. Staying away from Janeshia had been hard for him. He gave her space, hoping it would help her see him clearly as the man who truly loved her and hoped to win her heart.

A few minutes later there was an urgent knock at the door.
"Larissa open up the door. It's me Janeshia."
Walker opened the door and smiled. "Hi Janeshia."
"Walker, what are you doing here?"
"Won't you please come in and have a cup of coffee with me?" he said with a gentle authority, leading the way across the room to the fully laden table set up by room service earlier.

Reluctantly she entered and gazed at him uncomprehendingly. As she sat down at the table, she noted how Walker, who was tall and handsome, seemed to electrify the room.

The two of them sat there without speaking for what seemed like minutes.

Finally Janeshia broke the ice. "Okay, what are you doing here, in Alexandria Louisiana I mean?"

Walker looked at her with a deep intensity. "I'm a native of this place. Besides, I found I needed to go back into the swamp to, shall we say, meet my spiritual guide and renew my spirit," he said quietly.

Curse the man she thought. He still had the power to rile her emotions. "Okay that answers that question so what are you doing in Larissa's room?"

"What?"

Slowly Janeshia looked around the room. Hysteria welled up inside of her like the swelling wave on the ocean. Outrage slid bitterly off her tongue. Her chin shot up in the air. "Walker tell me now, are you and Larissa having an affair? This is her suite. You're a pig if you're sleeping with my best friend."

Walker roared out with laughter. "Let me try to explain," he softly laughed in disbelief. He touched her shaking hand gently. "I've been calling you leaving messages on your phone just pouring my heart out and you think that." He took a gulp of his coffee and ginned." Anyway Larissa just called me a few minutes ago and said to give you the message that she had to leave. And she told me to tell you she gave you the wrong room number last night. You can check with the hotel manager to verify it or call Larissa if you like."

The touch of his hand almost undid her, nervously she reached for her coffee. "I'm acting stupidly aren't I?" Her body relaxed. "I've got no right to act like this. It's just that Larissa told me you weren't seeing Phoebe Wright anymore. But she was so secretive and wouldn't tell me who you were seeing," her words tumbled out.

"You asked about my seeing Phoebe?" he questioned.

"Well yes, I did," she sighed heavily, as her words tumbled out uncontrollably. "You see, when I saw you and Phoebe together that time. I thought things were serious. I thought you to were the real thing, in love I mean."

He leaned in with a keen determination. "Phoebe and I were never a serious item," his voice reassured her. "In fact she was a bad dating suggestion made by Adam."

"Never? Ever?" she questioned reaching out to touch his hand.

"Never," he tenderly smiled.

She looked back into his eyes with a powerful intensity capable of reversing the spinning earth. "So you're not seeing anyone?"

He shook his head. "No, I'm not seeing anyone."

Janeshia had a deep yearning to kiss him right now.

She willed herself and pulled away. "God I must look terribly foolish and stupid right now. It's just that there's so much I want to talk to you about."

"I like how you're acting right now. I like it a lot."

"No in fact you look like a goddess." His eyes lovingly studied hers. "A very beautiful goddess. You're my idea of the real thing and someone I would very much like to have breakfast with right now."

Nervously Janeshia smiled and sipped her coffee. "Walker, I don't know what's come over me. But I have to be honest with you," her smile faded. "These last couple of months since that time at your parent's house have been really stressful for me."

His eyes shown with deep adoration. "That was the night when we made love," he said grinning. "And we fell asleep together under the moonlight."

Janeshia breathed out slowly. "Yes, that time. When your mother caught us having sex, I was just so embarrassed and afraid," she lifted her gaze and met his. "Well, I guess I sort of got scared of the thought of being with you because of our working relationship, and well, I just up and started dating the first guy that asked me, and well, anyway things didn't work out between us, the guy I mean" her words tumbled out. "Anyway he and a few other things are the reasons why I've been having a real stressful time lately."

Walker squeezed her hand. "Yes, I know about that."

"You knew about Ramsey….I mean the guy and me, how?"

"Adam St. Charles told me."

"What?"

A shadow fell across his face. He looked up and caught her staring. For a split second she saw the pain he felt for her.

A few months ago, she hadn't even known Ramsey Montgomery existed. She didn't know why she had pursued him. Her voice shook as she tried to explain. "I thought I liked Ramsey. But I guess I didn't."

He smiled softly, concealing his hurt as best he could. "I don't care about Ramsey, you're my dearest friend. The only person I would love to have a relationship with. I guess I'm just destined to be the guy that wants a girl name Janeshia to love him."

Her eyes met his. She could no longer put off what she must say. She hoped she would find the right words. "But…What if there's something.....I mean something I need to explain?" she asked.

"I trust you."

Her hand relaxed at the sound of his words. She reached over and traced her hand over his. Her heart went out to him. A weariness that was bone deep engulfed her.

They looked at each other for a split second before he hesitantly reached out to her. He lightly touched her face, and then threaded his fingers into the hair at the nape of her neck.

"Janeshia I've never felt this way before for anyone," he said rising and pulling her with him.

A whimper of surprise escaped her lips. "Walker I want you."

With a groan he swept her up into his arms and carried her toward the bed. He lowered her slowly. The two of them quickly fought breathlessly with zippers and buttons, until their clothes were scattered around them.

He lowered her beneath him. His lips possessively took her mouth. His hand traced her firm breast. His thumb flicked over her nipple

She moaned with urgency. In one moment, she pushed him away, sat up and swung astride him. The heated core of her body touched his belly. "Walker, I want to ride you," she commanded bending her knees, taking his penis and guiding him in to her.

Walker felt his body jerk against the onslaught.

"Don't stop.....Please don't stop," he said unable to take his eyes off of her.

"Never my love," she breathed out hoarsely.

Hands, mouths and bodies rubbed together in urgent need until their bodies surged up in surrender.

Chapter 37

Old friendships

After spending two days relaxing and renewing her love and friendship with Walker Perrault in Alexandria Louisiana, Janeshia returned home determined to face an old nightmare head on.

With high anticipation she drove her slick black Cadillac STS through the traffic in downtown San Jose, California. The traffic on East Santa Clara Street moved smoothly as she made her way to San Pedro Street.

San Pedro Street was known locally as San Pedro Square. Restaurants located here were known to be some of the best in the city.

She pulled into the parking lot and found a space. She took a quick look at herself in the rearview mirror. The eyes that stared back at her were sad and fearful. Even after all of this time she was still amazed at how Alice could make her feel like she was still that little kid confronting a bully.

She got out of the car and walked down the sidewalk. The building she was heading for was located in the middle of the block of San Pedro Square. She walked through the wrought iron gate that led down the small alley to the front entrance of the restaurant.

The young hostess that greeted her had kind blue eyes that twinkled. She gave her name and she took her to her seat.

Alice Couvertier-Trudeau's limp brown eyes flashed with

flecks of amber as she stared back at Janeshia. Her lips curved up into a smile.

"Hi Janeshia," she nervously breathed out. "I was beginning to think you were going to stand me up."

"Sorry I'm late Alice," she said taking a seat.

Alice nervously laughed. She was so grateful she hadn't stood her up. "Don't worry about that."

The moment was tense between them.

Alice took a sip of her water. "I see you still like coming to this restaurant."

"Yes, it's still my favorite," Janeshia slowly breathed out. She stared back at Alice.

Alice could see that their having a conversation wasn't going to be easy. She would have to work at making Janeshia continue to talk to her.

Alice shrugged. "Oh look, the waiter's here.

The waiter took their orders.

A short time later, Janeshia enjoyed another bite of her *Lasagna Vegetariano*. She took another sip of her wine.

The two chatted little during their meal.

Alice glanced at her and smiled. "So I guess this is as good a time as any to tell you why I wanted to have lunch and talk."

"I'm listening," Janeshia said.

"So how are things these days at the foundation?"

"Great," Janeshia said with an annoyed expression.

Alice took one look at Janeshia's annoyed face and knew she was about to tune her out. "Well that's good. I always knew you'd grow up and be a success. You were and still are a strong woman."

Janeshia looked back at Alice with an unreadable sigh. "What is it that you want from me, Alice?"

"Well nothing. Except ...." She hesitated and then took a big sip of her wine. "You see Janeshia, what I want from you most in the world is for you to forgive me," Alice's voice shook as she bowed her head. "I'm not proud of the things I've done to you. I want us to be friends again, like we were as kids, before I did all that stupid foolish stuff. I'm really sorry for any hurt I caused you."

Janeshia shook her head unsympathetically. She felt the pulse in her forehead pound with the force of her emotions. "That stupid stuff was your daily humiliations. Not to mention the time you punched me in the stomach and left me lying on a flooding basement floor. You hurt me bad Alice. Worst yct, I could have drowned."

Alice's voice cracked. "I know...I know," she murmured. "I hurt you and I'm so sorry. If it makes you feel better, my grandmother gave me the worst whooping in my life. I'll never forget it. I swear my butt still hurts until this day."

Janeshia smirked out a laugh. Her thoughts raced. She remembered hearing about the butt whooping Alice had gotten for what she had done to her. Still she was not ready to let Alice off of the hook so easily.

"Alice I was just a kid, a little kid for Christ sake and you were nothing but a bully to me. And for your information, I've always had a mother and a father. I was never illegitimate," she rubbed her forehead. "I've always known my mother wasn't my birth mother. I've never been ashamed at how I got into this world."

Alice's face reddened. "I was just jealous of you that's all. I'm very sorry about all that," she said sadly.

"Jealous? Why?"

"Because..... I mean is it okay if I talk to you about her? Your mother I mean?"

"Who? My mom, Aurore Allen-James?" Janeshia asked. Recognition dawned. "Oh, you mean my birth mother Sheba?"

"Yes." Alice's eyes grew wide.

Janeshia stiffened. "Okay I guess, why?"

"I don't know if you were aware of it," Alice said with a blank expression. "But your father....."

"Yes I know some people believe my father and Sheba were lovers. And I know my mother was her best friend," Janeshia's eyes narrowed.

"No....No...I'm not trying to say anything bad. Everyone in our family knows that Sheba had a mind like a child. My grandmother said so."

Curiously Janeshia raised a brow. "Oh really, what else does your grandmother know about Sheba?"

Alice's expression glowed with her interest. "My grandmother said that when Sheba was born the two chambers in her heart were not fully developed. No one thought Sheba would ever live as long as she did," Alice smiled gently so as not to give offense. "Did you know she had that clairvoyant super power gift thing like that comic book character, Jean Grey? My grandmother said Sheba was born before her time. This world couldn't understand her. My grandmother always says that the best thing that ever happened to her was having you."

"Do you know if Sheba died during childbirth? No one in my family would ever tell me."

"Oh no, even though she had that bad heart and all. It was like she willed herself to live. My grandmother said Sheba said she needed Aurore to forgive her. She didn't die until after your mother, Aurore came to her bedside and forgave her, and agreed to take you as her own. Sheba told your mother that that was the only reason she had been born to make sure that her best friend had the daughter she had always wanted. Once I knew that, I was determined to seek your forgiveness."

Janeshia fortified herself with a deep breath. "How does your grandmother know so much about Sheba?"

"That's the reason I've wanted to talk to you and apologize for all the years I bullied you. We're cousins. Sheba was my grandmother's baby sister."

Her words caused an instant reaction. Her heart beat raced. Her eyes swelled up with tears.

Alice reached over and touched her hand. "Don't cry. By the way I brought you a present," she reached and placed a box in front of Janeshia.

Janeshia cleared her throat forcibly. "A gift for me, why?"

"Well, it's really to make up for all those years." a little something to show you how I finally grew up and realized that all of that negative Karma energy I lavished on you as a kid was really just hurting myself," she hesitated.

Janeshia blinked back at her.

"Open it please."

Janeshia slowly took the top of off the box.

A stunned gasped escaped her lips.

"Alice why? How did you get it? I saw you tear up the original."

"I was lucky my grandmother had a copy. She let me make a copy of hers, once I told her how much; I regretted tearing up your copy. I know it's not much but I hope it shows you how sorry I am and how much your friendship means to me."

The old photo made Janeshia's voice catch in her throat. It was a photo of her two mothers hugging each other and holding a small blanket wrapped bundle. It must have been taken when her mother Aurore had agreed to take her, just before Sheba died.

Her voice shook. "Thank you Alice."

Alice's giving her back the photo healed her wounds and her heart softened. "Well, I want to tell you something Alice, a woman… I mean an old friend of my family told me recently that I shouldn't give up on an old friend. Thank you for my photo, Alice, my old friend, my cousin."

Alice's eyes glassed over with pure happiness.

Janeshia put the photo in her purse. "Wow, I forgot you were a wealth of information growing up. I should ask you about any people I need to find."

"See, now you can see being friends with me has its advantages," Alice said. "I know all of the old families that settled here. If I don't know them, my grandmother does. Ask me about anyone I can tell you their family history, secrets and where they buried their relatives and their enemies."

Janeshia lifted a brow. She always knew Alice's family was well connected. Maybe having her as a friend and a cousin was better than keeping her as an enemy.

Alice lifted her glass of wine and regarded Janeshia, "You know I mean it, whatever you need just ask."

Janeshia's thoughts turned to that time long ago. "Okay I'll take you up on your offer. Remember when you left me in the basement. Who was that boy that carried me out? He was my hero," she murmured out in a slow breathe. "Boy was I ever in love with him. I know I was only four years old. But he was the nicest boy I ever meet."

Alice shook her head in disbelief. "Don't you know who that boy is? He's Walker Perrault. I thought you always knew he was the boy that carried you out of the basement?"

Chapter 38

Pssssst…..We've got problems at work…

Janeshia got up the next morning with determination and headed into work.

She got off the elevator and headed to her office.

A whispered voice sliced the air. "Pssssst, Janeshia we need to talk before you go into the office," Tamara Bell, her assistant, whispered and motioned for her to join her behind a large palm fern pant.

Janeshia strolled over. "What is it?"

Nervously Tamara looked around. "I've been hiding here trying to catch you. We've got problems. Big problems."

"Tamara why didn't you just call my cell?"

"Because, I had no choice. There is a strange man sitting at my desk. I think he was placed there to keep me from alerting you. Besides, I was too frightened to retrieve my purse. They just called an emergency board meeting," she whispered.

"What?"

"Janeshia, all of the board members are there."

"Oh my goodness that can't be, Tom Craig never comes to a board meeting," Janeshia said. "Tell me, who else showed?"

"Well let me see," Tamara shrugged. "I've seen Ulysses Portillo, Bertie Mills, Dave Redland, and that sleazy smarmy weasel looking Nate Trent."

"Nate Trent?"

"Yeah that guy. Oh yeah, those back stabbing dizzy blond twins Janet and Linnet Mann are here. And Kate Martin and David Creek made it too. But that was only when I was at my desk. Since I've been hiding out here I don't know who else showed."

Janeshia looked puzzled. "That's strange; I wonder what's going on?"

Tamara nervously sighed. "I think they are trying to stack the deck against you Janeshia," she paused. "Oh I forgot Adam St. Charles is in there too. He is acting like he is running the show."

"Interesting," Janeshia sighed. "What about Walker Perrault? Has he arrived yet?"

Tamara sighed. "No, and he is the only one not here."

"Maybe I should give him a call."

"I thought of that too Janeshia, per Walker's secretary he's out of town. She can't reach him."

"Janeshia? There you are." Adam St. Charles' voice called out.

She turned around. A cloud of uncertainty strained her thoughts. What was Adam St. Charles up to? She wondered.

"You weren't trying to leave were you?" He asked.

"No Adam, I just arrived."

"Perhaps I should escort you to the conference room," he suggested.

"Janeshia doesn't need you to escort her anywhere Adam St. Charles. She's a woman of integrity, class and high moral standards. Things you can't even understand, comprehend or probably can't even spell or look up in the dictionary, you slimy sleaze ball jerk!"

"Tamara its okay," Janeshia said moving to place herself between the two of them.

"Look Adam, It won't be necessary for you to escort me. I was just on my way there. Tell everyone I will see them in a few minutes."

Adam sneered. "Very well, don't keep us waiting too long."

Janeshia watched him walk away. She thought about the past week. How strange everything had seemed. And then she remembered her visit to Miss Mary Mackeey and the encouragement her grandmother Lena Mae Allen had given her. *"The future belongs to you. Use your instincts. You must. If you do not, you will lose something you love very much."*

With renewed confidence Janeshia straightened her shoulders.

A few minutes later, Janeshia knocked softly at the conference room door. She didn't wait for an answer and strolled right in. She quickly scanned the room. Adam St. Charles was not in sight.

"Ladies and gentlemen, I believe you requested the honor of my presence," she announced as she marched over and took the head seat.

Weasel faced Nate Trent was the first to say something. "Janeshia you should have waited until......"

With an acid tone in her voice Janeshia said, "Oh I'm so sorry Nate, you wanted to put me in my place and tell me where you wanted me to sit? Am I right?"

Janet and Linnet, the back stabbing Mann twins smirked loudly.

Kate Martin giggled openly. She had a petite rail thin frame. Her hair was shining black bobbed-cut short, with precision cut bangs that made the eyes in her head look sensually alluring.

The conference room was filled with chaos.

The voice that roared and sounded like an African King as it sliced the air took control. "Let Janeshia sit wherever she wants to Nate," Ulysses Portillo bellowed. "For God's sakes this isn't a trial of law. And Nate Trent you'd better act like you've got some manners."

Caught like a mouse in a trap. Nate loudly cleared his throat and lowered his gazed.

Startled by the directness of the man's voice, Janeshia took a quick glance at Ulysses Portillo. The deep creased jowls on his face reminded her of a country hound dogs. His slanted dark eyes stared back at her. He had the face of a man that was used to being obeyed.

He had always been a mysterious man to her. She'd had never known him to show any kindness to anyone. Now she looked on amazed at something she had never noticed before. His eyes were truth seekers.

"Janeshia, I'm sorry but we – all have summoned you here today because we have a matter of grave concern that requires immediate attention," he hesitated. "Since we are not fully staffed today with our fierce leader right now, no permanent decisions can be made. We must say that this is a fact finding mission," he assured her. "And because we have reason to believe someone may try and leak this story to the Silicon Valley News, we feel its best that you are removed as director until this matter, all inquiries and a full investigation is done."

A chilled insensitive voice added. "Yes Janeshia," Nate Trent said, determined to have the last word. "We believe you have abused your position as Director of the Silicon Valley Diamond Foundation and we will make a full investigation into the matter immediately."

The room erupted in soft chatter.

Janeshia eyes looked back at Nate with an unreadable sigh. "And what matter at hand would that be Nate? You've been talking very loud but you haven't said a thing about exactly what this investigation is about."

Nate let his eyes roam over her face and body as his stubby fingers played with an ink pen. "You know what you did Janeshia. You had hot passionate sex with an employee," he smiled viciously. "With a man who was obviously not your type, or class level."

Janeshia sat motionless.

"What would you know about Janeshia type, Nate?" Adam St. Charles' voice sliced the air.

All heads turned in the direction of Adam St. Charles' voice. He walked out of a hidden door and crossed the room with a murderous look in his eye.

Nate Trent's eyes bulged wide. "Nothing….Nothing at all," Nate said disarmingly. "Here, Adam, I saved you a seat by me."

Adam sat down and leaned in close. "So Nate," he whispered. "You thought I wasn't listening. You backstabbing little…."

"Shhhhh Adam, someone might hear you. I was just trying to put Janeshia on the spot like you wanted," Nate said testily.

Adam rolled his eyes and whispered with a jealous glint. "You were trying nothing of the sort. You and I both know you've always wanted her."

"Don't try any of your bullying on me Adam. Nate's brow lifted as if signaling an alert.

All eyes watched the two men whispering.

Ulysses Portillo cleared his throat and took charge of the situation. "Adam St. Charles, where did you come from?"

Janeshia waived her hand. "Ah that door leads to a very small hidden copy room. We hardly use it."

Kate Martin shook her head. "Wow a secret room. This just gets better and better."

"Well that brings us to my next question Adam, where you eavesdropping Adam? Ulysses Portillo asked frankly. "As I recall we did ask you to leave the building."

Adam shook his head. "I wasn't eavesdropping. I'm sorry. I must have misunderstood. As I recall, you said the meeting was adjourned. No one said I had to leave the building."

"Hmmmm," Ulysses Portillo gruff out. "Well this is an investigation and our bylaws require that this board of directors conduct our investigation honoring the privacy and confidentiality of all parties involved."

Adam flashed a brilliant grin. "But you have the lecherous harlot vixen of a director present right here,' he pointed. "Why not conduct your investigation now?"

Janeshia was mortified at the names Adam called her.

Kate Martin regarded Adam with an expression of disdain.

"I can't believe he just said that!" She blurted. "Ulysses do something, this meeting is getting out of hand."

"We agree," echoed the Mann twins.

"There will be no name calling Adam!" Ulysses Portillo shook his head impatiently.

David Creek, silent throughout the whole matter, finally spoke up. "Ulysses, I believe we should hold this matter over until Claire Marie Perrault can join us. She is the majority shareholder."

Adam's angry gaze went around the table. "What kind of investigation is this? You need to get on with this matter now!"

Nate Trent mused. "Adam's request sounds reasonable to me," he said. "Don't you all remember why we've called this meeting?"

David Creek's large head shook lightly. "But Marie Claire isn't here," he protested loudly.

And I'm sure Adam St. Charles would like things concluded as quickly as possible," he frowned. "Besides, if Adam had done something like what she did, his being a man and all, we wouldn't even have had this meeting. We would have suspended him without a glance," his attention drifted back toward Janeshia. We don't owe that harlot any operations of protocol."

"Nate, you act like a stupid bastard sometimes," Kate said.

"Nate, I warned you about your manners," Ulysses Portillo's robust voice growled through the air. "And for your information that little scene you just played out with Adam might have been lost on everyone else in this room, but remember Nate I have a deaf relative," he paused to let his meaning sink in. "Maybe there are others here we need to investigate also."

Janeshia listened intently.

Ulysses' eyes gazed around the room. His words flowed like a deep river. "And for the record Adam, I must disagree with you. This investigation is being treated with the upmost fairness for all concerned. If you would let us continue our investigation in a fair and just manner, we will soon gather the truth!"

The room erupted in soft chatter.

"Now hold on just a moment here," Adam interrupted. "If you don't ask this slut a few questions I will."

"Ulysses, I'm sure the Mann twins will agree, we woman won't tolerate Adams behavior much longer," Kate bellowed.

Janeshia shivered. For a few seconds she seemed to feel a darkness engulfing her. Her whole mind ached with what was happening right in front of her eyes. She wished she could just run from the run and hide. Slowly, deep within, she heard a voice. Her grandmother's words echoed in her mind. *"The future belongs to you. Use your instincts. You must. If you do not you will lose something you love very much."*

A smile crept to Janeshia's face. "Adam St. Charles. I am not a slut. But then a natural born predator like yourself, wouldn't know what a real lady looked like if she walked up and slapped you in the face."

Kate Martin gave a soft snort. "You tell him Janeshia!"

Janeshia's eyes sparkled wickedly as she studied Adam. Something flashed in her mind. "Adam, since its story-time and you've had the floor making up your stories. How about I tell one of my own? I heard that there was a story about how you got that cut under your eye," she surrounded up a professional smile. "The story goes that some woman gave it to you. After she told you to stop but you didn't know what the word stop meant. The story says she slapped you hard and her ring left you with that ugly small scar just below your left eye."

"You bitch!" Adam hissed.

Kate Martin blurted. "Whew! Sounds like there is more to this story than just what Adam has been telling."

"Silence," Ulysses Portillo demanded. This meeting is totally out of control."

"I'll agree to that," Kate said. "Take control of this mess Ulysses."

Ulysses Portillo's eyes narrowed. It was obvious he was annoyed. "Okay, right now Janeshia it isn't necessary that you stay and answer any of our questions. We will be in touch with you privately."

Furiously Adam St. Charles clenched his fist and hit the table.

"Are you planning to use that thing to solve your problems Adam?" Ulysses glared at Adam's clenched fist and then back to his face.

Adam took his meaning and unclenched his fist.

Ulysses folded his hands and continued. "Janeshia this decision is unanimous I….We the majority do hold you in high esteem; and we know that the best and safest thing to do at this time, is to ask you to kindly remove yourself from the premises until we conclude with our investigation."

Janeshia rose to leave. She drew in a deep breath as she slowly walked to the door.

"Now hold on just a moment here……" Adam interrupted rising from his seat. His eyes held a dangerous jealous rage. "There's something more this board needs to know. Janeshia is carrying my baby!"

The last thing Janeshia heard was the conference room being awash with startled utter amazement.

Chapter 39

An invitation to Breakfast....

The green and black checkered taxi cab pulled to the curb on Market Street just in front of Plaza de Cesar Chavez Park. The little old lady emerged from the taxi and paid the driver. Her Chanel Boucle plaid suit had been the height of fashion in her day. The pin pleated skirt matched perfectly with the jacket.

She walked into the small park and sat on a bench in front of the public fountain. Watching the water gurgle and spurt into the air was an old favorite past time of hers. She squinted over the rim of her glasses and checked her watch. It was half past nine. She had plenty of time to relax. From her spot on the bench she could see the Tech Museum and the San Jose Convention Center across the street.

"Rose Olsten?" Is that you?" A thickly accented voice called out.

Mrs. Olsten turned around immediately. She knew the voice. Jovially she smiled. "Dolly? Dolly Couvertier-Trudeau, I haven't seen you in ages."

"Oh my God Rose you haven't changed a bit," Dolly Couvertier-Trudeau cried out with joy and throwing her arms around her.

Dolly Couvertier-Trudeau was dressed in a fine small brim black hat with a green trim and a green pantsuit with matching purse and shoes.

"Rose you remember my granddaughter Alice Couvertier-Trudeau?"

"Yes I do," Mrs. Olsten said.

Taking her cue Alice nodded greeting.

"Well now," Mrs. Olsten gushed. "Where are you and Alice off to, this fine morning Dolly?"

"We're having a late breakfast at the Fountain Restaurant at the Fairmont Hotel."

"Oh that's wonderful, Mrs. Olsten smiled. "You've been missed at the Pearl Palmer's bridge games."

Dolly frowned with a shrug. "I vowed to stop going until that card cheater Lamina Symons apologizes. Did you know she had the nerve to tell me she didn't want me as a partner? She said I was incompetent as her partner. Me Dolly Couvertier-Trudeau!" she exclaimed. "I've played cards with the best. I know how to play cards."

Mrs. Olsten smiled sympathetically and checked her watch.

"Oh Dolly I'm sure you were on your way some place important. I wish you had time for a cup of tea so that we could catch up on old times?" Mrs. Olsten suggested.

"You're in luck, I do have some extra time this morning," Dolly said. "Mrs. Olsten have you had breakfast yet? If not you should join me and my granddaughter, at the Restaurant," Dolly suggested. "We could catch up on old times."

Mrs. Olsten looked at her watch again. "It's early enough, I could have a cup of tea or something," she said and raised a concerned brow. "But I wouldn't want to inconvenience your granddaughter Alice; she looks like she has someplace important to go?"

Dolly threw back her head and laughed. "Alice is stuck doing her grandmother's bidding today and for the rest of this week. I might add. That girl has been out of town for ages. And she promised to spend today with me no matter what," she smiled softly taking Mrs. Olsten's arm and leading the way.

"Alice darling be a dear and walk a head and get a table for three at the Restaurant,

"Okay sure, grandmother," Alice said strutting ahead of them. She crossed Market Street and walked headed for the lobby of the Fairmont Hotel.

Chapter 40

The Faint, then the Battle....

"Wake up Janeshia."

Someone's hand was shaking her shoulder.

"Come on wake up, you're missing all the action," the voice roared in her ear.

Janeshia opened her eyes and realized the voice belonged to Tamara Bell, her assistant. She looked around. She was lying on the sofa in the ladies room.

"Tamara? What happened?"

"Your guts and your brains told you to faint and you did. I don't blame you. I would have too," Tamara said helping her up. She straightened her suit. "I was told to stay with you and make sure you're okay."

Janeshia recovered her equilibrium. "Wait a minute I was in the conference room when....."

"When they told you to leave, and you did. And then you had to go and walked out the door saw Claire Marie Perrault standing there and then you fainted from the shock of it all. It's a good thing David Creek caught you in time," Tamara excitedly said. "Come on. We've got to get you back into that conference room. "I can't hear a thing out here."

Janeshia stood and Tamara steadied her as they made their way out of the ladies room.

"Come on Janeshia, stay strong. The conference room is straight ahead."

Ready to do battle, Janeshia put one foot in front of the other and marched ahead.

Chapter 41

A Geek Knight, some shining amour & the Angel

"Walker! Well what a surprise to see you here?"

Dolly Couvertier-Trudeau turned to see where her friend Rose was looking. A good looking man in a beautifully tailored deep navy suit smiled brightly at them as he walked over.

"Hello Mrs. Olsten?" How are you doing?"

"I couldn't be better Walker," Mrs. Olsten grinned and tilted her head. "Walker, this is a very good friend of mine Dolly Couvertier-Trudeau, and her granddaughter Alice Couvertier-Trudeau."

"It's a pleasure to meet you Mrs. and Ms. Couvertier-Trudeau," Walker said. "I'm sorry but I'm kind of in a hurry. I just dropped in to pick up some coffee and breakfast to go."

Alice reached her hand up and piped into her grandmother's ear. She murmured in a whisper. "He's the one grandmother. Walker's the man that is in love with Janeshia."

"Well I'll be damn," Dolly said. Her mouth opened and then

closed back again. She stared back at Alice and whispered. "My Janeshia?"

"Yes, Grandmamma," Alice shrugged.

Dolly's eyes narrowed. She leaned over and whispered. "He's the spitting imagine of his brother....Except for his eyes and his hair. No wonder Janeshia got confused with the two of them."

Mrs. Olsten peered over the rim of her tea cup. "There's nothing wrong with my hearing. Why are you whispering about Walker and Janeshia, Alice?"

Dolly Couvertier-Trudeau rolled her eyes in appreciation. "Make no mistake about it Rose; we are not saying anything bad about Walker or my...... I mean Janeshia. In fact I am much honored to meet you Walker," she said extending her hand.

Walker looked perplexed. "You look very familiar Mrs. Couvertier-Trudeau."

"Call me Dolly," she said favoring him with a brilliant smile. All at once her finger clasped tight around his hand. As her fingers glided over his skin. "Walker you have an enlightening aura about you like you just recently returned from the Kisatchie forest of Louisiana? How did you find my sister Mama Moue Redbones?"

"You are?" Walkers' voice carried a curious tone.

"Yes, Sheba was my baby sister," Dolly replied. Boldly she cocked her eye in a knowing way. "Don't you have a brother?"

The gravity of her voice transfixed him. "I....No....Ah" Walker hesitated. His instincts told him Dolly had a knowing spirit. His brows pulled together. "I've just learned of the possibility of a brother," he said stating the truth. "That's one of the reasons I'm in a hurry."

Dolly's deep green eyes sparkled. "Walker you are in an awful hurry," she hesitated. "And I feel it has to do with Janeshia. I can tell. Is my Janeshia alright?"

Walker hesitated and nodded. "I don't know, but I do need to be someplace important right now."

"Alice, your cousin needs our help," Dolly said reaching for her purse. "We need to leave immediately."

Dolly tilted her head. "Rose I believe I must shorten our little get together. But I promise you a rain check."

Rose Olsten put down her cup of tea. "Huh, I smell trouble Dolly."

She turned her attention. "Walker if you don't mind. my

granddaughter and I would like to accompany you?"

Mrs. Olsten cleared her throat. "I'm going too. In fact I was planning to have lunch with Janeshia today."

"Rose, you never told me that you were having lunch with Janeshia?" Dolly adjusted her hat.

Rose put her tea cup down gingerly. "The subject never came up Dolly," she said. "But that's where I was on my way to. I just arrived early to enjoy the park for a couple of hours," Rose shrugged.

Walker looked between Dolly and Rose.

Rose caught Walker staring. "Walker I can see you had no idea my first name is Rose. Rose Olsten." she smiled leaned forward and took his arm. "Come on Walker, I have a proposition for you. I believe it's time for you to go into your Geek Knight in shining amour routine. It's needed for doing battle and I'm the Angel you need to show you the way."

Chapter 42

The Drama King performance....

The Conference room door seemed enormous as Janeshia helped Tamara push it open.

She held the door opened for her. And Janeshia walked through the doorway of the conference room.

All eyes turned on her.

"Now what is she doing here?" Weasel faced Nate Trent's jowls quivered. "We told you to leave."

"I want her here," Claire Marie Perrault's voice roared. She did not get to her feet. She sat in the seat at the head of the table like a royal queen.

"Sit here by me. We can share the throne," Claire Marie commanded.

Ulysses Portillo cleared his throat and chuckled loudly. "Now that our Queen and her princess are seated, I guess it's time for our little fray to begin."

Nate Trent interrupted. "Surely you cannot be serious? That woman is present;" he pointed his hand in Janeshia's direction."

Kate Martin leaned and jeeringly whispered "Be quiet Nate. We already know whose side you're on."

Nate's eyes swelled in fear and his voice died in his throat as his met Kate's gaze.

Ulysses Portillo's robust voice heralded drily. "We are present here for the purpose of gathering evidence." He turned and looked straight at Nate Trent. "I need to add that this is a confidential matter, if anyone is suspected of leaking any of what is said here today to the press or anyone, you will face expulsion."

Everyone in the room was silent.

Janeshia sat transfixed and glued to her seat.

"Now that our illustrious founder, owner and major shareholder is present, we can begin," Ulysses Portillo said with urgency.

"Thank you Ulysses," Claire Marie said, waving a graceful hand. "You are quite right. We should get started."

"This meeting is now called to order," Ulysses bellowed. "Adam St. Charles you've made numerous serious accusations today. I hope that you can support them. You now have the floor."

Nervously Adam rose cautiously. He cleared his throat. "I have a report here that will show Janeshia James has been stealing from this foundation!"

Soft murmurs went around the room.

The corners of Adam's lips curved up into a crooked smile. His mood was like a raging tiger ready for the kill. His voice was pure acid when he spoke. "My report will show Janeshia has systematically been sending monies to an off shore account in her name and solely for her use!"

"Stop lying Adam!" Janeshia snapped out in protest. "Adam, how could you do this to me?"

"Silence!" Ulysses bellowed. "Janeshia please calm down."

Adam's eyes gleamed as he honed in on his prey. His tongue was as shape as a blade. "My report will show the monies she took belong to this foundation and she deposited them in an off shore account in her name. My charges are that she knowingly set up these accounts, falsified the existing reports for this foundation and that she knowingly has laundered monies through these accounts for some unscrupulous people," he observed his prey scathingly. "Furthermore I also charge that Janeshia James is a cold hearted shrewd harlot, who on several occasions tried to proposition me into performing sexual services for her in order to secure my loyalty and to hide her deceit from this illustrious board of directors."

Janeshia choked back a sob.

"Adam, may I see that report sir?" Claire Marie commanded.

Adam slid the report across the table.

Adam's eyes met Janeshia's. "Yes, you may. In fact I have enough copies here for everyone," he said passing out the extra copies.

Janeshia's eyes watered as she looked at the report placed in front of her. She closed her eyes willing the report to disappear.

Claire Marie put on her glasses and slowly flipped through the pages.

Adam observed her. He licked his lips and moistened his tongue to ready itself to strike the final blow for its intended victim. "I gave Ms. James every chance to change the outcome of things here today. Prior to this hearing today, I asked her to come forth and admit her guilt," his eyes held anger and rage. "And instead of heeding my advice, in a fit of rage she cut me with a wine bottle. I had to have ten stitches to close up the wound," he said rolling up his sleeve and exposing his stitches. "Here are the photos of Janeshia accompanying me to the emergency room," Adam said passing the photos out. "Even then she was trying to persuade me not to tell anyone what she did. Look at my injuries in the photos. A creature that would do this would never admit her guilt."

The photos Adam passed out where quickly passed around the room.

Janeshia took a brief look. Confusion clouded her thoughts. The woman in the photo looked exactly like her. Someone was doing a really good job of trying to frame her. A sob choked out of her.

The room held an awkward silence.

Adam produced a thin smile as he looked back at Janeshia. He held her gaze with a steel confidence as his eyes gleamed like crystals, as he watched her.

Kate Martin tapped her pencil on the table. "What I would like to know is what she did with all of the money. I don't see her driving a new car or taking expensive trips."

Nate's tone was precise when he spoke. "Janeshia took control of the money deposited to her accounts in the Cayman Island and brought an office building in lower Manhattan," Nate added. "It's all there in the report."

Adam turned and looked at Kate. "Janeshia's crime was high larceny. Her crime was simple theft with the intention of permanently depriving this great organization of its monies. Janeshia stole from this organization for her sole benefit," he said, finishing his presentation with a stone face, like a tiger that just made his kill. "The moment I was sure Janeshia was stealing this foundation blind I reported my findings to Nate."

Nate cleared his throat. "Yes Adam did. He delivered his report to me just yesterday and immediately I arranged for this board to meet. This report shows that Janeshia James is not the honorable and exemplary person we thought," he grimly looked around the conference table. "The photos alone are conclusive proof this woman has been throwing herself at this man like a harlot."

"You liar! You....You... You crazy lying drama king! Stop it! I am not a harlot and I'm not a thief!" Janeshia's voice shook as it sliced the air.

"Quiet please." Ulysses' voice commanded as softly as he could.

Nate wiped his hand across his mouth. "We cannot let a woman like this continue to run this organization. In fact if I had my way, she would be locked behind bars for her loose moral values, just like we lock up all women in this country caught in the act of prostitution!"

Ulysses shrugged, his face hardened as a shadow of doubt filled his brow. "Adam St. Charles I will assume you have concluded with your presentation?"

"Yes I have," Adam said smugly.

Nate Trent rose and cleared his throat. "Based upon the testimony given by Adam here today and this report and as those pictures indicate, we have some grave, important matters to deal with here today," he said. "I purpose this document alone shows enough evidence to ask Janeshia James to step down as director of this foundation."

A thin smug smile showed on Adam's face as his eyes beamed staring back at Janeshia.

"So does this board have mutual agreement that we will ask Janeshia James to step down as director of this board?" Nate asked.

Confusion, anguish and tears clouded her eyes. Janeshia stared up at the ceiling trying to figure out what she must do. At the moment all she could think of was looking at the door and praying for a miracle.

All at once Kate Martin's voice sliced the air. "Hang on a minute. Adam those scratches…"

"Yes? Adam asked.

"Did the hospital run any test? You know like check for DNA? And the woman in the photograph she looks like Janeshia, but there is something strange. Do you have any clearer photos or a report from the hospital?"

Ulysses chuckled softly. "Go head Adam please answer?"

Adam was furious. His hand clenched in a fist. He saw Ulysses staring. He released his grip. "I don't have to provide this board with a doctor's report. You have my word."

"That's because you don't have a doctor's report or any other report that you didn't make up yourself," Janeshia said staring back at Adam unbelieving. "You're a filthy stinking villainous, lying bastard!"

Adam raised a brow. His face frowned into an extorted expression of revenge. "Yes, but you're the nasty little pregnant tramp, that's going to jail for stealing this organizations money. I hope that bastard brat of yours will be taken from you the minute it's born," Adam laughed through clenched teeth. "Who's the villain now bitch?"

"Oh my God Adam why are you doing this to me?" Janeshia's voice shook.

"Don't you know? Because you're a thief and a whore!" Adam murmured.

Horrified Janeshia choked back on a sob and buried her face in her hands.

"Recess!" Ulysses yelled. "Half hour, we all need a damn

bathroom break."

The room quickly emptied.

Cautiously Claire Marie walked over and touched Janeshia on the shoulder.

Janeshia looked back at her with tears streaming down her face.

"Stay strong and calm yourself," Claire Marie said squeezing her shoulder. "We're going to get through this, I promised an oath to take care of you many years ago and I won't undo that oath now."

Chapter 43
Walker to the rescue!

An hour later, the conference room seemed interminable as Janeshia sat and stared back at the room full of people.

The atmosphere of the room was intense as the group whispered around her.

She didn't know how much more her stomach could take or her nerves.

She looked up and watched as Adam St. Charles whispered something to Nate Trent. It was obvious the two of them felt her defeat was at hand.

Adam stared back at her and made a hand gesture, thumbs down. She quickly averted her eyes.

Slowly the door of the conference room opened.

The atmosphere in the room changed noticeably as Walker Perrault strutted in. Immediately his vivid green eyes sought out hers.

Janeshia rose quickly and burst out. "Oh my God Walker I'm so glad you're here. Adam is telling lies about me," tears ran down her face. She looked as helpless as a small child. "I swear I haven't done any of the things he's accusing me of."

Walker quickly closed the distance between them. All at once his hand reached up and wiped the tears off her cheek. "Don't worry," he whispered low, too low for anyone else to hear.

The moment wasn't lost on anyone in the room.

Claire Marie removed her glasses. "Walker, it's about time you got here."

Janeshia looked around. Everyone was talking excitedly to each other. She looked back at Adam and saw the alarm in his face.

The conference room door opened again and three ladies walked in slowly, Rose Olsen, Dolly Couvertier-Trudeau, and Alice Couvertier-Trudeau. The three ladies quickly found seats for themselves.

"Walker said it was okay if we attended," Mrs. Olsen spoke up for the group.

Nate Trent swallowed hard. "Walker, and ladies. You're just in time. We were just finishing up here. This board has come to a decision."

"A very hasty decision no doubt," Walker said opening his brief case. "I have a true investigator report that I would like to present into evidence," he said passing the report around. "Please read it everyone, before you succumb to Adam St. Charles' greatest show on earth. A drama of deceit that contained the biggest fraud, theft and falsifying of business records this foundation has ever seen."

Adam St. Charles swallowed hard. His face broke out in a sweat. "You can't prove a thing!"

Walker shut his brief case. "Oh yes I can Adam. In fact I have a witness."

Adam's thin smile disappeared. He looked deeply troubled. "Witness?"

Claire Marie's voice was frosty. "You heard my son. We have a witness. And who knows Adam, we may have more."

Walker's voice was cool. "Ulysses, you are the chairman of this board. Would you be so kind as to call our first witness? I believe he is standing outside the conference room door."

Ulysses cleared his throat. "David Creek you are closest to the door. Would you be so kind as to open it for our first witness?"

The atmosphere in the room was noticeably changed.

David Creek was a quiet man. As usual he was wearing his signature tattered white jacket. Anyone looking at him thought the old white haired man with round rimmed glasses, was poor. This was far from the truth. David Creek was one of the richest men in the valley.

David rose and stiffly walked to the door and opened it.

Janeshia leaned up in her seat trying to get a look at who was coming through the door.

In walked a man wearing dark glasses. His looks were foreign.

Janeshia had never seen him before.

Marie Claire reached for the carafe of water in front of her and quickly poured herself a glass. "This guy looks like he's got a good story to tell."

Adam's steel confidence slowly faded.

Ulysses steel voice called out. "Sir, would you be kind and remove your sunglasses and then state your name for the record."

The man removed his shades. A slight accent escaped from the lips of the mysterious man's mouth. "I am Mr. Manitou Alexandre Grand."

"Mr. Grand what brought you here today?"

He grunted. "I guess you can say I was personally invited here today by Walker Perrault."

Janeshia felt her breath squeeze out of her lungs at the sound of Walker's name.

Ulysses cleared his throat. "So Walker Perrault asked you to be here today?"

Mr. Grand shook his head. "I wouldn't say asked. It was more like they persuaded me. In fact I was escorted here today by an attorney named Larissa London, who indicated to me that she works for this foundation. As well as a private investigator friend of hers, a Mr. Arthur Daily," he swallowed hard.

"Persuaded you, you say. How?"

"Let's just say I made a sizeable donation to the foundation," Mr. Grand drily said.

"Why would you do that?" Ulysses asked.

Mr. Grand cleared his throat. "To avoid my having to let us say, spend my time where I wouldn't be happy. If you know what I mean."

Ulysses chuckled. "Do you know Adam St. Charles?" he tersely asked waiving his hand in Adam's direction.

There was awkward silence.

Adam frowned.

The man sneered. "I am acquainted with him, yes."

"And are you acquainted with any information about Adam St. Charles?"

Mr. Grand cleared his throat. "I am aware that Adam falsely obtained Janeshia signature, for the sole purpose of setting up some off shore accounts to launder monies, as well as to steal monies from the foundation for his own personal gain."

"Just a moment, you can't believe a word of what this man says," Adam furiously interrupted. "This man is a liar. This is a conspiracy! A conspiracy!"

"Adam, I told you that your cover was flimsy," Mr. Grand protested.

Walker's eyes captured Janeshia attention. His eyes softened as they reassured her. His lips moved. She could have sworn he mouthed the words, *"See I told you there was no need to worry."*

Janeshia smiled back at Walker. In the distance she could hear Adam's ravings. She shook out her thoughts and returned to the present.

Ulysses was annoyed. It was obvious because his eyes had narrowed into slits. "Be quiet Adam, I have the floor and as long as I do, it would be best that I hear very little out of you."

Janeshia settled back into her chair. This was getting very interesting. She looked up and caught Marie Claire smiling at her.

For the next five minutes Mr. Manitou Alexandre Grand gave his account of how he was just a victim of Adam St. Charles' shrewd cold hearted scheming antics. "Adam even concocted the tale about sexual harassment. He knew it would be the nail in the coffin for Janeshia with the board of directors. His motive was he hoped to be appointed as the next board of director's member. And he knew all of you would agree to appoint him if he agreed not to pursue legal actions against the foundation."

With a terse expression Ulysses asked, "And why should we believe you Mr. Grand?"

"I don't lie!" Mr. Grand said sullenly.

Nate Trent rose. "Ulysses we can take this man's word for anything without proof."

"What did Adam offer you Nate?" Ulysses asked.

"What?" Startled Nate Trent slowly sat back down in his seat.

"Oh, you don't have to answer now Nate, I'm sure it will come out," Ulysses hesitated. "But then again, I may already know the answer."

Nate Trent swallowed hard.

Ulysses turned his attention back to Mr. Grand. "Mr. Grand did you provide any records of this information?"

He nodded. "I cooperated fully with that private investigator, Arthur Daily, and that attorney," Mr. Grand said. "I gave them the information they wanted. All of the records. I even gave them the laptop Adam used when he was with me."

"And why did you do that?"

"For immunity," Mr. Grand said. "I won't face jail time, since I gave back the money." He turned and looked at Adam. "Sorry Adam, I had to throw you under the bus. There's no honor among thieves."

Uncomfortably Adam shifted in his seat. "What?"

His statement was met with a hushed silence.

Ulysses chuckled softly and looked back at the witness. "Thank you Mr. Grand. I believe I'm finished with you for now," he turned and looked at Walker. Just last week they had met in private to discuss this same issue. He thought back. Now he knew with certainty that Adam St. Charles was a monstrous man capable of fiendish deed, just as Walker had said. But Adam was also a major risk, which needed to be taken care of. He could see it all now clearly. Now he knew it was time to wrap things up. He cleared his throat and came back to the present.

"Adam, your allegations are totally untrue. And you've wasted a lot of this board's precious time. I will exercise my executive power and conclude your allegations are fraudulent lies. All accusations against Ms. James are hereby unfounded and she will retain her rights as director of this foundation with the board's upmost apologies."

"What the hell do you mean?" Adam screamed.

"He means you need to get out," Kate Martin said.

"No, I need him here. Adam you will stay where you are," Claire Marie said. "At least until we call our next witness."

David Creek quietly rose, quickly walked to the door and opened it.

Ramsey Montgomery slowly walked in.

Hostility showed on Adam's expression. "You?"

Ramsey wasn't alone. He carried a young child. The child. The room was electric with excited talking.

"Silence!" Ulysses cleared his throat. "As the Board has heard the pervious witness, this whole scheme was fabricated by Adam St. Charles for the sole purpose of his selfish cold hearted desire," he firmly said. "Therefore we have exonerated our director and I move to close this matter now."

Kate Martin curiously asked. "What about the next witness?"

Ulysses shrugged. His voice was firm. "The next witness has to do with a private family matter; all board members are asked to vacate the premises immediately."

He turned his head and pointed. "Nate Trent, if that is lost on you, it means you are to leave and vacate the building immediately. If I so much as hear you stop to take a drink at the water fountain, I'll personally call you in for review. Now leave!" Ulysses commanded sharply.

"Claire Marie, I won't leave if you need me to stay," the soft diminutive voice of David Creek sliced the air.

"Thank you David for your concern, but I will be fine," she said softly. "Oh and David I expect to see you at Lamina Symons house for cards on Saturday."

David smiled and opened the door. "You do know old Lamina Symons chcats are cards don't you Claire Marie," he waived. "But don't worry I'll be there."

The Conference room looked empty with the few people that remained.

The small group stared between themselves.

Finally Claire Marie Perrault broke the ice and got up from her seat and walked over to where Ramsey stood. "So young man, you are Ramsey Montgomery?" She asked with a wry smile. "You remember me?"

"Yes," Ramsey nodded with a smile. "And this precious little girl is Coco."

The child in Ramsey's arms beamed when he said her name.

"The child's name is Coco," Claire Marie murmured.

"Yes," Ramsey smiled.

"Coco please say hello to Mrs. Claire Marie Perrault."

Coco shyly waived.

Ramsey hesitated and put Coco down. "Coco go and look out that window over there," he said pointing across the room. "I bet the view is really pretty from there."

He watched as Coco smiled and ran over to look of out the window.

Claire Marie closed the distance between them.

"Ramsey do you recall when I asked you to indulge an old woman and give her a hug?"

"Yes, I do."

"Can I ask again, for another hug?"

Ramsey turned holding up his arms.

Claire Marie walked into his embrace.

Ramsey hugged Claire Marie tight with a wide smile. "This time I say thank you for indulging me. I have wanted to hug you from the first moment I knew."

"Why are you smiling at her? And why are you letting her hug you?" Adam snarled "She never gave a damn about you?"

"Shut up Adam!" Ramsey flashed him an annoyed look. "You're in so much trouble right now. And I don't want you to upset Coco," he said through clenched teeth.

Janeshia stared between Adam and Ramsey. "You know Adam, Ramsey?"

Ramsey flashed a brief smile. "Sorry to say it, I do. I guess you haven't figured it out yet Janeshia, like Mrs. Perrault did. Adam is my brother."

Clair Marie fumbled to straighten her glasses. "Janeshia, I never understood why you couldn't see that my Walker and Ramsey Montgomery looked so much alike, they could almost be twins," she nodded. "They are almost the same height. And they have the same strong jaw, build and coloring. They just have different colored eyes."

"Walker's eyes are green," Janeshia said astounded.

Claire Marie continued. "My Walker has my family's famous green eye color. That's the Edmond's green, you know," she paused, turned and studied Ramsey. "Ramsey you have my late husband's Edward Perrault's strangely mysterious grayish brown colored eyes. Some folks call that color mystic hazel," she nodded. "Your eyes can change colors easily based upon your mood."

Defiant Adam smirked. "We're both the sons of the late Mr. Edward Perrault.

Claire Marie quietly studied Adam and then turned her head.

"Unlike my brother," Adam continued, "I have always

wanted my share of the Perrault family's fortune," he chuckled. "So mommy dearest, how about giving me my inheritance now, so that I won't have to take you to court."

An anxious expression bordering on belligerent resentment flashed in Claire Marie's eyes. "I beg your pardon Adam; but I am not your mother."

Ramsey chuckled softly. "Wrong as usual Adam, I am the son of Claire Marie Perrault and Edward Perrault. It appears mother lied to you. Just as she lied about the deceitful way she became pregnant with me, he shrugged.

"Ramsey you are a liar!"

"No Adam, I've seen the genetic testing results."

Annoyed Adam interrupted. "You're the one that stupid Ramsey. How can you say you're the son of both of them? Mother only took Edward's sperm, she told us."

"No mother stole both the Perrault family's sperm and eggs. But apparently she was only able to use it one time. And that was for me."

Hostility fled from Adam's expression. "What?"

"Yep little brother, it looks like you may want to ask Mother who your real father is. But you'll have to wait until she gets back from her cruise."

Ramsey shifted his gaze and stared back at Claire Marie. "Well, I guess you figured it out that my brother thought he was entitled to a share of the Perrault family's fortune. Adam always did want to get things the easy way."

Janeshia was confused. "Wait a minute. Adam, don't you have a sister? You applied for a scholarship for your sister."

Ramsey looked confused. "Sorry Janeshia, I know I put you through a bunch of crap behind my dating you for selfish reasons. But it looks like my brother has been unloading a trunk load of lies on you as well," he shrugged. "We have no sister."

"Selfish reasons, what are you saying?" she asked.

Ramsey looked at her sincerely. "I mean I was only dating you for some stupid idea my brother put in my head, that my being close to you could help him get a promotion. He lied to you and he lied to me. He was only interested in setting you up so that he could take over the foundation," he paused. "I don't condone his actions. In fact, I want to apologize to you for my part in it. I think Adam's actions were deceitful. Just as most everything Adam does is deceitful."

Claire Marie cleared her throat. "Is Coco my grandchild?"

"I consider Coco my child," Ramsey shook his head. "But the fact she is Adam's child.

"That little thing isn't mine. ….." Adam protested.

Ramsey turned on Adam with a rage. "Adam if you call Coco a name. I swear to God I'm going to punch you in the nose."

"Okay," Adam hesitated and shut his mouth.

"Damn," Janeshia muttered. "I never thought I'd see the day that Adam St. Charles respected someone. Let alone was afraid."

Adam gave Janeshia a mean look but kept his mouth closed. The moment was awkward.

"Coco's mother was a …. Adam's lips curved into a frown.

"Adam! I also meant for you not to call Coco's mother names either," Ramsey began giving him a look that stopped Adam cold.

Adam forced himself to speak coolly. He knew what could happen if he made Ramsey upset. The last thing in the world he needed now was to have his big brother mad at him. "All that I was going to say brother was that my relationship with Coco's mother was well, complicated," he laughed nervously. "I'm very lucky that my brother and my mother have taken good care of the child."

Adam stared back at his brother. He watched him staring at Janeshia. He watched Walker staring back at her too. He looked at the two men in disgust.

The day wasn't going as Adam had planned and now it looked like Janeshia had won. He looked at her. He could tell she only had eyes for Walker. He hated what he saw. Secretly he knew Ramsey really cared for Janeshia. That's why he wouldn't go through with the plans he'd had for her.

Stubbornly Adam turned and looked at Janeshia. He walked closer. "Well I guess you've won Janeshia. By the way I'm so glad my brother dumped you when he did. We don't like whores in our family. Now who are you going to get to be your bastard's daddy?"

Walker cocked his head and lean forward. He swung his hand connected to Adam's jaw. Before Adam finished his sentence he went flying. His body fell over a chair before he landed with a loud crash hitting the floor.

"Adam, I'll have you know my child has a father," Walker said shaking his hand.

Ramsey chuckled. "Adam....Adam," he said. "When are you going to learn to keep your big mouth shut?"

Adam lay on the floor clutching his jaw wishing he could take back the flippant words he just uttered.

Ramsey nodded stiffly. "Get off of the floor Adam, I've checked with Mrs. Perrault and an attorney and we've all agreed you need to go away for a while. He offered Adam his hand helping him up. "And maybe if you act real good, I might be able to keep you out of jail, maybe."

Janeshia strolled over to where Walker stood. She clasped the hand he punched Adam with. "Walker are you hurt?" A thread of fear echoed in her voice.

Walker shook his head.

Janeshia's expression was full of uncertainty as she searched his gaze. "You knew I was pregnant?"

"Yes," Walker replied.

"God I'm so sorry for all the trouble I've cause. You've saved my honor twice in one day. I owe you everything right now," she said massaging his hand. "God I've been such a fool not to see things clearly. All along you loved me and were watching out for me. And I was too blind to see it, that I loved you also."

The corners of Walker's mouth lifted into a smile. "I'm just happy knowing the beautiful Janeshia finally realizes she loves me and that she knows I want the child she's carrying."

She looked up and met his gaze. "You want me?"

"And our baby," Walker took a deep breath. "I want the whole package."

Epilogue

Janeshia hadn't thought life could get any better as she watched Walker staring out of the window of her office. She looked back at her hand and gasped again in surprise at the diamond ring, the ten carat cushion cut yellow diamond was adorned by smaller diamonds. The words Walker had said to her when he put the ring on her finger still echoed in her mind. *"I love you so much; I want to put a ring on your finger and make it totally legal."*

Walker slowly closed the distance between them. "Janeshia my love, do you want a bigger ring? Is that the reason you keep staring at it?"

"Honey, if you tried to take this ring off of my finger, you'd be in for a fight," she grinned. "But the makeup sex would make you forget all about any battle."

Smiling, Walker pulled her into his arms. "You promise?"

"Yes."

Walker pulled back. "Janeshia I need you to make me a promise."

"What?"

"Christmas is the most magical time of the year. Make my Christmas wish come true and marry me on December 1st."

"Oh my love yes," she whispered.

At that moment Walker's mouth covered hers in a lingering kiss.

The End

♥

Coming Soon......Next book in the A Geek, an Angel, Series....

A *Geek, an Angel, and a Bowl of Gator Gumbo* is a contemporary novel, bittersweet romance tale revolving around two star crossed lovers Lacey and Kienan. After growing up they grew apart. Kienan Egan dumped Lacey during college.

Gorgeous Lacey La Cour lost her hopeful playful spirit after Kienan dumped her. Now an adult she is strong and independent. Her life is perfect. Except that her manipulative, selfish older brother Nicholas loves money. He's spent his and he needs more. He plots and schemes his way into getting others to do his bidding. Then tragic forces are unleashed as Nicholas opens up doors to the past. The past were the dead never dies.

Come and enjoy the panoramic views of the breathtaking Mount Hamilton in Silicon Valley to the magical pull of San Francisco and Oakland California. A *Geek, an Angel, and a Bowl of Gator Gumbo i*s an extra ordinary tale of the real and the surreal.

About the Author J.A.JACKSON

J.A.JACKSON is an author who lives in an enchanted little house she calls home in the Northern California foothills with her husband and Big Sally an American scent hound. She fell in love with writing as a small child. She was born in Arkansas and comes from a family rich in story tellers. She spent over ten years working in the non-profit sector where she wrote grants, press releases and contributed many stories to their newsletter. She was their Newsletter editor for over ten years. She loves growing roses, a good pot of hot tea, chocolate, magical stories, suspense stories, ghost stories, and reading Jane Austen again and again in her past time. Please write her at P.O. Box 62323 Sunnyvale, CA 94088.

PSEUDONYM: J. A. Jackson

Media Contact: Rossi Jackson email rossijackson@comcast.net

Made in the USA
Charleston, SC
11 March 2015